"CAN YOU SEE ANYTHING ABOUT *ME* IN THAT CRYSTAL BALL?" VERITY ASKED.

The Great Lavengro put a hand to each side of his face and leaned forward. "You have a companion of great loveliness. Fair of feature and graceful of limb."

Verity basked in the tribute to his wife Bella's charms.

The clairvoyant continued, "She once displayed these beauties to all the world."

"*All the world!*" Verity bellowed.

"Displaying her arse in a penny gaffe," Lavengro said desperately. "You must have known!"

But Verity was scrambling to his feet, and as the scrawny clairvoyant snatched a chair in self-defense, Verity bunched his right hand in a hamlike fist and delivered a mighty smack to his antagonist's jaw.

Also by Francis Selwyn

CRACKSMAN ON VELVET
SERGEANT VERITY AND THE IMPERIAL DIAMOND
SERGEANT VERITY PRESENTS HIS COMPLIMENTS
SERGEANT VERITY AND THE BLOOD ROYAL

SERGEANT VERITY
AND
THE SWELL MOB

FRANCIS SELWYN

𝔰𝔇

STEIN AND DAY/*Publishers*/New York

FIRST STEIN AND DAY PAPERBACK EDITION 1984
Sergeant Verity and the Swell Mob was first published in hardcover in
the United States of America by Stein and Day/*Publishers* in 1981.

Copyright © 1981 by Francis Selwyn
All rights reserved, Stein and Day, Incorporated
Printed in the United States of America
STEIN AND DAY/*Publishers*
Scarborough House
Briarcliff Manor, N.Y. 10510
ISBN 0-8128-8050-1

The Shah Jehan Clasp

In those ever-famous days of September 1857, when our infantry and light horse stormed the rebel city of Delhi, the treasury of the Mogul Emperors was broke open. Its masterpiece was the rich clasp of Shah Jehan, or Sháh Jahán, ruler of India two centuries since. This great clasp formed a *sarpesh* or turban-ornament, a fine tall plume cut in white jade and encrusted with gold. It bears a perfect galaxy of diamonds of the first water, a leaf-pattern of emeralds with precious stones. But who shall describe that blood-red ruby at its base, that most exquisitely carved Burmah stone?

Tradition avers that Shah Jehan's curse shall fall wherever unlawful hands despoil his treasure. For this, his *sarpesh* was nicknamed 'The Devil's Clasp'. Of its recent history, but little is known. It was sold for an unnamed vendor in 1858 by Dubouq, Rivery & Fils, in Paris. During two weeks it was displayed at the Crystal Palace among souvenirs of the late Sepoy rebellion. Where it now rests, or what fortune attends its owner, I am not able to discover.

—Captain J. H. Monck-Learmont
A Rider with Hodson's Light Horse
London, 1860

CONTENTS

STUNNING JOE

1

Stunning Joe O'Meara hung by his fingers in the high star-light, like a thin black spider. Fifty feet below him, the shaded cobbles of the stable yard held their promise of shattered bone, the lingering death of a body broken on the wheel. He pressed himself gently against the rose-coloured brickwork of Wannock Hundred. Even in naming a Sussex mansion, Baron Lansing had given it an air of bogus antiquity.

Stunning Joe's bony fingers were hooked over the dressed stone of the highest window ledge. His spread legs had found lodgements for his toes where the mortar of the Georgian bricks was loose and crumbling. Lean and light-boned as a child, he was hardly visible in the night, wearing his black breeches of tight moleskin, his dark vest and thin canvas shoes.

He worked his way along the high mansion wall, the cold memory of a drop to the cobbles always behind him, the tiled eaves a few feet above him. Holding the ledge by one hand, he stretched the other out, caressing the rough brick surface to one side. The little file between his fingers dug at the mortar. Tiny fragments rattled on the stones far below. Stunning Joe tested the finger-hold, trusted it, and slowly moved his other hand along the stone window-ledge.

Clamped like a limpet against the wall, he drew a deep breath of air in the crisp November night. Below him a light breeze stirred the remaining leaves of the park elms. A fox barked clear and cold on the moonlit flank of downland. Further still, where the starlight struck a flat pale reflection, he caught the distant shell-sound of the flood tide running between Seaford and Beachy Head. In the shadow of the eaves his head moved in sharp brief glances. The slick black hair shaped a skull that had the narrow keenness of a ferret.

Alone in the cold silence of his spider-perch, he touched the toe of a canvas shoe along the line of mortar, feeling for his next foothold. A stable clock in its white-painted cupola chimed the half hour. Time was not important to him just then. What mattered was that he should achieve complete surprise. The window of the Baron Lansing's library would be armed against any upward attack. But it was beyond imagination that a thief could walk round two sheer walls of the house and come from above. No other spiderman in London would have looked at such a route.

Two men had tried the simple method of scaling the house front. But razor-sharp glass was set cunningly in the mortar and the pipes and ledges coated invisibly with tree-grease at a cruel height. The first man was now serving a ten-year sentence in the penal colony of Parramatta. His companion was in the hospital of Clerkenwell prison, his shattered body held in the agony of an iron brace.

Clutching the tiny crevices of the sheer wall, Stunning Joe glanced aside and saw the next window ledge almost within reach. His fingers touched it, the other hand moved to the niche vacated by the first. As his weight shifted, he snatched hand over hand and swung easily along the stone projection.

Round the next corner of the building, though at a lower level, was the library window. The room contained the Lansing emerald, and diamonds to the value of £10,000. Its other treasure was beyond price. The Shah Jehan clasp, *sarpesh* or turban-ornament of the Mogul emperors, had been seized by the British army during the sack of Delhi in 1857. How it came to be sold in Paris, or what the Baron Lansing had paid for it was a mystery. With infinite patience Stunning Joe edged his way toward such treasures as no other Bramah safe had ever held. Old Mole and Sealskin Kite, the putters-up of the robbery, had promised him it should be so.

And neither Old Mole nor Mr Kite had ever been mistaken before.

The corner of the wall posed the greatest danger, though there was a pipe running up to the gutter on the near side. Lower down the smooth metal would have a lethal smear of grease. At this height, Stunning Joe tested it with his fingers and found it clean. Gripping it with his knees, he could just see the outline of the darkened library window beyond the projection of the wall. He adjusted the canvas strap on his shoulder, feeling the weight of the small bag on his back. The thin metal frame of the jack-in-the-box and the other tools which it contained would be more than equal to any safe which Joseph Bramah could construct.

Immediately above the library was a 'blind window', a decorative relic of the days of the window tax. It was a shallow recess, matching the shape of the one beneath to complete the symmetry of the façade. Stunning Joe looked down and saw the broader stone of the sill below. He knew that to set hand or foot on it would probably be the end of him. Instead, he hung by his hands from the upper recess, then released his grip and fell. For a fraction of a second the wind roared at his ears and then the rough coping stone above the library window smacked into his hand like a blow. His other fingers stung with the coldness of torn skin, but the grip of one hand was all that he needed.

He worked with great care, though he knew that the Baron Lansing himself was at his town house in Portman Square and would not be expected at Wannock Hundred for two more days. The tiny diamond in the ring on Stunning Joe's finger took out the little square of glass above the window catch. The glass itself fell on the carpet inside without a sound. In a moment more the top half of the window glided down and the agile bony legs swung in over it, dropping to the floor of the room like a gymnast.

With the curtains open the moonlight of the clear November night was all the assistance he required. First and most important, he went to the door of the room, putting his eye to the crack and seeing that it was unlocked. He slipped off the canvas shoulder straps and took from his bag a small picklock with a hooked end. So much ingenuity was given to preventing locks being opened but closing them remained relatively simple. Stunning Joe eased the tumblers gently, one at a time, and heard the metal bolt click home under the pressure of its spring. He took a steel watch-pin and jammed it in the space where one of the tumblers had been. It would take a locksmith to move it now. Turning round, he went to work undisturbed on the safe.

The Bramah stood behind a green velvet curtain next to the Baron Lansing's desk. Old Mole had told him that much. It was the usual iron box which trusted to the weight of its bolt rather than to the strength of the mechanism. It was a job for the jack-in-the-box.

Stunning Joe took out the heavy brass stock of the instrument. Into one end he fitted a steel wedge, like the blade of a huge chisel. Into the head of the shaft at the other end went a steel lever, a foot long and an inch thick. By winding the lever round, the steel wedge was driven slowly forward with a pressure between three and four tons. Ignoring the lock, Stunning Joe applied the thin edge of the steel to the crack on the hinge side of the safe door. Kneeling at his task, the veins of his forehead contoured with exertion, he wound the steel lever like a mill-blade. There was no sound but the shrill scraping of metal. Several times he stopped for breath. Then at last he felt the door of the safe start, as one of the hinge screws jarred loose. When that happened, he knew he had won.

Patience and effort brought the screws out, one by one, each easier than the last, until the safe-door was free on that side. Stunning Joe laid the door aside and inspected the interior. There were several jewel cases in dark red or green leather and a diamond pendant in a nest of black velvet. He scooped them out and put them in a square of thick cloth.

There were half a dozen wash-leather bags of sovereigns, and he added these as well. Then he did the cloth up, like a workman's lunch, and put it in the crossed webbing of his shoulder-straps.

He was about to leave when someone rattled the china handle of the door. There was a spoken exchange between two men outside. He could not make out the words, but the tone was one of irritation rather than alarm. Their footsteps receded.

He tightened the shoulder-straps again and pulled himself out over the window frame. By standing on its wooden top he could just reach the lower ledge of the sham-window above him. And that, for Stunning Joe, was enough. It was hardly midnight. There were six or seven hours of darkness before him with no more to do than retrace his route and walk away into the Sussex lanes. As a final precaution, he released his grip with one hand and pulled out the thick cloth with its bundle of jewel cases. It was no larger than a pineapple and just as light. Gently he lobbed it out into the darkness, so that it fell into the yew hedge beside the drive. He followed the gentle parabola of its descent with his eyes, knowing that he could find the bundle again within a few seconds.

After that, it was a matter of patience and infinite care. If he should lose his hold or disturb the guardians of Wannock Hundred, at least there would be no evidence upon him. Not that Joe O'Meara had any intention of doing either. As he told himself, he was now a very rich man. Caution was the best policy. His only unease was over the Shah Jehan clasp. It was famous, repeatedly illustrated in the picture papers after its capture at Delhi. For two weeks it had even been on public display. A man could neither eat it nor sell it — except to some rummy cove who would gloat over it in secret behind his locked door.

Old Mole and Mr Kite had abler brains than his for such matters and Stunning Joe was content to leave the disposal of the heathen *sarpesh* to them.

He edged his way round to an angle of the mansion wall, where two sets of windows rose at right angles to one another. Their upper and lower ledges were as easy to him as a ladder. With a speed which any circus acrobat would have envied, he made his descent. Standing on the upper ledge of the highest coping, he sprang sideways and downwards across the right angle, catching the lower ledge of the opposite casement in his strong fingers. With hardly a pause Joe launched himself sideways again to seize the next upper ledge of the first flight of windows. Side to side, he dropped nimbly down the levels of the dressed stone, his hands finding their hold with the lightness of a cat.

At last he hung from the upper ledge of the ground-floor window, barred like a prison cell. He listened intently to satisfy himself that the house was still in silence. Not a dog barked in the stable yard. Soundlessly he dropped to the cobbles, turned with his back to the wall and listened to the quiet November night.

From the shadows of the house about six feet beyond where he stood, a figure stepped into the starlight. It had the heavy shoulders of a fighter and a tall chimney-pot hat. There was just enough light to show the ginger mutton-chop whiskers.

' 'ello, Stunning Joe,' said Sergeant Albert Samson amicably. 'Come a bit early for the house party, ain't yer? Guests isn't invited till Saturday.'

Joe O'Meara, cornered in the angle of the wall, looked desperately about him, the beaked nose and the ferret-eyes yearning for escape. But there were other figures coming out of the darkness now, half a dozen burly shapes. With the instinct of panic he turned back to the wall, leaping for the upper ledge of the barred window.

'Come on, Joseph!' said Sergeant Samson firmly. 'We ain't got all night to watch you capering about on the roof. You'll only be fetched down in the end. And I shan't half be in a wax over you!'

As though to chafe his fingers, he was kneading one set of large knuckles in the palm of the other hand. Stunning Joe turned slowly to face him.

'All right!' he said savagely.

' 'at's the boy, Joe!' Samson clipped the metal cuffs on O'Meara's wrists until they almost bit the skin. 'What *would* you a-done next?'

'I'd a-got in, most like,' said Stunning Joe quickly. 'I was just going to find a better way. 'eard there was a cove going to crack the crib tonight. Thought I'd steal a bit of a march on 'im.'

Samson laughed indulgently and turned to one of the shadowy figures who handed him the cloth bundle, which Joe had lobbed into the bushes. He clapped a friendly hand on the prisoner's shoulder.

'You ain't half a caution, my son!'

They turned him about and marched him into the kitchen of the house. Samson, Stunning Joe and three uniformed constables stood round the scrubbed pine table. There was also a tall dark man with the air of a senior clerk.

'Mr Bunker,' said Samson, for Joe's benefit. 'London Indemnity Assurance. You might a-cost his firm a penny, my lad!'

The cloth bundle was opened and its treasures spread upon the table. Bunker stooped over them, one by one. Finally he stood up, holding a dark green jewel case of polished leather.

'Just this one, sergeant,' he said sharply. 'Broken open and emptied.'

Samson's composure vanished, the blue eyes filling with deep apprehension.

'What should be in it, then, Mr Bunker?'

Bunker drew himself up with the air of an actor about to deliver the concluding lines of a melodrama.

'The Shah Jehan clasp!' he said softly.

The sense of grievance which Stunning Joe had felt ever since Samson's appearance was overwhelmed by a feeling of physical sickness.

'It can't be missing!' he squealed, frightened for the first time. 'Unless it fell out p'raps!' He was now as eager to recover the jewel as any of his captors. Bunker turned his back on Joe and addressed the explanation to Samson.

'The locked jewel cases were placed in the safe as soon as the intended robbery was heard of. The Baron Lansing has the key to the safe with him, in London. The safe was not opened again until its door was forced by the thief.'

Samson nodded and turned to Stunning Joe.

'Right, my son. Where's that bleedin' jool to?'

'Not on 'im, sarge,' said a uniformed constable helpfully.

'Where is it, Joseph?' The left palm was kneading the right-hand knuckles again.

'I never had it, Mr Samson!' said O'Meara shrilly. 'I swear I may be damned if I so much as saw it!'

Bunker and the three constables looked pointedly away.

'Don't play me up, Joseph,' said Samson gently. The bunched knuckles came up, short and fast, into the narrow stomach. There was a start and an abrupt retching sound from the handcuffed prisoner.

'Now then,' said Samson pleasantly, 'where d'you say that jool was?'

Stunning Joe, his wrists locked behind him, was bowing over the table with perspiration starting on his forehead. His words came breathlessly.

'If it ain't there now,' he said miserably, 'it never was in the safe.'

And then, to the embarrassment of the others, he began to weep silently. Samson laid a hand on his shoulder again.

'You mean, Mr Bunker ain't telling the truth? Or Baron Lansing's been having us all on?'

'I don't know, Mr Samson! I don't *know*!' There was no mistaking the abject howl of despair.

Samson sighed.

'Well then, Stunning Joseph, I'll tell you how it looks to me. I been brought all the way from the Private-Clothes Detail in Scotland Yard. And I ain't that partial to country-side, meself. What I see is all the Lansing jools locked up snug in the safe. And then, with me own eyes, I see you, going in through that window and coming out with the spon-doolicks. Course, you had a few minutes to make away with any little trinket, before you and me struck up our acquain-tance in the stable yard. That emperor's clasp, what was sworn to as being in its box before your game began, ain't anywhere to be seen. No one touched that box but you, my son.'

O'Meara made his last defiance.

'They must a-done! They bloody must!'

Samson ignored the outburst.

'I ain't got more time to waste, Joseph, seeing the grounds'll have to be searched presently. So I'll put it to you like this. When the business comes to court, who's going to be believed? Banker Lansing with more money in Pall Mall than you ever dreamt of? Or a bleedin' little thief like you?'

2

Stunning Joe gave his gaolers no trouble in the weeks before his trial at the Old Bailey sessions. Once before he had been lodged briefly in the grim neo-classical fortress of Newgate prison, next to the Central Criminal Court. They brought him in apart from the other prisoners, through the lodge, with its iron-bolted doors and window grilles. The way led along a narrow gas-lit passage, lined with the plaster death-masks of the murderers who had been hanged on the public platform outside the press yard. At the end of this was the great nave of the prison under its glass roof, five floors of cells rising on either side with their iron balustrades and spiral ladders.

He was locked into the last reception cell on ground level. Only the two condemned cells lay beyond his. The iron door slammed and the lock turned. They left him to himself in the high cramped space, the lower wall painted with green disinfectant lime, the upper half whitewashed.

From time to time he heard the shuffle of feet in the yard outside, the rattle of iron, and the warder's voice, 'Step out there! Will you step out!' Hoisting himself to the bars, he saw the slow circling of figures. These were convicted criminals, dressed in coarse brown uniform. The 'Scotch cap' covered their faces, as well as heads, leaving only two circles for the eyes. Each man was identified solely by the numbered disc sewn on the breast of the woollen tunic.

Day by day, O'Meara swore that he would not give way to despair. Old Mole and Mr Kite might do something for him. At least they would find a lawyer to present his case. There would be times when escape, or even rescue, was possible. A prison van transferring men to the hulks at Woolwich or Portland might be successfully attacked. But the memory of betrayal at Wannock Hundred and the mystery of the Shah Jehan clasp began to sour his hope.

One morning, in the week before his trial, he heard the marching tread of several warders and their rhythmic shout of 'Governor-r-r!' calling the prisoners to attention on the governor's approach. The footsteps seemed to halt outside his own door. But it was the condemned cell next to his which was opened. He heard the governor's voice reading a document to the convicted man.

'James Jacob Fowler, your case has received Her Majesty's most gracious consideration. However, the circumstances of your crime utterly preclude the possibility of mercy being extended to so hardened a criminal. You are therefore ordered for execution in fourteen days from the present, by Her Majesty's gracious command.'

There was a pause as the condemned man recovered his composure, and then a roar from him as the warders slammed the door shut.

'She can kiss my bloody bum, blast her eyes!'

It was less than ten minutes after this when two warders opened the door of Stunning Joe's cell.

'O'Meara! Consulting room! Quick-sharp!

Old Mole had got him a counsel for the trial! He followed the passageway with the warders beside him, his heart pounding at the thought that he had not been abandoned after all. As each iron gate was unlocked, its keeper shouted, 'One off!' when Joe left the near side, and then 'One on!' when he entered the next area of the prison.

The consulting room was at the centre of the administration buildings in an area of double pillars and vaults, like a cathedral crypt. The little room itself almost resembled a private chapel, with low walls to waist height and glass above. The warders could watch the lawyer and his client without hearing what passed between them.

There was a table in the room and a painted line about three feet in front of it.

'Stand on the line, prisoner!'

Stunning Joe obeyed. The warders stepped outside, watching through the glass, and the man who sat at the table looked up.

'It won't do, Joseph,' said Sergeant Samson sadly. 'It really won't do at all.'

'You stinking jack! You got no right coming here! I want a brief!'

He started forward to the table and the warders stepped to the door. But Samson waved them away.

'You couldn't have a better brief than me, Joseph. I'm the only one left who could say a good word.'

'Much chance!'

'You think I come about that trick of the Shah Jehan clasp? So I have. I want to know, Joseph. I do. But I never come empty-handed. I got a present for you. The name of the party who gave your game away.'

Stunning Joe swallowed and the little eyes fastened expectantly on Samson.

'You were bouncing a little trollop called Vicki Hartle,' said Samson cheerily. 'Cigar divan and oriental massage, off Haymarket. After you went down Sussex way, Miss Vicki prigged a toff's watch and notecase. Turned out to be Inspector Garvey, over "C" Division. Anyway, Vicki being lined up for a real smacking from the beak, she lays out the goods on you at Wannock Hundred. Garvey let her go.'

'She never!'

'I got no cause to lie to you, Joseph. 'ow else d'you think I happened to be there?'

'The damned bitch!'

'Yes, Joseph. Now, in course, you'll want Vicki Hartle's hide off her. If we was to find that heathen clasp before your trial came on, why you might be able to knock Miss Vicki one side of Haymarket to t'other in seven years. P'raps five. But if you will be obstinate, my son. I'd say that little whore won't get her licks for another fifteen years.'

'I never *seen* any bloody clasp, Mr Samson!'

'Then tell us who might have done. 'oo put you up to it, Joe?'

But now they were back to the rules of a game which O'Meara knew well.

'I can't say no more, Mr Samson, nor I won't.'

Samson released a long breath.

'All right, Joseph. Let it be. Any last words for Vicki Hartle, then? 'ere, they reckon Mr Garvey was prodding her when she took his things! Still, you know what minds them jacks down "C" Division got!'

As Stunning Joe lunged vainly at his tormentor, the warders threw open the door and dragged him away. Alone in his cell, he wept with the misery of his plight.

Sergeant Samson predicted the outcome well. One morning in the following week, Joe O'Meara was put up in the dock of the Central Criminal Court for trial and sentence. From his vantage point he looked down into the well of the little court, the wigs of counsel and clerks below him. Opposite him, the elderly judge, red-faced in robes and wig looked, for all the world, like a little old lady. Somewhere above his head was the public gallery, which he detected only by the smell of orange peel, the rattle of nutshells, and an occasional buzz of conversation. He doubted that there were any faces there which he knew, though he was in no position to see.

In any case, his trial was of little public interest. There was no chance of an acquittal, no thrill of suspense as to the outcome. Only once was the murmuring in the gallery stilled, when the judge, with the royal arms of England on red leather behind him, looked up to pass sentence. Stunning Joe heard the thin judicial voice deploring the accused's hardened and unrepentant attitude. None of this concerned O'Meara. He listened only for the final words, when they came. 'Transportation to a penal colony for a term of fourteen years.'

The murmuring in the public gallery began again, and the two warders took him down the steps of the dock. The trial had barely lasted ten minutes.

So far, Stunning Joe had resisted even the thought of winning favour by betraying Old Mole and Sealskin Kite. Now it was too late for that. Mr Kite was an astute old exchange broker with no criminal record. Any attempt to accuse him at this stage must be dismissed as the last desperate falsehood of a condemned felon. In a few days more, Joe O'Meara and the other transportees would be taken down to the prison hulks in Portland harbour. From there a contractor's vessel with armed guard would convey them to the prison depot at Port Jackson, Australia. A man might live through fourteen years of privation and brutality, but he knew it was not likely.

Two days after the trial, a pair of escort warders opened his cell again.

'O'Meara! Visitors' corridor!'

In his coarse brown uniform he glanced at them suspiciously.

' 'oo'd want to visit me?'

'Parish priest,' said one of the officers sharply. 'One visit you're allowed. This is it.'

He walked between them, not understanding. He had no parish priest. The last Irish O'Meara had been his grandfather, who had found his way to Southwark thirty years before. Certainly he had not expected a prison visit from anyone.

The visitors' corridor was about four feet wide with grilles down either side of it. Prisoner and visitor faced one another through meshed windows, separated by the width of the corridor in which the warders stood, listening to each conversation. Stunning Joe peered across at his visitor, making out first the cassock and biretta, then the plump pale face. For the only time since his arrest, he almost laughed. Now he guessed that Mr Kite had not forgotten him.

The figure beyond the other grille was 'Soapy Samuel', nicknamed after a man whom Joe understood to be a famous bishop. Soapy Samuel's speciality was that of posing as a clergyman — generally of the Church of England — and collecting at the doors of middle-class homes for non-existent overseas missions. Samuel was a past-master in deception, with solemn owlish face, unctuous voice, the dry-washing of the hands, in an impressively realistic performance. With episcopal cross and gaiters, he had effortlessly lightened an archdeacon of twenty-five guineas on two occasions.

As a Roman priest, he was less convincing. Stunning Joe, taken aback by the vision before him, spoke as though the warders could not hear him.

24

'What the hell might you be doing here?'

'My son!' said Samuel, gently reproving. 'While yet of mortal breath, seek to repent your crime. Such is the message I bring.'

The tongue licked over the fat lips, the sole indicator of Samuel's nervousness in the prison confines. Stunning Joe furrowed his brow, knowing that Soapy Samuel must have come on Kite's errand, seeking some message in the fatuous platitudes.

'Remember,' said Samuel, 'that you are now to expiate your offence. You must do so with a glad heart. You will — at all times — obey implicitly, without question, the orders of those put in command of you. That is now your first and most important instruction. Do you understand me?'

'Yes — father,' said Stunning Joe. If this was the best that Mr Kite could do, he had better have kept his money in his pocket.

'We are taught,' said Samuel woefully, 'that man must die to live again. Take that message to your heart, my son, for it is the good news I bring you from one who cares for us all.'

O'Meara took the message to heart and glared uncomprehendingly across the space where the warder stood.

'And thus,' droned Samuel, 'shall you be reunited at last with your loved ones, and with those who have been your friends in the past.'

'You tell my friends I ain't forgot 'em!' said Stunning Joe sullenly. 'Specially I ain't forgot my young person!'

Samuel nodded gently.

'Sorrow and repentance will be hers to share, my son. There is one who watches over such matters.'

O'Meara's eyes brightened.

'Supposing I could have confession?' he said hopefully. The warder roused himself.

'Confessions to be heard by Her Majesty's prison chaplains only,' he said. 'No disrespect to your reverence.'

Soapy Samuel nodded.

'A very proper arrangement. And now, Joseph O'Meara, I leave you in good hands. Think of my words, and seek to throw off the bonds of sin.'

It was evident that Samuel had no clear idea of the proper pastoral procedure for a Roman priest in this situation. He began to make a sign in the air, thought better of it, stood up and turned away. The warders led Stunning Joe back to his cell.

For two more days he lay on the wooden bunk and thought of Soapy Samuel's words. Obeying those in authority. It needed no visit to remind him of that. Dying to be born again was an easy cant term which meant nothing to him. He had every intention of being reunited with his friends but, he thought, they had better be quick about it. The one certain comfort was that Sealskin Kite knew of his betrayal by a young bitch called Vicki Hartle. And Mr Kite was a hard man in such business.

At last the iron tiers of the cell echoed to the warders' shouts of 'Lags away!' and the time had come for the transportees to leave. Stunning Joe's wrists were handcuffed before him and a pair of steel manacles was locked on his ankles. The steel was much lighter than he had imagined it would be, enabling him to move at a shuffling walk. The line of men, like a file of sinister monks in their brown uniforms and caps with eye-holes, moved slowly across the yard. The prison van which was to take them to the train at Waterloo was like a black hearse.

As the van lurched and jolted over the paved roads, Joe O'Meara waited for the sudden halt and the thunder of wooden staves on the doors, which would signal his rescue. But at Waterloo the doors opened and the prisoners, now linked in pairs by chains between their fetters, moved slowly towards the carriage which had been attached to the waiting train. They occupied every compartment of it, with two warders to each felon. Many hours later the long journey ended under a barn-like structure covering both railway tracks and the platforms on either side. It was the new station at Weymouth.

Another van carried them out along the narrow Portland isthmus, the great sweep of Chesil Bank curving away to the north-west. Stunning Joe caught a glimpse of blue water glittering in the summer evening. For the first time he realised the change of seasons which had passed during his months of confinement in the unvarying gloom of Newgate.

The long-boats were waiting at Portland quay. A file of warders armed with rifles marked the way. In the semi-circle of the great harbour lay the rotting fleet of hulks. These were the old wooden warships of Nelson's navy. With their rigging cut away, their hulls anchored by rusty mooring chains, they lay like grim and diseased symbols of retribution.

In groups of six the new prisoners were helped down into the long-boats, the oars manned by good-conduct prisoners under the guns of the warders. Two weeks more and the new arrivals would be transferred to the hired transports, with not even a glimpse of the great limestone rock of Portland to remind them of their country.

There was a shout of 'Oars away!' and the blades cut the harbour swell with smart precision. Stunning Joe listened to the ripple of the water and the rhythmic creak of the wooden locks. Ahead of him, dripping with weed and encrusted by shells, the hulk of the old 74-gun *Indomitable* rose like black doom, blotting out the evening sky. He saw now that Soapy Samuel had been used to keep him sweet. Surely, Sealskin Kite had forgotten him after all.

A TAME JACK

3

In the hot July morning there was a stillness over the narrow pavements and the dingy shops of Trafalgar Street. The road ran upward like a canyon between high rendered walls to the dark tunnel of the iron bridge which carried Queens Road overhead from the railway station towards the sea. Beyond the glass-roofed splendour of the platforms with their cast-iron pillars, a dozen engines were coaled-up in the yard, high above the level of the little street. In a few hours more, they would return to London with the excursion trains which offered 'Brighton and back for three shillings and sixpence'.

The noon silence which hung like a cloud over the cheap summer lodgings and homes above the shops was shrilly broken. First there was a burst of song from the caged birds on the wall outside one of the shops. Black painted letters on the stonework promised: 'Foreign and British Song Birds. Parrots. Canaries. Nightingales.'

The cause of the disturbance was a pair of ragged boys in torn coats and shabby caps pulled down almost to their eyes. One of them was bouncing an india-rubber ball as they ran out of a side street and up towards the dark iron tunnel of the station bridge. Just before the archway of the bridge a more imposing shop with a painted board announced that Mr Suitor's Emporium 'respectfully solicits an inspection of spring and summer modes'.

Silks and taffeta with wide sleeves and gold buckles shone in the darker interior beyond the glass. On the pavement outside a row of wax dummies was paraded in the latest male fashions. Some had the faces of young gentlemen, gloved fingers stuck out like bunches of radishes, the wax limbs draped in long Oxonian coats, baggy Sydenham trousers, Talma capes and fancy vests. Beyond these figures of fashion were several stouter effigies of countrymen, whose suits were matched by red plush waistcoats and wide-awake hats. At the far end were the figures of young women in servants' costume or the new 'riding trousers'.

The two ragged boys drew level with the open doorway of Mr Suitor's Emporium. The one who was bouncing the rubber ball gave it a vigorous slanting pat. With a long bound, the ball disappeared through the opening among the contents of the shop itself. Their caps well down, the youngsters ran after it. In a moment more the shopman and his assistant were intent on finding the ball themselves and preventing the boys from rifling the contents of the shop during their search.

With hardly a sound another pair of boys, ragged as the first two, ran out from the opposite turning. They moved with their heads kept down, as if below the line of vision of the occupants in the shop. They began at one end of the row of dummies, their quick fingers unbuttoning and stripping off the clothes. Two of the Talma capes came away, then one of the Oxonian coats. Because of their lightness it was easy enough to turn the dummies up and strip off the trousers too. Even if the shopmen had seen them, Mr Suitor's dilemma was pitiful. Either he could remain to guard the valuable silks or go out to prevent the stripping of the dummies. It was impossible that he and his assistant could do both.

Two more boys ran out into Trafalgar Street from the same turning. Those who were bundling up the dummies' clothes now lobbed the bundles back along the line of what appeared to be a human chain. Coats, trousers, capes and fancy waistcoats passed down the road with incredible dexterity, then turned the corner and were lost to sight.

Inside the shop, the two boys who were searching for

their rubber ball dived here and there, overturning the piles of folded silk, knocking the rolls of worsted to the floor. Suitor and his man struggled to hold them as a female dummy in the shop itself fell across the counter and broke into several pieces. But the lads were far too nimble for the outstretched arms of the men. Ducking and dodging, the ragged boys seemed less intent on finding their ball or even robbing the shop than on creating havoc with its contents.

Little Billy, the leader of the chain of boys outside had denuded four of the dummies when Mr Suitor looked up and gave a cry of anguish. But it was better to suffer the pavement robbery than to leave the other pair of boys to smash everything in the shop itself. However, he went so far as to stand in the doorway and utter a shrill cry for help to the world at large. At this, one of the boys in the shop leapt upon his back, clamping Suitor's arms to his sides. Little Billy, turning from the dummy upon which he was engaged, then kicked the proprietor deftly between the legs.

'Stash yer gab!' he yapped in his harsh treble voice.

With Suitor groaning in despair as he supported himself over the counter, and his assistant wringing his hands in token of abject surrender, Little Billy and his ragged boys worked with great thoroughness along the pavement. Billy had finished the section of dummies which represented smiling young gentlemen and was now beginning on their stouter country cousins. The first of these was a plump effigy of a well-covered man in frock-coat and tall hat. Its round red face was ornamented by black moustaches, waxed at the tips, the black hair beneath the hat itself flattened for neatness.

Little Billy looked down to the button which held the frock-coat across the broad midriff. His nimble fingers began to free it. Then, to his dismay, the dummy's hand clamped itself like the collar of the pillory round the back of his neck. The effigy spoke.

'Right, my lad!' it said. 'You done your thieving for today!'

Billy attempted to struggle but he felt himself lifted bodily in a pair of brawny arms. Sergeant Verity, as though holding a mere baby, handed him to the uniformed figure of Constable Meiklejohn who now stepped out of the corner beyond the Emporium. Wrenching himself round in Meiklejohn's arms, Little Billy bawled a desperate warning to the other ragged boy who had been stripping the dummies with him.

'Run Todger! It's the bloody law!'

Todger looked up from his preoccupation with wrenching a pair of Sydenham trousers off the legs of an upturned wax figure. What he saw was the stalwart figure of Sergeant Verity, fixing him with a scowl of disapproval. And then Verity took a strange little stick from the capacious pocket of his private-clothes frock-coat. Attached to the stick was a flat square of wood. Still scowling, he raised the stick above his head, twirled the wood rapidly and set up a raucous grinding sound with it. Todger knew the sound only too well. Verity had sprung his rattle.

Dropping the bundle of Sydenham trousers, Todger sprinted away down Trafalgar Street like a champion, driving the rest of the human chain before him. Verity positioned himself, glowering, in the doorway of Mr Suitor's Emporium. His bulk effectively blocked the escape of the two ragged boys who had gone in there after their ball. One behind the other, they now charged at his belly with heads lowered.

What might have seemed like blubber proved to be solid muscle. The first boy appeared to bounce straight back, losing his footing and tripping over a bale of silk. The second one ran his nose and mouth against the hard base of Verity's palm as the sergeant handed him off. Both got to their feet, swaying dizzily from the impacts.

Without a word, Verity strode forward. He jerked the two youths upward by the scruffs of their necks, holding them off the floor. Next, as though they weighed nothing at all, he held each of them to one side of him at arm's length. Only then did his face grow a deeper red with exertion, as he brought the two dangling boys together. Their two heads, each bowed by the way he held them, met with a crack that was audible in the street outside. When he dropped them, they remained cowering on the floor. Verity took a step backward.

'Right, Constable Meiklejohn!' he called. 'In 'ere! Two sets o' handcuffs and a truncheon just for safety's sake.'

Leaving Meiklejohn to deal with the disorder in the shop itself, he went out into the street again. The last of Little Billy's human chain was disappearing round the corner of the side street, Todger bringing up the rear. It was precisely as he had expected, and he knew that he had sprung his rattle at the required moment. Just as Todger and the last of the young thieves reached the corner, they paused, jigged uncertainly on one leg for an instant, and then turned about. Todger and his followers were pelting back in a rout towards the Emporium. Their forearms worked like pistons in an effort to gain more speed.

The cause of this change in direction was not yet in sight, but Verity could hear the heavy boots of the uniformed men, whom he had positioned behind a door in Tidy Street. Six of them rounded the corner, stalwart figures in belted tunics with truncheons drawn. At Verity's call, he and Meiklejohn stepped into the roadway, cutting off the retreat of Todger and his companions.

After that it was almost routine. Several of the ragged boys stopped running and gave themselves up. Most of the rest had hesitated for too long on seeing Verity and Meiklejohn in their path. Before they could recover their wits, the uniformed men had overtaken them. With wrists handcuffed behind their backs, they stared dumbly at the scene of their defeat.

Only Todger fought on. He came towards Verity at a run, ducking and weaving, though avoiding the error of trying to

knock his adversary down. Verity lunged at him, but
Todger was under his arm and sprinting away up Trafalgar
Street towards the dark iron bridge and the station. Within
minutes he would be lost in the crowds, perhaps even on his
way back to the Lambeth slums from which the gang had set
out at dawn.

Verity and two uniformed men plodded after him up the
hill. But Todger was far nimbler and had a good start.

'Stop, thief!' Verity bellowed after him. Todger was running along the pavement past the Emporium. As though to
impede his pursuers still further, he was knocking down the
wax dummies as he passed. Under the feet of Verity and his
men, the slope of the street began to fill with rolling limbs
and trunks.

All the dummies stripped by the thieves were down. Just
ahead of Todger were those still displaying female fashions.
The first of these was a striking example of portraiture. Its
profile had the golden enigmatic beauty of Pharonic funeral
sculpture, a fine arch of brows above expressionless eyes.
The gloss of scented hair was drawn back in an elegant coif-
fure from the line of the forehead and nose. In casting the
figure the artist had given it a straight back and narrow
waist, of the best fashion, underemphasising the breasts and
making the thighs firm and trim. His only erotic licence appeared to be in a certain tight cheekiness of the rump. The
result was displayed in a linen blouse and a pair of close-
fitting American riding trousers made of pale blue cotton.

Todger had no time to appreciate such details. He raced
up the pavement, making no further effort to delay his pursuers by throwing down the models displayed. As he approached the female effigy, the beautiful eyes under their
fine brows looked quickly in his direction and were still
again almost at once. It was only when he sprinted past the
warm-skinned figure that Miss Jolly thrust a neat foot between his own, and Todger went sprawling into the gutter.

Even then the hunt was not over. Picking himself up,

Todger pounded onward. If anything, his lead over Verity
and the other officers was increasing. But Jolly was close
behind him. Though the American riding trousers were
tighter, they were better suited to running than skirts would
have been. More to the point, Todger and his pursuers were
far more winded than she. So long as she ran, as if walking,
with a tight little swagger of her hips, the young thief would
gain on her. Abandoning decorum, she began to stride out.
After a few steps the shoddy stitching burst and the seam of
the breeches opened with the rhythm of her steps in a smooth
golden smile across the seat of the garments. The sun caught
this warm silken texture of skin. By now even the uniformed
men who had retired winded were taking heart once more.
Open-mouthed and eager-eyed, they set off once again, racing after their youthful quarry.

It was not to be expected that the girl could match
Todger's strength. Instead she kept pace just behind him,
waiting keen-eyed as a cat for his first error of judgement. It
came when his foot slipped backward on a cobble through
sheer fatigue. He might have regained his balance, but Jolly
was too quick for him. A deft two-handed push to one side
sent Little Billy's lieutenant sprawling for the last time.

Ten minutes later the dark shape of the police van turned
into Trafalgar Street from York Place. Verity had assembled
Meiklejohn, the six other uniformed constables and Miss
Jolly. Handcuffed and dejected, Little Billy, Todger and
eight juvenile accomplices were put aboard the Black Maria.
The six Brighton constables and Miss Jolly went with them,
Verity and Meiklejohn walking behind.

Only then did the man who had watched the entire inci-
dent from the dark tunnel of the iron bridge move from the
shadows, walking in the opposite direction. A thoughtful
scowl marked the set of his features. Contrary to this appearance, Old Mole was unusually pleased by the events which
he had just witnessed.

*　　*　　*

Meiklejohn, like Verity, was an officer of the Private-Clothes Detail from Whitehall Police Office, Scotland Yard. He, too, had once been a sergeant. But then there had been an unfortunate matter of grievous bodily harm inflicted on a member of the public during a raid on a brothel in Langham Place. Thanks to the complaints of a tall blonde whore, Helen Jacoby, he was now a mere constable again. But in his private conversation with Verity, as they walked back through the warm Brighton streets, he showed an easy sense of equality.

'You sure it's right?' he asked for the twentieth time. 'Using a young bitch like Jolly? She's thieved, she's whored, she's perjured herself. If I was to pick myself a copper's nark, she'd be last in the list.'

Verity set his tall hat more firmly on his head, patted his moist cheeks with a spotted handkerchief and blew the ends of his moustaches with the effect of summer heat.

'Trustworthy, Mr Meiklejohn,' he said smugly. 'I'd vouch for her — word and deed.'

He gave the dreamy smile of a high-flyer on seeing a sinner brought to redemption.

'P'raps you would,' said Meiklejohn sceptically, ' 'cept she could have my neck in a rope as well as yours, if you happen to be wrong. What's she ever done but sing Queen's evidence a couple of times to save her own pretty skin?'

'Saw the error of her ways, Mr Meiklejohn,' said Verity firmly. 'Twice she gave information regarding Lieutenant Verney Dacre and his deeds of darkness. Railway gold robbery here and the matter o' the American mint in Philadelphia. That's repentance, Mr Meiklejohn!'

'Only when Mr Dacre tanned Miss Jolly's bare backside with his pony-switch!' said Meiklejohn sourly. 'Repentance be buggered!'

'All different now, Mr Meiklejohn. 's all different now.'

'Blessed if I see how.'

They passed under the cast-iron colonnade of the Theatre

Royal in New Road, the oriental onion domes of the Royal
Pavilion rising like a fairy palace beyond the lawns. Verity
paused to read a theatre bill, advertising *The Colleen Bawn*.
Then he turned magisterially to his companion.

'Law of 1838, Mr Meiklejohn. That's what's different.'

'Law of *what*?'

'Conditional pardon. That's what Jolly got for all her
crimes. Means she don't serve time in gaol but commits herself to an institution for the reformation of offenders. But she
got to stay there the rest of her sentence, keep its rules and
take its punishments. Any running off or contrariness to her
keepers and it's back to gaol again. The whole sentence
begins again from the first day, as if she'd never started it. I
think you'll find her trustworthy.'

'But Jolly ain't in an institution.'

'She was till a few weeks since.'

'Where?'

'Mrs Rouncewell's Hygienic Steam Laundry, down Elephant and Castle. Old police-matron Rouncewell. Cor, the
rules she got there!' Verity chortled at the enormity of it.
'Brimstone and birch-rod for sneezing out of tune! Sergeant
Samson goes down one day and Jolly keeps on desperate to
him. Swears she can't stand another seeing to from Ma
Rouncewell. On her knees she begs to be took for a copper's
nark if the justices 'll approve. And so she was. Mind you,
Mrs R. took on something awful about it. Said she was just
getting a taste for the little piece.'

'And you trust Jolly on account of all that?' Meiklejohn's
freckled face was contorted with anxiety.

Verity chuckled again as they turned into Market Street,
the summer tide sparkling beyond the fish-stalls.

'Not just that, Mr Meiklejohn. Mind you, one little
naughtiness and it's back to the female penitentiary at Millbank to start her time again from the first day. But there's
more, o' course. When robbery is prevented or goods recovered, like today, shops and insurance companies can be

unaccountable generous. You and me can't take such rewards, being officers of the law. But Jolly can. I saw Mr Suitor slip her a guinea or two this morning.'

'I saw him slip a hand in them riding trousers of hers,' said Meiklejohn sceptically. Verity ignored the innuendo.

'Reward hunter,' he said smugly. 'Copper's nark and reward hunter. That's Miss Jolly from now on. She ain't no cause to kick against the pricks.'

'Do *what*?'

Verity stopped in mid-stride and glowered at his companion.

'Mr Meiklejohn, you ain't a Scripture-read man, o' course. Nor you ain't a man that studies much at all. All things considered, there's a lot you might do to improve yer mind!'

And then, seeing that they were almost at the Town Hall, where the detail was based, he strode forward with military precision, eyes glaring and fists swinging shoulder-high, like the soldier he had once been.

The day ended quite as well as it had begun. Verity and Jolly were walking separately along Kings Road, as though unknown to one another. In her pink silk dress the straight-backed beauty moved with her habitual tight little swagger. To one side of them, beyond the promenade rail, the bottle-green afternoon sea rolled towards the graceful ironwork of the Chain Pier and the pale cliffs beyond. Ahead of them walked a tall, pale man, dressed in an expensive black suit with a mourning-band round his silk hat. Under the hat brim there was a glimpse of crisp blond curls. He turned the corner into Ship Street, and Jolly followed him.

By the time that Verity reached the corner, the young man had disappeared. But Jolly was standing helpfully outside number 34, the shop of Mr Ellis, whose board advertised Romford Ales and Golden Sherry. Verity hurried down the street and peered through the window. The young man had made his purchase, a bottle had been wrapped for him, and he was about to pay. It was time to enter the premises. Verity, with the girl behind him, pushed open the door and stood back from the wooden counter as if waiting his turn.

The young gentleman handed a gold sovereign to the shopman who, as a matter of habit, spun it on the wooden counter to see that it rang true. Satisfied, he dropped it in the till, then counted out the change: a half sovereign, which he also spun for the customer's satisfaction, and eight shillings in silver. The young gentleman was about to pocket the money when he seemed to have second thoughts. He handed back the half sovereign to the shopman.

'Let me have silver,' he said airily. 'There's a good fellow.'

The shopman took the half sovereign and counted out ten shillings in change. Verity stepped forward.

'Oh dear, oh dear, Mary Ann! You done it this time, ain't yer?'

The young gentleman spun round and the shopman looked up uncomprehendingly.

' 's all right,' said Verity to the man behind the counter. 'He's called Mary Ann up and down Haymarket. 'Cos of his way of walking and all that. He just caught you with the old twining dodge, sir.'

He showed his warrant-card to the shopman, who shook his head dumbly, the plump comfortable jowls shaking like dewlaps. Mary Ann began to move his hand to his pocket but Miss Jolly was too quick with him. With a dark avaricious gleam in her eyes she sprang forward and sank her neat little teeth into the fleshy junction of forefinger and thumb. A half sovereign fell to the floor as Mary Ann gave a shrill cry and his silk hat tumbled off.

'Cross-eyed little trollop!'

'Oh dear, oh dear,' said Verity humorously. He stooped to pick up the fallen coin, still barring Mary Ann's path to the shop door. 'P'raps, sir, you'd have the goodness to spin your half-sov on that counter again.'

The shopman dropped the little coin which now made a dull wooden sound.

'It's different!' he said with plump astonishment.

Verity chuckled again.

'Course it is, sir. That's the twining dodge! Mary Ann comes in with a real sov and a dud half-sov in his palm. You give him change for the sov including a real half-sov. He thinks better of it, asks you for silver, hands you back your own half-sov. You don't try it to see if it rings true. Why should you? You only just give it him yourself. Only, o' course, it ain't your coin but the dud that he's had in his palm. Right then, Mary Ann, p'raps we'll just try your size in bracelets, shall we?'

The shopman took in Verity's explanation slowly as the handcuffs went on the young man's wrists.

'I never heard of such a thing!' he said indignantly.

'You have now, sir,' said Verity reassuringly. 'There's a dozen other shops in Brighton reported slum coins being passed in the last couple of days. Being from London, I twigged it as Mary Ann's little caper. He's down here for the races really — or was — that's when he passes them by the hundred. He was just keeping in practice with you. Wasn't you, Mary Ann?'

He clapped the silk hat back on the young man's shaken curls. The shopman came round the counter, the full extent of his obligation clear to him at last. He grasped Verity's hand.

'My dear sir!' he said clutching the hand tighter. 'I am most inexpressibly indebted to you and to this dear brave young lady!'

From the shadows of the counter, Miss Jolly's odalisque eyes watched him with feline expectancy.

'Whatever I may do in return,' the shopman continued earnestly, 'only name it!'

'Nothing for me, sir,' said Verity firmly. 'A man ain't to be rewarded for doing his duty. However, I shall leave that young woman to your own generous instincts.'

'Who has destituted herself in the cause of justice,' said Jolly's lilting soprano from the counter.

The shopman returned to his till. His plump hand descended on Miss Jolly's nimble fingers with a chink of coin. He coloured self-consciously as he whispered quickly into her ear. Verity marched the tall pale figure of Mary Ann out into the street.

As the culprit and escort disappeared toward the Market Street lock-up, Old Mole turned from his furtive contemplation of the Ship Street vintners. In the sallow face the yellowed mouth now hung open in an almost dog-like expression of good humour. At the turning into Kings Road he so far forgot himself as to drop sixpence into the hands of a little beggar-girl who had come up from her knot of companions on the warm shingle.

The six men of the Private-Clothes Detail on summer detachment were paraded in the little yard to one side of the Town Hall with its pillared Grecian façade. Inspector Swift, their senior officer, addressed them as they stood at attention in tall hats and long belted tunics. Swift was a large Irishman, the favourite senior man.

'It is my pleasant task,' he said, 'to pass on to you a message forwarded to me by His Worship the Mayor, on behalf of the shopkeepers of Brighton. These gentlemen wish to express their admiration and gratitude for the manner in which you men of the detail have dealt with the enemies of law. The arrest of the youthful conspirators in Trafalgar Street and the apprehension of a notorious coiner are dramatic examples of your success. In consequence of the posting of your detachment in Brighton for the summer season, the incidence of crime committed is now lower than at any time in the past five years.'

Verity felt his face glow with the pleasure of hearing his

achievements recognised at last. But he was soon aware that the Inspector had passed on to another topic.

'Following certain arrangements to be made for the Volunteer Review in Hyde Park,' said Swift carefully, 'I shall be returning to London in a day or two. I shall be replaced as your commanding officer by Inspector Croaker, with whom you are all familiar.'

Even in the silence it was possible to sense the gloom which settled upon the six men.

'Rot his bloody liver!' gasped Meiklejohn from the corner of his mouth.

'Silence on parade!' said Swift sharply. 'You will, I know, extend to Mr Croaker that same sense of duty and obedience which you have shown to me. I am confident that by your diligence and application, under the command of so experienced an officer, you will continue to bring credit to the detail. Parade dismissed!'

4

'Come down, O Love Divine!' sang Verity lustily. 'Seek Thou this so-o-ul of mine! And visit it with Thine own ardour glo-o-wing!'

He stood in the gallery of the Countess of Huntingdon's chapel in North Street, among the superior servants. Below, in the main body of the building, was gathered Brighton nonconformity in its Sunday morning silks and suitings.

'O let it freely burn! Till earthly passions turn, to dust and ashes in its heat consu-u-ming!'

Around him several of the other occupants of the wooden gallery glanced at the bull-necked, red-faced figure, a scowl of determination on his brow as he thundered out the old Methodist tune. The power of his lungs was sufficient to cause one or two of the well-dressed figures below to look up apprehensively at the din overhead.

In a row, along the wooden bench, were the other members of his little family. By common agreement they had exchanged the shabby house in Paddington Green for lodgings in Tidy Street during his Brighton detachment. At the far end was old Cabman Stringfellow, his toothless mouth opening and closing in imitation of the tune as he supported himself on the wooden leg which had served him since the loss of his own at the siege of Bhurtpore in 1823. As he protested, he was not really a church-going man. But his son-in-law's righteous insistence had driven the old man into compliance.

Next to Verity was the plump blonde figure of his beloved wife Bella, the only child of widower Stringfellow. Between them stood little Ruth, a sixteen-year-old maid-of-all-work. The softness of her figure and her crop of fair curls made her seem almost like Bella's younger sister. Her attractively solemn little face with its wide brown eyes was cast bashfully down to the hymn book. Neither of the women sang. Bella held four-year-old William Verity against her knees while Ruth nursed his two-year-old sister Vicky.

Verity himself needed no hymn book. The great Wesleyan hymns of his Cornish childhood were secure in his memory. Even the Calvinism of the Huntingdon connection was falling before them. This one was what his father used to call a strong man's tune, and Verity loved every note of it. 'Let holy charity, mine outward vesture be!' he bawled. 'And lowliness become mine inner clothing!'

Presently it was over and the preaching of the Reverend Mr Figgis took its place. Verity listened with a frown of honest perplexity. Cabman Stringfellow fidgeted briefly until nudged by his daughter. Then he leant forward with an expression of open-mouthed anticipation, as though he had been in the balcony of Mr Astley's circus awaiting the entrance of the tumblers and acrobats.

Then they were standing again, and Verity launched himself into the final hymn.

'Away with our sorrow and fear! We soon shall recover our home!'

The necks of those in front seemed to incline forward, as if in anticipation of the coming blast.

'The city of saints shall appear! The day of eternity come!'

For his own day of eternity he would have been quite content to thunder out the great hymns of the Whitsuntide revival with Bella and the others at his side. Beyond that, his expectations were of a city walled with jasper and gold where those who were now lost to one another would be reunited in something like a great wedding breakfast. It never occurred to him that it could be otherwise.

For the moment, he luxuriated in righteousness. If he pitied more earthly comrades like Sergeant Samson with their flash-tails and shady acquaintances, it was because they never knew such joy and satisfaction as his. As he looked about him it seemed absurd that men should make such bother over their rights to choose gentlemen for parliament. He saw instead a great crusade with Methodism for its banner and the majestic hymns of the Wesleys as its marching songs. Before it, surely the power of the squirearchy and the established church would be broken at last.

When it was all over for another week, he stood outside in the noon sunlight. As he shepherded Bella and the others through the crowd on the pavement, his hand in his pocket touched a pasteboard card and he frowned.

The card had come to the Tidy Street lodgings two days before, in an envelope addressed to him.

THE GREAT LAVENGRO
Clairvoyant and Astrologer Royal
to the Crowned Heads of Europe
has the honour to request the presence of:

A TAME JACK

William Clarence Verity, Esq.
for a complimentary consultation
Sunday the 14th of July at 3.

Signor Lavengro's parlour stands
twenty yards west of the Chain Pier.
NB *A prompt attendance will oblige.*

Verity's first impulse had been to tear up the invitation with a sense of disapproval that such pastimes should be permitted upon a Sunday afternoon. It was Bella who had urged him to accept.

'Don't be so narrow, Mr Verity! Go on! 's only fun!'

But when he had yielded to her argument, it was not out of any desire for fun. Sunday or not, his curiosity was prompted. Why should the Great Lavengro, from his tented booth by the pier, bother to send such an invitation to *him*? He would go, he told himself, not with any genial sense of sport but with the trained suspicion of a detective policeman.

The Verity family turned out of Black Lion Street and walked ceremoniously along the flagstones above the shingle beach. At their head strode Verity himself, his rusty frock-coat brightened by a new red cravat. His plump face glowing under the brim of the tall hat, he walked as if on parade. Beside him, in her blue crinoline, was Bella, endeavouring to restrain young Billy Verity. Behind her was Ruth, the round little face under the crop of fair curls seeming solemn as ever. She was carrying little Vicky, though starting from time to time as though touched about the waist and neck. At the rear lolloped Stringfellow on his wooden leg. Verity noticed that from time to time Bella glanced back at Ruth's sudden movements. He himself had deep moral misgivings as to the precise feelings of old Stringfellow for the sixteen-year-old maid-of-all-work. Indeed, he had already tasted Bella's anger at his first attempt to suggest the undesirability

47

of allowing her father and Ruth to occupy adjoining attic rooms.

The bright green sea stretched glassily away in the still, languorous afternoon. Hardly a ripple seemed to break upon the shingle below them. Gulls hovered and dipped, as if to frustrate the aim of young men in boats whose guns pop-popped at them. On Sunday the bathing machines were deserted and most of the yachts drawn up on the shingle, like fish on a slab. Only the *Victoria and Albert* and the *Honeymoon* were afloat with their white sails hoisted and their groups of giggling passengers. A party of young women on bay and piebald hacks cantered along the firm sand below the shingle. The girls wore gold and silver beaded nets over their shining hair, with multi-coloured feathers in their jaunty little hats.

Despite the width of the promenade, the ballooning crinolines made it seem as impassable as the Haymarket or Regent Circus. The men in peg-top trousers and coloured coats appeared dowdy by contrast with the majestic shape of their women under full sail. Presently, Verity became aware that the tit-tupping of Stringfellow's wooden leg had stopped. He turned and saw the old cabman some way behind them. Stringfellow, open-mouthed and intent, was engaged in conversation with a plump, expensively-dressed man. Verity noticed the cabman's face set in an expectant grin. His hand came up, palm uppermost, and the expensive gentleman dropped a small gold coin into it. Stringfellow ducked politely and touched his forehead. Then he caught up the others.

'Pa!' said Bella furiously. 'How *could* you?'

'Asked if I was a sojer,' said Stringfellow defensively. 'Asked what me reg'ment was. Where I lorst me leg. Told 'im how we rode at Bhurtpore. Give me 'alf a sov! Look!'

'It don't excuse!' said Bella haughtily. She turned her back and they walked on. Stringfellow hummed to himself, as if to show how trivial the misunderstanding had been.

At five minutes to three the Great Lavengro's booth looked forlorn and deserted. It stood upon the bare stretch of sand by the long suspension-work of the Chain Pier, tall and narrow like a tent from a medieval crusade. Its canvas striped vertically in yellow and red, the booth seemed hardly large enough for the clairvoyant, his client and the crystal ball.

The rest of the family stood back uncertainly while Verity approached. At first he thought there was some mistake, that he had been invited on the wrong day. Finding the narrow entrance in the canvas he stood outside and listened.

' 'ello?' he said hopefully, ' 's me! Verity!'

There was a movement inside and the flap was pulled open. A small sallow man appeared. His cranium was tightly bound in a black scarf bearing the signs of the zodiac in gold, like a skull-cap. He bowed to Verity with hands pressed together in an almost oriental gesture of courtesy. Then he ushered his visitor into the tent.

There was just room for a small folding table with a chair either side, one for the Great Lavengro and one for his guest. On the green baize stood a glass ball in a black holder. The clairvoyant ignored it for a moment and gestured Verity to his seat.

'You honour me, my dear sir, by accepting my invitation!' the breath whistled slightly between his ill-fitting teeth. 'Useless to pretend that I know nothing of your public fame. Why, the world knows of your hairbreadth escapes in America and India, your skill in bringing criminals to justice!'

'Do it?' said Verity, frankly puzzled. 'You never invited me 'cos of that, Mr Lavengro. Did yer?'

The clairvoyant permitted himself a faint smile.

'No, my dear sir.' The thin hands washed together unctuously. 'You are here because I believe I can help you. And help the cause of justice.'

'You mean you been robbed or something,' said Verity cynically.

Lavengro shook his head.

'I mean, sir, that the public takes me as an entertainment, perhaps a fraud. I am no such thing. Sometimes in the depths of my crystal ball I see too clearly what time must bring. I see crimes committed which, as yet, are unknown in the minds of their perpetrators. Do you understand me?'

'Go on,' said Verity quietly.

'I ask nothing of you,' said Lavengro with the same sibilant breath. 'No reward and no thanks. Only that you will speak for my art in the future when you hear it maligned.'

'Course I would,' said Verity scowling. 'If it's right.'

Lavengro put a hand to each side of his face, as if to cut out the sunlight in the woven fabric of the tent. He bowed towards the glass ball.

'Close your eyes, Mr Verity. Think of nothing but what I say and the image which rises behind your closed lids. I see a time soon to come. It grows close. No more than the day after tomorrow. As the sun declines I see a grassy place, not five miles from here. Tents and booths in abundance. There is a girl who acts in a charade. I see a medieval joust. But see! Now she is among the crowds. She walks against a man and stuns him. A hand enters his pocket where his watch might be. She has a notecase in her hand. The glass is cloudy. I can see no more.'

Verity opened his eyes.

'All you got is a flash-tail hoisting watches at a fair.'

'Close your eyes again, my dear, dear, sir. I see a darker place. Just before midnight of the same day. It is close to here — so close. Not half a mile. There is a shop, full of the treasures of Asia. Sparkling stones and glowing jewels. There is a man. So dark I cannot see. I see him with an implement cutting a hole. A round hole in a wooden board. . .'

' 'ere, Mr Lavengro!' said Verity suddenly. 'Now that's something like! Keep on about it! Anything yer can see! Exact place and time!'

'It is so dark,' moaned the clairvoyant. 'So dark! The hour

is near midnight, before or after. I can make out little else. Only. . .'

'Yes, Mr Lavengro? Anything you can!'

'German,' said Lavengro, as though with a great effort. 'German. . . Duke. . . German Duke. . . Alas, the shadows come upon me. . . I can see no more. . .'

He sagged back in his chair, as if with total exhaustion.

'Right,' said Verity briskly. 'Greatly obliged. And if I should apprehend such villains on Tuesday, you may hear to your advantage.'

But the sallow little man raised both hands as if to ward off a blow. 'No, my dear sir! No! I take no reward or thanks for such things.'

Verity shook his head slowly.

'Still, if such persons should be took, this'll be a story for the Whitehall police office! They'll never believe it! Caught by a magician's art!'

'No!' It came almost as a shout. 'You must tell no one of this, my dear sir. No one. For they will *not* believe you. You will do harm both to yourself and to me.'

'Yes,' said Verity reluctantly. 'I s'pose I would.'

Despite his scepticism, he was impressed. There was no earthly reason why the clairvoyant should seek to deceive him. If there was no female pickpocket at a fairground on Tuesday, no attempt to rob a jeweller's, he would have wasted a little time but no worse. To catch two such thieves, however, would advance his reputation even further. Added to the apprehending of the Trafalgar Street gang and Mary Ann it would give the lie to Inspector Croaker's vindictive reports on his conduct. As for the Great Lavengro, he had absolutely nothing to gain from a string of falsehoods.

Verity sat quiet for a moment longer, as if to let the clair-voyant recover. He hardly liked to speak what was on his mind.

'Mr Lavengro, sir. Can you see *anything* in that crystal ball? What might you be able to see about me, sir?'

Lavengro seemed visibly displeased by the request. But he shaded his eyes again and bowed towards the glass.

'Gold,' he said presently. 'Gold being carried at great speed. A masked man at a safe. . . India, a great diamond, a heathen fortress. Beauties of the harem. . . The high seas, a mighty warship, death by water and sudden deliverance. . . The great cataract of Niagara. . .'

'Yes, yes,' said Verity impatiently. 'Not that. About me, I mean. At home!'

'Ah!' The Great Lavengro looked up, then glanced down at the ball again. 'You have a companion of great loveliness. Fair of feature and graceful of limb.'

Verity basked in this tribute to Bella's charms.

'You alone,' droned Lavengro, 'are now the happy master of those beauties which she once displayed to all the world. . .'

'All the world!' said Verity thunderstruck.

'No longer,' said Lavengro hastily. 'No longer does she flaunt her pretty legs and comely thighs before her expectant admirers. . .'

Verity was on his feet, face reddening still further with anger.

'Now, you see 'ere, my man. . .'

'*No longer!*' insisted Lavengro desperately. 'No longer does the fair charmer waggle her voluptuous hips before an audience of costers. . .'

Verity's incoherent roar of rage on Bella's behalf filled the confines of the canvas booth. All his gratitude for the hints of robbery to come was now forgotten. He could think only of the foulnesses about his beloved wife which were spouting from the mouth of the obscene little man with his black and gold headscarf. The table was between them, but Verity smashed it aside, wrenching the clairvoyant to his feet with two ham-like fists grasping the man's lapels. Terror filled Lavengro's dark little eyes.

'Flashing her arse in a penny gaff!' he squealed desperately.

'Oh gawd! You must a-known! Haymarket! Regent Circus! Ma Hamilton's Night 'ouse!'

Verity withdrew a right hand in order to deal vengeance. But the Great Lavengro, awakening suddenly to the inevitability of suffering, kicked him sharply on the shins. A dull agony invaded the bone. Verity lost his footing and blundered back against the canvas wall of the little tent. It bulged under his weight but held firm.

He lunged away from it, clawing for the elusive Lavengro. His foot trod on the fallen crystal ball and he felt the cheap glass crunch to powder under his boot.

'I'll bleedin' have you in the infirmary for this!' he roared. Never in all his dealings with the most hardened criminals had he felt such a degree of fury. To hear his pure and beloved Bella — the mother of his children — spoken of in such a manner drove him almost demented.

The cheap furniture and the two men's bodies seemed to fill almost every available space in the booth. But Lavengro, in his frenzy to avoid serious injury, was scrambling for the door. Verity blocked the way. The scrawny clairvoyant snatched a chair and raised it in an attempt to smash the frame down on his antagonist's head. Verity's tall hat had long ago vanished into the debris and he was now unprotected against such a blow. But as Lavengro raised the chair with both hands, Verity bunched his right hand into a hamlike fist again and delivered a meaty smack to the clairvoyant's jaw.

The Great Lavengro sagged. Yet in doing so he brought the chair down gently but firmly. Imprisoned under it in the narrow space, Verity struggled to fight clear. He stepped back against the single pole of the tent and, to his dismay, heard a loud crack. Swathes of canvas began to enfold him until he was kneeling under the mass of it. Those outside, who had gathered when the tent walls began to bulge with the impact of hurtling bodies, now watched the flimsy structure subside like a deflated balloon.

Staggering about in the folds Verity found a tiny gap where the top of the tent should have been. It was too small to escape through, but large enough to give him a view of the Great Lavengro. Blood was trickling from a corner of the clairvoyant's mouth as he scrambled away in his torn clothes, racing across the shingle in the direction of Shoreham.

At last he found the hem of the canvas, struggled under it, threw it clear, and stood up. He was surrounded by a ring of spectators. Looking round for Bella and the others, his eye fell first of all on a stern figure. In its tall hat and long belted tunic, handcuffs and rattle at the side, it was unmistakeable. Worse still, its face was unfamiliar, not one of the uniformed constables of Brighton with whom Verity had so far struck up an acquaintance.

'Well then,' said the figure aggressively. 'What's all this?'

'Quick!' Verity gasped. 'Him! Running away over there! He's the one you want!'

The constable looked at him disdainfully.

'We can find him any time,' he said gruffly. 'It's you I want!'

Verity shook his head.

' 'm police officer,' he panted.

'Oh yes!' said the constable. 'Forget your uniform? Get them hands behind your back! You're a bloody hooligan, that's what!'

Verity was too winded to resist the handcuffs. In any case two stalwart volunteers from the crowd had his arms behind him and the metal cuffs bit into his wrists.

'Listen!' howled Verity. 'I gotta warrant card somewhere! I'm here to keep the peace, same as you!'

The uniformed constable looked round at the crumpled tent and its shattered contents.

'Oh yes?' he said again with the same casual disdain. 'This your idea of peace, is it? Get walking!'

And then, to crown Verity's wretchedness, there was a cry as Bella pushed her way through the crowd with the rest of his little family following sheepishly behind her.

The procession to the Market Street lock-up was a public humiliation which lived long in his mind. Behind him and his captor walked an interested crowd. Bella a few paces away was weeping silently. Billy in his leading-reins and little Vicki in Ruth's arms were bawling in unison, as if divining their father's disgrace by their mother's tears. Ruth, her pretty brown eyes wide with dismay, followed with Stringfellow. Of all the family, it was the old cabman who took the reverse of their fortunes most calmly. From time to time he fetched out the half sovereign and looked at it thirstily as it lay in his palm. Presently he turned to Ruth beside him. Finger and thumb took a soft fold of her face gently and shook it with roguish familiarity. He glanced back for the last time at the ruins of the Great Lavengro's premises. Then he patted Ruth forward again.

'No good do come of these things as a rule,' he said philosophically. 'No good whatsoever!'

5

'Aggravated assault!' Inspector Henry Croaker looked up from the chair in which he sat. With his small dark eyes, his face yellow as a fallen leaf, his leather stock buttoned up tight, he almost laughed in his glee. Verity, bare-headed and red-faced, stood rigidly at attention before the desk. The room, in the police office of Brighton Town Hall was unfamiliar, but the routine was one which he had undergone a dozen times during Croaker's command of the Private-Clothes Detail.

The inspector was swallowing greedily, in anticipation of

his triumph. This time, at least, the matter was beyond doubt. The Great Lavengro had been beaten by the fat sergeant before a crowd of witnesses, including a member of the local constabulary.

'Dismissal!' cried Croaker. 'Proceedings on a charge of felony!' In his total rapture, he almost sang the words to his victim. Verity struggled to retain his composure, though he knew well that his future in the detail had never seemed as black as now.

'Wasn't like that, sir. With respect, sir.'

'No?' said Croaker softly. 'Then tell me how it was, sergeant.'

'He said things about Mrs Verity, sir. Things about her having behaved in a indecent manner before marriage, sir! Dancing in them penny gaffs, sir!'

'Indeed?' The words were almost chuckling from the inspector's lips. 'And was he right, sergeant?'

Verity's flushed cheeks darkened to a port-wine shade.

'Mrs Verity is a pattern of purity and womanhood, sir. And anyone who says or thinks otherwise is a foul-mouthed scoundrel, sir. With respect, sir.'

Croaker paused, with the air of one who has committed a tactical error but for whom victory remains assured.

'As to that, sergeant, the matter will no doubt be fully aired when the public proceedings are brought. And since Mr Lavengro will presently be here, he may enlighten us even before then.'

'He got nothing to enlighten anyone about, sir. And if he knows what's good for him, he'll stay away! Else. . .'

'Or else, sergeant, you will give him another good drubbing, will you? That is what you were about to say, is it not? I strongly advise you, before the charge comes to court, to keep a tight rein on your tongue. Mr Lavengro will be here, have no fear. He is this moment being fetched by two uniformed constables.'

Verity stood at attention, as smartly as on parade. In his

mind were the other two items of information which he had received in the clairvoyant's booth on Sunday afternoon. The two crimes to be committed upon the following day. It had first occurred to him that he ought to mention these prophecies to Mr Croaker. But then he thought that Lavengro might now deny having made them. In that case, they would appear merely as his own falsehoods, the last measures of a desperate man.

From outside the room there came a sound of approaching voices. Two of these were the calm insistent tones of the escorting officers. The third, high and shrill, was evidently that of the outraged clairvoyant himself. There was a tap at the door. Croaker barked out a challenge and the door opened. Verity had his back to it but he saw Croaker rise and heard the other men come in.

'Mr Lavengro!' said Croaker unctuously. 'It is indeed so good of you to come here and assist us in so distressing an affair. Permit me, my dear sir, to offer you the profoundest apologies on behalf of the Private-Clothes Detail for the ruffianly assault to which you have been subjected.'

Like a trusted companion offering assistance to an invalid, Croaker took the Great Lavengro's arm and led him round the desk so that they both faced Verity from the far side.

'There!' said Croaker, gesturing with a finger which would have done credit to the Hoxton melodrama. 'There is your attacker, sir! Lay what charges you please! You shall make no enemies here for doing so!'

In the morning light, Lavengro looked less sallow than he had done in the canvas booth. His hair, released from the black and gold skull cap, now formed a short tumble of dark, oiled curls. He looked malignantly at Verity, and also at the others in the room. Then he shrugged.

'Never saw him in my life before.'

'Look again!' yapped Croaker. 'This is the man who brutally assaulted you in the middle of yesterday afternoon and brought down your tent into the bargain!'

Lavengro shrugged a second time.

' 'f you say so. Only thing is, I was out cock-fighting at the Dog and Duck in Preston village, and there's a dozen gents or more that was with me. Bleeding ask 'em!'

Croaker's sickly yellow features were immobile in a moment of terrible realisation. The dark little eyes froze with a deep, unfathomable agony.

' 'nother thing,' said Lavengro irritably. 'There was dancing. That Janet Bond, the Female Hussar. Her with the dark hair done up in a top-knot and that big bum. Split 'er fleshings when she kicked her legs. I was there all right.'

'Your tent!' shouted Croaker. 'It was destroyed!'

'Nothing wrong with it Monday morning, however. Tents don't destroy easy. They falls down and you puts 'em up again. P'raps someone put mine up again.'

'Why weren't you there on Sunday afternoon?' Croaker's tone was almost pleading in his exasperation.

' 'Cos the watch-committee don't approve of the magical arts being exercised on the sabbath. Even young Janet can only flash about before a audience of private gents. Any case, I likes a day to meself. Me and Janet got a bit of an understanding just now, and that takes up a man's time rather.'

Inspector Croaker's lip quivered, as though he might weep. His voice sank to a softer, imploring tone.

'Then who was telling fortunes in your tent on Sunday afternoon?'

'Dunno, do I? That's your bloody silliness.'

At last Croaker turned on the Great Lavengro.

'Very well, my man,' he breathed. 'You think yourself clever. Yes you do. But let me tell you this. My eye is upon you from this moment. Infringe one by-law, cause one complaint, and I shall be upon you like the wrath of God! I neither know nor care why you practise this present deceit. But you shall hear more of me, sir! Depend upon it!'

'Tell you what,' said Lavengro reasonably, 'I'm going from here to swear an affadavy of all this. And then, if so much as the shadow of one of your tall hats falls on my tent, I'll be round the watch-committee with a copy. Saying how I was brought here forcible to perjure meself over things that never happened. They'll have your privates off you and mounted over the Town 'all porch.'

There was an ill-suppressed snort of mirth from one of the uniformed constables behind Verity. The Great Lavengro, with a sense of theatrical dignity, swept from the room. Verity decided that the time had come to disclose the other predictions of the man who had posed as Lavengro on the previous afternoon.

'Sir,' he said smartly, 'there's one thing I gotta say, sir. With respect, sir.'

But Croaker was surveying the room with eyes which seemed blinded by his own interior humiliation. Suddenly aware of the sergeant's voice he brought his gaze into focus on Verity's smug red face. And then his agony became insupportable.

'Get out!' he cried. 'This minute! Get out! Get out!'

Above the glitter of the afternoon sea, the dry summer turf of the downland was covered by fairground tents and canvas booths. Banners fluttered from their tops and a great painted placard in red and blue announced 'Newsome's Alhambra Palace Circus! A Brilliant Assemblage of Equestrian Novelties! Lessons in the Polite Art of Equitation Given Daily by Madame Pauline Newsome!'

Elsewhere, the same information streamed from long strips of printed bills. A single flag proclaiming 'Newsome's Equestrian Novelties!' drooped in the warm air. Newsome himself stood in a wooden box by the entrance, like a saint in a niche, his leather purse ready to receive the coppers. From within a small braying band of brass instruments was playing 'All Among the Barley'.

Verity stood before the entrance with Miss Jolly a few paces behind him. She had equipped herself for whatever might occur, the pink crinoline concealing the riding trousers, in which she could move with improbable speed. Verity surveyed the other young women outside the tent with a red-faced scowl. Jolly watched with an occasional flash of her eyes to right or left, eager for her prey.

Newsome with his broad-brimmed farmer's hat and hoarse voice was haranguing the crowds.

'This way, ladies and gents, for the equestrian novelties, incorporating for the first time in this town Rowley's medieval tournaments! See two fair damsels joust for the love of the same knight! See the winner in her bride attire. . .'

Verity's eyes narrowed. He knew something of Rowley's medieval tournaments and the girls who made up its retinue. A troupe of light-fingered young sluts, he thought. Far and away the most likely to make the bogus Lavengro's prediction come true. He was watching the rear entrance of the tent, where Newsome's 'artistes' assembled. A deep satisfaction filled his heart.

The girl was no more than fifteen years old, but he knew her well enough. She was a sturdy tomboy, one of Newsome's jousting maids. The fair hair was combed from its central parting to lie loose on her shoulders, the snub nose, narrow eyes and thin mouth giving an impression of wilful insolence. Her figure was tightly cased in a white singlet and riding trousers of a smooth lavender blue cotton.

'Who's she, then?'

He was aware of Miss Jolly's high-pitched voice.

'A young person known as Miss Elaine. Made trouble for me and Mr Samson once. Don't take your eyes off her.'

Jolly at once joined the little band of admirers, upon whom the young suspect had turned her back. A tight broad belt at the waist drew in the smooth trousers, so that the robust seat and the swell of Elaine's young hips seemed to form an almost perfect circle. The little knot of men, now realising that a girl had joined them, looked quizzically at Miss Jolly. They were answered by a sharp glare from dark brows and then her profile turned away in sphinx-like imperturbability.

Verity walked in a slow circle round the tent without seeing any of Newsome's other girls. It was absurd, of course. How could the Great Lavengro himself, let alone an imposter, know that a girl would pick a man's pocket at the fairground on this particular afternoon? Trusting Jolly to keep watch on Elaine, he walked slowly among the other tents and booths. But as the moment came for the circus to begin, the customers drifted away. Outside the Punch and Judy box, the proprietor vainly blew his little trumpet to summon public attention. A man with a pair of dancing dogs stood in the shade of his canvas awning, staring malevolently towards the marquee in which Newsome's horse-girls performed.

Alone in his grassy space the Salamander Fire-King was practising his art, dressed in green tights, his green silk tunic embroidered with a gold lion. With head thrown back, he held the lighted link in his hand. Verity watched him, fascinated. The flame on the long wick seemed to dance always an inch or so beyond the man's lips. Yet he fed it slowly into his mouth, the fire sometimes glowing within his cheeks. He tucked the black, extinguished cotton into the side of his mouth, like a monkey storing nuts in his pouch. Suddenly the wick touched the man's moustache and there was a momentary fizzing sound. He gasped, drew the link away, and turned with his hand clapped over his face.

'You got no call to injure yourself for idlers to gape at,' said Verity sternly. 'They only come hoping to see you burnt.'

But he dropped a penny in the man's hand as he walked away.

There was no one who looked remotely like a pickpocket as he walked back to the circus tent. Jolly and the little group of men were still observing Elaine. Presently Elaine tossed back her hair, looked sullenly round at them and shouted belligerently, 'Seen all you want? P'raps you'd like to leave your entrance money in the box now!' And she strode away into the tent, with a final toss of her fair tresses.

Verity glanced about him. The downland outside the marquee was almost deserted. There was not another young woman, let alone a pickpocket, in sight. He took Jolly by the arm as Newsome's trumpeters began a discordant fanfare to announce the commencement of the riding.

'It's that young Elaine I fancy for number one,' he said softly. 'S'posing there *is* a number one and I ain't simply been made a fool of!'

Her eyes flickered in a silent predatory understanding. Verity led her to the entrance and deposited two coins in the money-box. They passed into the tent.

A rope on iron staves marked out the arena, the grass yellow under the canvas shade and sparse from the hooves of Newsome's ponies. Round the barrier was a crowd of ribboned bonnets, the pot hats and tall hats of the men, while Newsome in his red coat and white collar presided in the ring. A wag shouted, 'Evens the favourite!' above the murmur of the crowd as half a dozen ponies ridden by Elaine and the other girls cantered in from the far entrance. A man in front of Verity roared out 'Elaine on the grey! Let him laugh who wins! Hoo-ray, there! Hoo-ray!' He beat his topboots with a little whip and clanked his brass spurs.

Verity's eye passed over the assorted bonnets, searching for the face of a probable thief under each brim. There were bonnets in crêpe, bonnets in straw, or silk and satin. Some were garnished with fruit or flowers, others with feathers and beads. But not one of the pretty faces beneath seemed intent upon anything other than the antics in the ring.

Presently the first canter was over and the pony riders had withdrawn. Pauline Newsome herself came out on Rameses, the Dancing Horse, a dappled stallion which pawed the ground in time to the music of the band. Suddenly, Verity felt Miss Jolly's hand tighten on his arm and heard the shrill whisper.

'Look at her! What's she doing?'

He turned to find Elaine, but she was apart from the crowd, standing aggressively over a smaller girl with whom she was arguing.

'No-o-o!' Jolly's voice rose in protest. 'There!'

He followed the direction of her arm and saw the other young woman. She was seventeen or eighteen years old, dressed like a servant. Her brown hair was combed loose to her shoulders, falling aslant her forehead. Verity watched the narrowed quizzical eyes, the pert features, and the thrusting movements of her robust young figure. The girl was forcing her way through the crowd, as if to regain the entrance. From time to time the press of spectators obliged her to push herself tightly against a man or woman in order to make her way.

'Well, I never!' said Verity contentedly. He made no movement. The girl pushed her way through, coming closer to them. From time to time she seemed conscious of having thrust herself too roughly against a man who stood in her path. On these occasions she would pause and smile an apology. Verity noticed that she was generally forgiven by an answering smile, dismissive or hopeful as the case might be.

A moment later she stepped clear of the throng, reaching the more open ground just within the entrance of the marquee. Verity let her come on, and then he barred her path.

'Why!' he said amiably. 'If it ain't young Vicki Hartle! And what's a frisky young piece like Vicki doing so far from home? You was to pick rope at Mr Dredge's factory down Ratcliffe Highway for five years. Condition o' your release from Brixton Reformatory. . .'

Like Elaine, Vicki was a robust young woman but Verity caught her easily as she tried to evade him. The metal cuffs clicked shut.

'What was it, then?' he inquired conversationally. 'Them

corns that the hemp do bring out on the fingers? Being phys-
icked with sulphur by old Ma Dredge? Or just plain friski-
ness?'

'You've no cause. . .' The voice was high and urgent.

Verity patted the side of the plain brown dress and heard
a dull metallic clatter.

' 'ere!' he said admiringly. 'I'd say you prigged every watch
in this bloomin' tent, not to mention notecases! What with
that, and having to go back to the beginning of your first
little penance, you'll be making them other prison ladies
happy for ten years or more.'

The horror of it was reflected in her eyes. She twisted
against the cuffs.

'I'll be old!' she wailed imploringly. 'It'll be the end of me!'

'Old or not don't signify,' said Verity sternly. 'An honest
heart and a clear conscience. That's what you need. Any
case, you'll only be coming out to go back to Mr Dredge.
What's it matter down there if you're old or not? Mr Dredge
ain't fussy.'

'You're cruel!' she sobbed. 'Hard and cruel!'

'And you're a thief,' he said philosophically. 'A thief and a
whore, Vicki Hartle. There's proper places for such as you.'

'Two whole guineas,' said Verity firmly. ' 's quite enough for
a young person of your class.'

Even in the darkness he was conscious of Jolly's features
turned sharply upon him and the glittering resentment in
her eyes.

'They wanted to give me more!' she shrilled. 'They'd have
taken up a subscription but for you. Two guineas was
nothing to what I saved them!'

Verity scowled down the length of the gas-lit street.

'You're not here to make your fortune, miss! You got
repentance and amendment to show. That's what.'

Ever since the afternoon, when the grateful owners of the
watches and notecases had dropped their coins into Jolly's

64

hand, she had complained intermittently of Verity's mean-ness. He had insisted that none of Vicki Hartle's victims was to give a reward greater than two shillings. And when the total reached two guineas he had forbidden all further contributions.

He and Jolly now stood in the shadows of Duke Street as a church clock chimed the quarter before midnight. There was a stillness, broken only by the flaring of an occasional gas-jet and the more distant rumble of breakers on the shingle. German Duke. It had not taken him half an hour to find that the only jeweller's near the Chain Pier which corresponded with these words was the premises of Mr Germain in Duke Street. It was just the sort of clue which Lavengro's imposter would use, knowing that Verity could hardly fail to discover the truth behind it.

By no means were all the gas lamps lit in Duke Street. He and the girl stood in a pool of darkness outside a milliner's shop which effectively concealed them from view. On the far side of the street and a little further up the slope, there was another patch of shadowy obscurity. It concealed the locked wooden shutters of Mr Germain's shop-front.

There was no sign of a burglar, nor did Verity really ex-pect that there would be. To have caught Vicki Hartle that afternoon was nothing. Female pickpockets abounded in such places and any policeman who could afford the time would catch one sooner or later. Had Vicki not been there, he might have caught Elaine half an hour later. It was clear to him that they hoped to lead him on. Having seen the first 'prophecy' come true, he was now supposed to waste his time watching Mr Germain's premises in the hope of witnessing the second. No doubt they wanted him in Duke Street so that he could not be somewhere else. But this time he was the unseen watcher, and he had Jolly with him as a witness against stories which might be fabricated. Perhaps the shop had been burgled already and he was there to be set up as the dupe of the men who had done it.

The clock which had chimed the quarter now struck the hour. Duke Street remained deserted. It was a minute or two later when there was the sudden noise of a plank moving, as though perhaps a cat had jumped on a piece of loose wood and caused it to fall. The sound came from somewhere at the back of the shops on the far pavement.

Softly as a shadow, Verity moved forward, motioning Jolly to remain on watch where she was. There was no entrance at either side of the jeweller's shop. But, two doors along, a narrow alleyway led behind the buildings. Its cobbles were slippery with the night's condensation as he followed it. At the rear of the buildings it passed between the high walls of two back yards. Keeping his boots clear of the brickwork, Verity hauled himself by the strength of his powerful arms so that he was on top of the wall, two doors along from the rear of Mr Germain's. Gently he stood up, towering above the level of the ground, and peered towards the back of the jeweller's premises. He could see nothing, but he was certain that a faint rhythmic scraping was coming from the dark space.

Whoever was doing the scraping might not hear his soft footsteps above the insistent rasping. He decided that if the sounds stopped, he would remain immobile. So long as it persisted, he was safe in moving towards it.

He dropped softly down, crossed a patch of grass, and pulled himself on to the next wall. Having negotiated that, he had only to cross another area and then he was looking over the rear wall of the jeweller's shop.

Like the front of the building, the windows here were barricaded by locked wooden shutters, bolted as well on the inside. Though it was dark, Verity was just able to make out the shape of a small grey-headed man crouching by the lowest of the shutters. At the top of the shutter there was already a neat round hole, some four inches across. The little man was now working at a point which would enable him to reach the lower bolt. He was using the cracksman's favourite device for this, a centre-bit which operated on the principle of a pair of compasses. A centre spike held the tool in position. Then, turning a large handle in a clockwise direction, the burglar drew the cutting bit round and round the perimeter. In ten minutes a practised criminal would reach the bolts. If necessary he would cut out the lock as well.

The man's face was hidden at first, but then he paused and mopped his cheeks with a handkerchief. Verity knew him at once as Blind Charley, so called from his habit of working at night and also from a begging dodge which he had once resorted to when times were hard.

Charley cleared the second hole and his hand had gone through to find the bolt when Verity tapped him on the shoulder.

'If I was a cruel man, Charley, as some think I am, I'd a-let you get in there and then nabbed you coming out with the sparklers. As it is, they can't give you more than *attempted* robbery. Looking at it all sides up, you got a lot to be thankful for that it was me come along just now.'

Stringfellow spat on a harness brass and polished it with his sleeve.

'Prophecies!' he said disdainfully. 'No one ever prophesied anything for me. Nothing of any bloody use, that is. You might a-asked this cove which of them nags is going to win Lord Bristol's plate at Brighton races. Now that's something like!'

'But if it ain't real fortune-telling,' said Verity persistently, 'where's the point? Villains is always ready for a caper, but not this. See Vicki Hartle let herself be caught hoisting watches so's someone's prophecy can come true? Six years of it if she gets a day? Course she wouldn't! And Blind Charley? Shaved head and oatmeal diet for seven or ten? He let himself be took to fulfil someone's predictions? It don't answer, Stringfellow! It never don't.'

Stringfellow pummelled the brass against his sleeve. He

paused to draw a long sup from the glass of dark beer on the kitchen table of the Tidy Street lodgings.

'What do rile me,' he said, 'is them things said about Miss Bella! I don't let that pass!'

'I seen through that, Stringfellow,' said Verity calmly. 'They got it wrong. My consort, he called her. You know what? They seen me working with Miss Jolly and took her for my young person!'

'Well I never!' said Stringfellow, visibly impressed.

Verity dropped his voice to a more dramatic tone.

'And what it do mean, Mr Stringfellow, is this. I been watched ever since I come to Brighton. That's how they twigged me with Jolly. More 'n that. Two cunning villains have gone to gaol for years and years, just so's bigger fish than they can pull some caper or other. And look at the bother they go to so I can have me future told! I dunno yet what's behind all of it. But I ain't been set up like this unless it's worth a king's ransom to someone.'

Stringfellow nodded and thought about the problem. Presently he looked up, toothless and expectant.

'Course,' he said, 'you might hear no more. But if you should have to do with that fortune-telling cove again, there weren't no harm to ask him about them runners in the Bristol Plate.'

6

Verity, Meiklejohn and four constables of the Brighton force stood in the high-walled yard of the Town Hall. They were all dressed in the frock-coats and plain hats of 'private-clothes'. Positioned at ease, awaiting the arrival of a senior

officer, the men talked surreptitiously to one another from
the corners of their mouths.

'Meiklejohn!' said Verity, keeping his eyes in front of him.
'What the 'ell's this Brunswick Square detail, then?'

'Dunno,' said Meiklejohn innocently. 'Standing outside
them big houses where the swells live. Seeing they ain't disturbed. Touching yer hat and opening the carriage door for
persons of quality.'

'That ain't work for detective officers, Mr Meiklejohn,
and you know it! Why us, anyway?'

'Mr Croaker,' said Meiklejohn. 'We're in his little book.
Me for causing a rumpus over that bitch Helen Jacoby. And
you got right up his nose a few days back, didn't you? Mr
Croaker been narky about it ever since. Last time I see him,
he give me a look that'd turn a pint of fresh cream sour on
the spot!'

'We weren't fetched down here from London just to stand
sentry-go for a few nobs, Mr Meiklejohn. And there's another
thing. . .'

'Parade! 'Shun!'

Six pairs of boots stamped to attention as the door leading
into the police yard opened. Verity looked for Inspector
Croaker but there was no sign of him. The grand white-
haired old figure who entered was Superintendent Gowry,
the 'Old Governor' of the Private-Clothes Detail. He was
accompanied by a well-dressed stranger. Verity's features
contracted in a frown of perplexity. If Mr Gowry had come
all the way from London to take the parade, there could be
nothing less than royalty behind the Georgian façades of
Brunswick Square.

'Stand – at – ease!'

The six sets of boots thumped again in unison. Verity
heard the superintendent introducing the stranger as Mr
Bunker of the London Indemnity Insurance Company of
Lombard Street.

'On the 8th of November last,' said Gowry presently,

'there occurred a robbery at Wannock Hundred, the country seat of Baron Lansing, the banker. Prior information was received by the Metropolitan Police who were able to frustrate the crime. The thief, one Joseph O'Meara, was apprehended after he had taken the Lansing jewels from their safe but before he could make his escape. This plan was agreed between the Baron Lansing, the London Indemnity Company who bore the insurance risks and the Commissioner of Police.

'Among the gems was one piece, heavily insured and unique in the world. The Shah Jehan clasp, the ancient turban-ornament of the Mogul emperors, taken from the rebels at the sack of Delhi, four years ago.

'The thief was apprehended outside the room. But the case which had held the clasp was already empty. He denied all knowledge of it, even though a confession might have eased his sentence. At his trial, O'Meara was sent to transportation for fourteen years.

'An intensive search of Wannock Hundred and its grounds has failed to locate the Shah Jehan clasp. The London Indemnity Company paid a claim of £5,000, not the full value of the clasp but a settlement agreed with Baron Lansing. The company's investigators are now led to believe that the jewel was never stolen but that a gross fraud had been perpetrated.

'Several weeks later, Baron Lansing died. Nowhere among his effects was there any trace of the clasp. However, it was discovered that he had for almost a year been keeping a young mistress, first employed as a governess. That young person was installed in a house in Brunswick Square, Brighton, of which the Baron had given her a lease. Knowing that he would be unable to leave her his estate, which was entailed upon his family, there is reason to believe that he made her a present of the clasp and that it remains in her possession.'

The sun was shining directly upon the row of men standing at ease. Verity felt a droplet of perspiration run slowly down his forehead and gather on his eyebrow. But with a sense of military propriety he kept his hands clasped behind his back.

'The evidence,' said Gowry, 'though strong enough to warrant careful surveillance, is not sufficient to obtain judicial authority to search the premises in Brunswick Square. That surveillance will therefore be undertaken, day and night, by the officers of this detail. It will be maintained until there is evidence of the presence of the Shah Jehan clasp, or at least sufficient grounds for an authorised search. The houses of Brunswick Square, though large, are easily watched. They are built as terraces and have only front and rear entrances. The rear entrance of number 33 will be surveyed from a hired room in the stable mews known as Brunswick Street West. This watch will be kept by Inspector Croaker and two senior officers of the Brighton Constabulary. A second watch, covering the front door and the area steps to the basement will be kept by the six of you in the square itself. This scrutiny will be maintained, day and night, on every day of the week until further notice. Stand easy!'

The six men shuffled their feet and eased their shoulders a little. Verity felt a sense of deep injustice. After all that he had done, the arrest of the Trafalgar Street gang, Mary Ann, Vicki Hartle and Blind Charley, this was to be his reward! His round red face grew warmer still with a sense of affront. To stand like a porter outside the terraces of white mansions which graced the western end of the promenade! And to what purpose? Banker Lansing's doxy would hardly flash the heathen clasp about with two stalwart figures standing permanently outside her front door! The whole idea was what he called 'dead lead'.

He roused himself from indignant self-pity, just as Bunker, the smartly dressed director of the London Indemnity came along the line, handing each man two pieces of card with pictures or diagrams upon them.

In the background Superintendent Gowry was still talking.

'A fraud upon an insurance company may seem a lesser crime. Yet it is as grave as any robbery or assault upon the person. For it attacks the very basis of trust on which commercial confidence and probity must rest. You will treat this as a conspiracy of the most serious kind. You will use your best endeavours. . .'

Verity looked at the first card. It was a splendid coloured engraving of the Shah Jehan clasp done at the time of its public display in the Crystal Palace. The turban *sarpesh*, shaped like a proud eight-inch feather, seemed to glow and flash with ruby red and emerald green. The quill was carved of white jade. The plume was gold, set with a tight-packed galaxy of gleaming gems. It rose from a diamond the size of a small egg. A pattern of green leaves was carved from emeralds, whose buds were twenty deep maroon rubies. The crowning glory was a ruby-flower so large that a man's finger and thumb would not circle it.

Its value, Verity guessed, was beyond calculation. The jewels alone were worth far more than the London Indemnity's compromise settlement of £5,000. The craft and history of the great Mogul clasp made it unique and without price.

'We are confident that the heirloom remains in Brunswick Square,' said Gowry. 'The young person who lives there was German governess in the Lansing family before she contracted a — er — closer acquaintance with the late Baron. She has no associates in the English criminal world. No likely accomplices here. She must therefore take the clasp out of England, if she chooses to profit by it. And there she knows the Customs and Waterguard will search her, every stitch. We seek not revenge but her honest confession. It will come when her position appears plain to her. You will take over surveillance from the London Indemnity inspectors this afternoon. The young person will be watched every hour

72

and every minute, at home and wherever she may travel. Mr Croaker will assign your duties at two o'clock. Parade! Shun! Dismiss!'

As the men turned away Verity glanced at the second photographic card which Bunker had handed out. His eyes bulged a little and he gave a rich chortle of excitement.

'Don't prose so!' said Meiklejohn wearily. He and Verity were alone in the room which served as office for the men of the Private-Clothes Detail during their Brighton secondment. The noon sunlight, heavy with dust, fell on a pair of counting-house tables and two high stools.

'I tell you I seen her before!' Verity whispered insistently. He glanced back nervously at the closed door, as if fearing interruption. 'She was one of them young persons bred up at Miss Lammle's in Cheyne Walk. Bred up to be a governess. Me and Mr Samson had an eye on the house after a young beauty called Judith Perry was sent there. German governess this one was. Name o' Cosima Bremer. She's no more 'n eighteen or nineteen now. Bit flighty but no real harm in her. Will yer look at that likeness again, Mr Meiklejohn!'

Meiklejohn glanced unenthusiastically at his copy of the photograph which Bunker had handed to each man of the detail. He saw a girl who looked no more than seventeen, the dark governess skirts still delineating in their folds the long agile legs and firm hips. There was an animated prettiness in Cosima's face with its blue eyes and the fair hair which was worn loose, though tightly shaped as it waved to shoulder-length.

'Banker Lansing's fancy!' said Verity triumphantly.

Meiklejohn shrugged.

'All right. You know her then. What I wouldn't give for a pint of gin-shrub!'

'Can't yer see it, Mr Meiklejohn? I know her!'

'Rum-shrub, even,' said Meiklejohn. 'If I was in London now, I'd be sitting in Ma Freeman's with a warm belly and a glass on the table.' He sighed at the unfairness of it all.

'Listen to me, Meiklejohn! I had dealings with this young person! It's me that can make her see reason!'

'You tell Mr Croaker, then.'

'You gone stoopid, 'ave you?' said Verity, reddening with exasperation. 'Old man Croaker 'd have me off this detail so fast I'd never know I'd been on it. No, Mr Meiklejohn. What I got is a stratagem!'

Meiklejohn looked up, the apprehension clear in his face, and Verity snuffled humorously.

'Ain't the first time I've brought such young persons to see reason, Mr Meiklejohn. First chance I get I'll have Cosima in a corner and put it to her good and straight. Let her hand over that heathen ornament and every good word shall be spoke for her. Else she'll be took for handling stolen goods. Ten years under lock and key in a place where beauty fades remarkable sudden.'

Meiklejohn appeared thoroughly alarmed.

'You listen, Verity. . .'

' 's all right, Mr Meiklejohn! Trust me and we'll all be shaking Mr Gowry's hand tomorrow.'

'*Verity!*' Meiklejohn's shout interrupted his plump companion's enthusiasm. 'What's going to happen to us all when Croaker finds you scared the bird off the nest and she can't be found this side of Christmas? Have some sense!'

Verity thrust his large head forward, glaring pugnaciously.

'Won't be like that, Mr Meiklejohn. I *know* her!'

Meiklejohn became reasonable.

'Look, old friend,' he said gently, 'I'd rather have Whitehall or Haymarket. Who wouldn't? But Brighton ain't a bad billet for now. 'f you want to end up down Mr Croaker's privy, that's your affair. But me and four other poor bleeders on the detail don't fancy it. Act sensible and we'll all have a bit of a jolly here with the races and the chits on the promenades. So you just leave her be and proceed as instructed. All right?'

'You forgot something, Mr Meiklejohn,' said Verity solemnly.

'Have I? What's that, then?'

'I ain't one to say it without some cause,' said Verity, 'but since that unfortunate affair in Langham Place over Miss Helen Jacoby, you been reduced to the ranks. I'm your superior officer. In fact, I'm superior to anyone else that'll be watching the front of the house. What I say goes.'

Meiklejohn let out a breath of forceful exasperation.

'See here, Verity,' he said gently. 'You take a single step towards Miss Cosima whoever-she-is. Say one word to her. That's all. I'll be in Mr Croaker's office there and then. And I'll tell him that you know the young person and she knows you. An officer that can be recognised has no use in surveillance. Why, you won't be on this detail then. You won't even be private-clothes any more. They'll have you wearing your legs out, up and down the Waterloo Road in a tall hat and uniform. Can't say I should like to have your feet when that happens.'

Verity's face fell. Under the flattened black hair and the waxed moustaches his round red cheeks went slack as if in a token of surrender. He seemed bereft of any answer. Then he pulled himself together.

'You ain't a man of confidence, Mr Meiklejohn,' he said reproachfully. 'Not a man of confidence at all.'

Meiklejohn's triumph was not marred by this.

'P'raps not,' he said thoughtfully, 'but I know a soft billet when I see one. And I seen one here. Mind you, though, I wouldn't say no to a pull or two of shrub before we all got Mr Croaker's harness on our backs.'

It was the following morning when Verity and Meiklejohn took their first watch in Brunswick Square. Verity himself had not previously walked as far west as this during his time in Brighton. After the narrower streets of the town, the market area still reminiscent of an old fishing village, the grandeur of Brunswick Town, as the neighbourhood was called, seemed undeniably impressive. The square was built on a slight incline, the lower side open to the promenade and the sea. At the top end there was a gap between the buildings where Brunswick Place entered. The fine white houses of the square thus formed two L-shaped blocks. Baron Lansing's love-nest was in the corner of the western block.

Verity stood at ease in the morning sunshine which danced on the bottle-green waves where the buildings opened out to the sea. He had begun to take a proprietorial interest in the majestic sweep of Georgian façades. Against the tall cream houses, the black paint of area railings and drawing-room balconies shone with an immaculate gloss. Behind the long sash windows of the first floor, veiled by silk curtains, he could almost imagine the swish of evening gowns and the strains of a waltz or a quadrille.

Below the handsome bowed windows of the principal apartments, flights of steps led up from the pavement to the brass-furnished doors of each house. A gate was set in the pavement railings, giving access to the basement steps which led down to the kitchen and servants' quarters.

While Inspector Croaker and his colleagues of the Brighton Constabulary watched the rear of the house from their hired room, Verity and Meiklejohn surveyed the front. It was easily done. At first, Verity had been apprehensive that they would have to stand immediately outside the building, or at least directly across the square from it. Even a helpless young woman like Cosima Bremer would soon have recognised them for what they were, even if she failed to identify Verity himself. But the design of the square enabled them to watch without being seen.

They stood a few yards up Brunswick Place, which divided the two blocks of houses as it entered the square from the hill above. This gave them an oblique view across the front of the corner house. Anyone entering or leaving must cross their gaze, while they themselves could not be seen from the windows of the Lansing mansion. If the girl who lived there wished to scrutinise them, she would have to come down the steps as far as the pavement to do so.

In any case, Verity and Meiklejohn had a pretext for their guard. The house outside which they appeared to be standing watch was one of the grandest of all, tall Corinthian pilasters rising between its long windows. During the summer recess, the mansion was the home of the Right Honourable Henry Layard, lately appointed Under-Secretary of State for Foreign Affairs upon Lord Palmerston's insistence. The Right Honourable gentleman had been greatly flattered when offered a private-clothes guard upon his front door. To the entire neighbourhood, as well as to the Queen's Messengers arriving with despatch cases, his newly acquired grandeur was advertised unchallengeably.

Verity and Meiklejohn stood either side of the front door with its polished brass, their boots planted firmly astride, hands behind their backs, the rear of one hand resting in the palm of the other. It was the approved posture for a private-clothes detective on surveillance duty. Only one feature betrayed their purpose. The eyes, which should have stared unswervingly ahead, slanted sidelong at the opening of Brunswick Square and the view across its north-western corner.

Verity shifted apprehensively as a young woman came into sight, walking from the dazzling sunlight of promenade and sea. She was making for the top of the square, accompanied by a child in red velvet carrying a hoop. It was the oldest dodge in the business, a pickpocket or a flash-tail who used a child to give a semblance of innocence to such movements. But before she reached the shaded corner of the square, she crossed to the green space of its private central garden. On the long sweep of grass, stretching down to the promenade, a dozen lime trees, warped by the prevailing sea-wind, rose among the paths and flower-beds. The child gave a cry of delight, produced a stick and began to bowl the hoop vigorously. Verity sighed.

The morning passed in heat and stillness, broken only by the distant surge of breakers and the shouts of children on the beach itself. A milkman, pulling his little cart with several churns upon it, passed the two policemen and turned into the square. He stopped outside the corner house and leant over the area railings.

'Milk down below!'

Presently he returned to his float, carrying a jug, ladled out milk from a churn, and went back to give it to someone on the basement steps.

'Bloody useless!' said Meiklejohn, breaking the silence between the two men. 'He could be going off now with that Shah Jehan clasp in his milk churn! There's a hundred ways!'

'No he couldn't, Mr Meiklejohn.'

'Course he bloody well could.'

'No he couldn't, Mr Meiklejohn.'

'Why couldn't he?'

Verity turned his plump face smugly upon his companion.

' 'Cos he's one of Mr Bunker's men from the London Indemnity, Mr Meiklejohn. That's why. And so's the baker, and the cat's meat man. They got this square sewn up tighter 'n a curate's pocket. What a curse that jool brought on Miss Cosima! A legacy o' doom, Mr Meiklejohn! She can't admit having the clasp without a charge of stolen property or fraud. And she can't trust a living soul with the story. And she ain't a wicked girl, as such. Not reely bad.'

Meiklejohn was silent for a moment, as though something had begun to weigh upon his mind.

'P'raps you was right, Verity. P'raps the best thing would be to have it out with her, face to face.'

Verity chortled indulgently.

'No, Mr Meiklejohn. *You* was right. I thought about it after.'

'About what?'

'That jool ain't just a jool, Mr Meiklejohn. Can't be. If it was Banker Lansing's inheritance there was more to it. And the trouble someone's taken to try and sweeten me! What for? That jool 'd be the biggest give-away a thief could have. Ain't a magsman that would touch it, unless he was to throw it in the sea. I don't suppose Miss Cosima got the least idea what it's worth, nor why.'

'Ten thousand, old Bunker reckoned.'

'Double it, Mr Meiklejohn. Treble it. Put a nought on the end and double it again. Banker Lansing's fortune, that's what it was. This whole thing got a real rich aroma about it. A real ripe smell.'

He broke off suddenly as a figure scuttled out from the little gate above the basement steps of the Baron Lansing's mansion. It was a servant, a girl in a green cotton dress. The girl had a cloth in her hand. She flapped it vigorously in the air, as though to shake dust or crumbs from it, and then scuttled back again. As she turned, Meiklejohn let out a gasp of surprise.

'Blimey!' he said. 'Jolly!'

'Tighter 'n a curate's purse, Mr Meiklejohn,' said Verity firmly.

The sun was at its zenith, turning the sea to molten silver.

'Ten thousand,' said Meiklejohn presently. 'Ten thousand on the open market, Bunker said. That's your Shah Jehan clasp.'

Verity shook his head.

'No, Mr Meiklejohn. I don't see it. Three villains has gone to their reward. And there's a lot that never came to light. There's a 'ell of a sight more to this than ten thousand. More than a heathen clasp that the stoopidest magsman in Seven Dials would look at and run.'

'My eyes is hurting,' said Meiklejohn plaintively. 'Looking sideways into that square all the time! I'll have a bloody squint like two gobstoppers by the time this lot's over.'

'It ain't just for ten thousand,' said Verity, ignoring the complaint.

Meiklejohn lowered his voice to a growl of exasperation. 'How can a jool be worth more than a jool is worth?'

Verity settled his burly shoulders. Under the tall stovepipe hat his eyes were set, his red face round and belligerent. He puffed his black moustaches up, as if to dislodge an insect which might have landed upon them.

'I dunno, Mr Meiklejohn,' he said fiercely. 'I dunno why I been seen off, nor how a jool can be worth more than it is. But I bleeding well mean to find out!'

TICKET OF LEAVE

7

Pale daylight began to penetrate the barred portholes of the *Indomitable*'s lower deck, where Stunning Joe lay motionless and watchful in his coarse brown hammock. He knew by the gurgling of water round the wooden hull that the tide had turned and was now on the ebb. Two more days, he thought, and the contractor's vessel would take on board its human cargo for Port Jackson. Then, even the familiar sounds of Portland Harbour would be lost for ever.

The convict decks of the *Indomitable* were each divided into two long prison dormitories running fore and aft. They were railed off by iron bars from floor to ceiling, like animal-cages, with a narrow gangway between in which the warders kept their vigil. A hundred men slept in each cage, the line of hammocks packed so closely that there was no space between them. In the misty light some of the sleepers had already begun to stir, groaning, coughing and yawning.

Stunning Joe could just make out the figure of the warder in his narrow corridor, lit by a glimmer of little lanterns fastened in a row to the bars of the two cages. The oil-light caught the polished buttons of the dark uniform, the crowns stitched upon the lapels, the glazed peak of the officer's cap. The warder had put down his bull's-eye lantern and was splashing the deck around him with chloride of lime from a tin bucket. Joe O'Meara caught the harsh acrid smell in his nostrils. If statistics were to be believed, the third-class felons on the lower deck would die at the rate of forty a year from what was called 'general infirmity'. It was rare for a warder to catch the prisoners' contagion but the officers of the night-watch took no chances.

Somewhere overhead a deep-toned bell was struck three times. On each of the fetid decks the warders took the bright bunches of keys which hung at their belts and drew them jangling along the iron bars.

'All up! Turn out! Move yourselves!'

Following his neighbours' example, Stunning Joe slid down from his hammock and began to dress in the convict's uniform, rusty brown with red stripes in a hoop-pattern. There was nothing to be gained by defying authority. Soapy Samuel had preached obedience and dying to be born again. Joe dismissed the promises of Samuel, but they were the only hope offered to him since he had come face to face with the officers of the law at Wannock Hundred.

Between two lines of warders the third-class convicts shuffled up the companionway to the top deck. Each man carried his hammock, now rolled and trussed like a large sausage. The upper deck of the old wooden ship had been built over with square huts, the so-called 'hammock-houses' where the prisoner's bedding was stored during the day. The masts of the *Indomitable* were cut down to a height of a dozen feet. The stumps had been left as clothes-props between which the lines of washed linen and bedding were hung to dry. The garments suspended there looked as if they had been sprinkled with pepper but this was merely the infestation of lice and fleas which prison laundering never removed.

Standing in the single file of men, waiting to hand in the bundled hammock upon which his number and the ship's name had been stitched, Joe looked about him. The dark ferret-eyes measured the distance to the ship's rail and the expanse of water, beyond which the Dorset coast grew yellow in the early sun. Warders with carbines and short bayonet-blades attached to the barrels stood between the felons and the ship's side. He would be dead before he could cross the deck.

With his hammock stacked in its place, he followed the

shuffling prisoners down the steps again, to the lowest and dampest level of the old wooden ship. The first men were already scrubbing the floor of the cage and arranging canvas cloths on the white deal tables which now stood where the hammocks had been slung. Each table accommodated a dozen men, sitting on benches at either side. An inverted bowl of brick tin, polished like silver, was set at every place, a matching basin at the table's end.

'Stand! Stand at your places!'

The warder's hoarse shout was followed by the obligatory grace, uttered in the same military shriek.

'Bless this food to our use and us to Thy service! A-men!'

The benches scraped as the men moved them to sit down and eat, under strict rule of silence. Prisoners deputed as messmen doled out a single hunk of bread from the laundry baskets and a ladle of rust-coloured cocoa from the tin pails. This portion twice a day, plus a ladle of boiled meat at noon made up the diet of the hulks. In the first few weeks Joe had endured a hunger that was like torture to him. Now he felt only the numbness in his belly which followed the keen torment of his initiation.

Five minutes later the duty warder's voice came again, in a shrill yap.

'All up! Stand at your places! Will you stand when I order you!'

Then came the muster, each felon saluting like a soldier and shouting 'Yes sir!' as his name was called. Stunning Joe wondered how Sealskin Kite and Old Mole could ever have believed that they would spring him from such a crib as this.

After the muster each cage was unlocked in turn. Under an escort of warders the men were marched up to the top deck once more. This time they wore glazed, broad-brimmed hats over their cropped hair as they waited docilely in line to go down the gangway steps to the cutters below. A queue of these little boats waited to ferry the labour gangs to the Portland quarries. Rocks broken under their hammers

were used in building the new quay and prison. The oars-
men were first-class convicts, indicated by the two red bands
round their right arms, their black leather patches on the left
sleeve. Stunning Joe looked for no assistance from them. A
first-class man had too much to lose by being implicated in
escape or mutiny. Many of them were more vicious than the
most brutal warder.

Beyond the convict hulks, the hospital ship *Iphigenia* and
the little washing-sloop *Lydney* rode at their mooring chains.
Even from these auxiliary vessels, Joe thought, there was no
prospect of escape. He sat with the other men in the cutter,
cowed and despondent, while the sun shone on the polished
bayonets of the warders in the stern. Many of the new officers wore the Alma and Inkerman clasps upon their breasts.
A man who had fought hand-to-hand in the bloody skir-
mishes of the Crimea would not hesitate to use bullet or steel
on a condemned felon.

Stunning Joe's detail was marched up the hill from the
quayside, through the streets of the little town, to the stone-
yards on the far side of the peninsula. The men were halted
while the contractors detonated another section of the whit-
ish rock-face, providing the boulders upon which the prisoners worked with their hammers. Joe O'Meara glimpsed
again the long crescent of Chesil Bank below, its banked
pebbles curving away towards the mainland and freedom.

A man who could once get clear of the work detail might
make a run for it when darkness fell. During daylight, of
course, it would be impossible. A figure on the long stretch
of pebbles connecting Portland with the coast would be as
conspicuous as a bluebottle on a whitewashed wall. The
sharp brain in the neat little head thought of darkness. Darkness, or perhaps a sea mist.

The men worked in groups of six to a dozen, standing in a
ring about the pile of chalky boulders, swinging the heavy
stone hammers and smashing them down on the cracking
masonry. In an outer ring, their carbines at the ready, three

warders faced inward, watching the men at their labour. Each officer had a notebook, in which from time to time he made a note on a man's enthusiasm for work, or his lack of it. On Joe's arrival, the senior officer in charge of the detail, MacBride, had explained with relish the penalties of sloth. A warder who 'took a shine' to a prisoner could reduce his life to a living hell. MacBride had only to make an unfavourable page of notes for Joe O'Meara to find himself on bread and water, in solitary confinement in the suffocating little cell which stank of the ship's bilges, even tied to the gratings for the cat o' nine tails. Had circumstances permitted, Stunning Joe would have gone to the gallows with a song on his lips for the murder of Officer MacBride.

By the end of the morning the smooth wooden handle of the hammer was slipping in Joe O'Meara's hands. He was still a novice, only six weeks in the yard, and his palms were not yet calloused. After several hours of labour the blisters burst and his hands bled. It happened at the end of every morning and every afternoon, often before the end. Mac-Bride's voice was at his ear as he paused.

'To your work, O'Meara! To your work, sir!'

The cold blue eyes under the polished peak of the warder's cap glinted with rage, as though the felon had offered Mac-Bride some personal insult by his idleness. Perhaps he had. It was a rule of any warder's employment that he should be fined a shilling of his pay every time that one of his convict detail was caught malingering.

A noon gun from Portland Castle was the signal for work to end. The trim cutters took the convicts back to the *Indomitable*. In the cages below deck there was another muster roll before the men sat down to their silent dinner. Stunning Joe's meal consisted of a potato and a ladleful from the tub of meat. Like all the provisions for the hulks the meat was supplied by private contract. Rotten before it reached the vessels, it had been boiled to a thin stew. On three days of the week, as a measure of economy, it was replaced by gruel, consisting of barley boiled in water without the addition of salt or any flavouring. Salt and pepper were included in the supplies, but were used exclusively on daily dressings applied to the backs of men who had been flogged. It was held by the prison medical authorities that this prevented putrefaction of the culprit's wounds.

After fifteen minutes, the warders in the corridors between the cages began to jangle their keys along the bars.

'All up! All up! Stone-yard details to your places! Move! Stir yourselves, you damned scoundrels!'

Joe O'Meara joined the file of men. They shambled without fear or resentment. It was MacBride's boast to new arrivals that a month of prison diet and discipline would leave them as quiet as gelded stallions. In this, at least, Mac-Bride had always been proved right.

The summer heat of the afternoon seemed to strike back at the men of the labour details from the white surfaces of new stone. Some of the parties were permitted to strip to their blue shirtsleeves, but not MacBride's. The sweat ran into Stunning Joe's eyes and he felt as though his strength was draining from him with the moisture. He knew, beyond doubt, that they were going to kill him. Unless he fell suddenly, from a seizure in the glare of the stone yard, he would not die at Portland. But only a fool would believe that he could survive fourteen more years of this in Parramatta where the heat would be twice as fierce as England in July.

Somewhen, about the middle of the afternoon, he knew that the chief officer was making his rounds of the details. As the senior warder approached each detail it was the duty of the guard to shout the official strength of the party followed by the number of men who were actually present. Sickness and the departure of transports generally caused some discrepancy. Joe O'Meara heard the voices getting closer.

'Ten-eight, sir! . . . Six-five, Mr Patterson! . . . Seven-seven, sir! . . . Six-three!'

The dust in the lower part of the stone-yard seemed thick

as smoke, rising from the fractured rock at the hammer blows of the men. Joe O'Meara choked suddenly as he drew a lungful of it. Dust was the only cover he would ever have, enough to make it worth the chance. He would run and run. Of course they would fire at him but they might miss. If not, he would as soon die here and now as suffer what lay ahead of him.

He had nerved himself for the dash across the quarry, up the rock-face and over the turf beyond. Then he heard MacBride's 'Seven-six, sir!' not two yards behind him. And even in his desperation, Joe held himself in check.

Once the chief officer had made his rounds, MacBride and his two subordinates relaxed. There would not be another check upon them before five o'clock. One of the warders went off behind a corner of the quarry to relieve himself. The other subordinate was far away, not looking in Joe's direction. But MacBride was at his back. Then, to Joe's astonishment, MacBride spoke to him, very gently.

'You, O'Meara! Lay your hammer down and step to me!'

Joe propped the long-handled hammer against the rock and turned about. MacBride stood over him, dark whiskers clipped short, the pale blue eyes watching keenly under the polished cap-peak.

'Obedience!' said MacBride softly. 'Obedience to those put in authority over you. Y' have have that lesson by heart, have you!'

The voice was that of the Celt, overlaid by the intonation of an industrial slum. MacBride laid down his carbine, as if to tighten the belt of his tunic. Joe stared back at him, not daring to believe that the most savage of all his guards could be Sealskin Kite's man.

'Don't mess me about y' focker!' A bitter resentment of O'Meara and his own complicity sharpened the tone of the words.

'No, sir!' Joe's heart beat faster, his eyes measuring the distance to the rock-face. He knew that he could climb fifty feet of it in less time than it would take some men to go up a flight of stairs. MacBride's voice grew softer.

'Hit me, Stunning Joe!' he said. 'Hit me, and run!'

In a few seconds more the warder who was relieving himself behind the rock would reappear. MacBride's other subordinate might turn round at any moment. With his hands hanging beside him, MacBride faced the little spiderman impassively. Joe locked his hands together, as if in a gesture of indecision. Hardly raising his head, he brought his double grip up, like a rock from a catapult, to connect with the angle of MacBride's throat and jaw. It was not at all what the warder had expected. With a long choking sound he stumbled forward, going down on hands and knees. Joe's locked fists smashed downward on the exposed nape and MacBride lay still.

For a split second, Stunning Joe thought of the carbine, but he knew it would impede him. If they got close enough for him to use it, he would be taken anyway. Already he was racing across the quarry, through the clouds of hot dust and the glare of the white Portland stone. The wind roared at his ears and the scarred face of the quarry was twenty yards ahead of him, rising to the open turf above. He glanced back once, long enough to see MacBride still lying motionless and the other warder unslinging his carbine. Joe ducked his head and began weaving across the remainder of the quarry. A single *twing-g-g-g*! sang past him like an insect and he saw the bullet smack into the rock-face ahead of him with a spurt of pale dust. It was no easy matter to hit a man at this range, a target moving as quickly and erratically as he had done. On the rock-face itself it would be a different matter.

The broken wall of limestone came under his fingers, and he began to pull himself up, the deft little hands and feet finding their crevices as easily as a monkey. Behind and below him the shouting had begun, the warders holding their carbines over their heads with both hands, which was the signal of an escape. MacBride had risen to his knees but only the officer who had fired the first shot was still taking aim at the fugitive. The carbine cracked like a whip as Joe seized a sharp ledge of rock above and his feet trod the crumbling limestone into a shower of fragments. A bullet chipped the white surface a dozen feet to one side. At first he thought the officer with the carbine must be Mr Kite's man too, firing deliberately wide of the mark. But as Joe pulled himself to the rim of the quarry, where the turf began, he saw that his escape had been well timed. In mid-afternoon, the July sun was directly over the quarry face, shining into the eyes of those below. Shooting into the colourless glare, the marksman would be lucky to get a bullet anywhere near his target.

In any case, Stunning Joe now had the turf under his hands, as he wriggled upward over the final ledge and lay for a few seconds on the high downland to fill his aching lungs. The softness of the turf was like a carpet under his feet after months of stone floors and the decking of the hulk. As he ran onward the sounds of voices and pursuit died away. It would take them a good while to follow him by the quarry path.

He looked to right and left. On the one hand was the glimmering sweep of Chesil Bank. When darkness came he would follow its shore, wading waist-deep, his movements concealed by the roar of the tide. The other way led along the cliffs, towards Portland Bill and the end of the peninsula. A man who was running for freedom would hardly be expected to choose that direction. With the glittering channel stretching away into the horizon glare, Joe followed a path which skirted the cliff edge. His pursuers would search the more likely escape routes first. It would be dusk by the time that the armed warders and the dogs began to drag the cliffs on this side.

Stunning Joe knew that there were two lighthouses at the tip of Portland Bill, constructed on the high ground. They were known as the Upper Light and the Lower Light from the difference in their locations. From conversations among other prisoners, Joe understood that they were not manned, merely visited by a Trinity House engineer once a week. The Lower Light was on sloping ground, where the land dipped towards the sea. It was almost the last place that the hunters would reach. By then it would be dark. Stunning Joe would have slipped out, retraced his route to the start of Chesil Bank and begun his eight-mile walk to the mainland at Abbotsbury. By the next day he would have stolen clothes and money, reaching the safety of Dorchester or one of the market towns. On the following night he would be back with Mr Kite and Old Mole.

He devised the plan as he ran, with the quicksilver of the afternoon tide below him. Not more than ten minutes later he saw the two lighthouses before him. At the end of the peninsula the expanse of turf sloped gently towards the last cliff, and the tall finger of the lighthouse tower was clearly visible. The Lower Light was sixty or seventy feet high, the glass lantern rising above deserted fields and distant white-washed farms. Stunning Joe was alone under the summer sky, knowing that he was free at last. The lock of the light-house door was so simple that he could have picked it with his finger-nail. He was studying it, thinking that he would lock himself in and make them believe he had never been there, when he heard a movement behind him.

Joe turned slowly, dreading to see a dark uniform with crowns on the lapels. But it was an unshaven man in an oatmeal-coloured smock and leggings, his grey hair dishev-elled. There was a shotgun in his hands as he bared his gums and grinned at the fugitive.

'You'm a runner!' he said humorously.

8

Stunning Joe looked blankly at the ragged man in the smock. There was no hint of intention behind the yellowed teeth in their shrewd smile. Joe, bracing his narrow back against the lighthouse door, met the eyes of his adversary and found them expressionless.

The man passed his tongue slowly across his lips, as though he found this an aid to thought.

'You'm a runner,' he repeated quietly, 'from the hulks! You'm took your ticket o' leave!'

'Stop a bit,' said Joe reasonably. 'You've no cause to take a part. Act sensible and you shan't suffer by it. A week or two shall see you richer than you are now. It ain't your quarrel.'

The ragged man's mouth widened in amusement.

'See me rich?' he sniggered. 'You don't look to me like a man of substance, my friend. Where's the proof?'

Joe measured the distance between himself and the barrels of the shotgun. He slid his right foot forward and the man drew back at once, keeping the aim of the gun steady.

'You stop that nonsense soon as you like, young shaver,' he said quietly. 'Right then, Mr Will and Master Harry! If you please.'

Two more figures stepped round from the far side of the lighthouse, where they had been concealed during the brief conversation. One was a fair-haired man in a smock similar to the first. The other was a boy of seventeen or eighteen with weak limbs and blotched complexion. They both carried guns, blunderbuss muzzle-loaders. Stunning Joe knew all too well that they fired a hail of metal fragments at each shot, enough to drive a dozen iron fragments into his body at this range. The ragged man turned to Will, speaking as though Joe O'Meara could not hear them.

'Ten sovereigns was give for the last,' he said thoughtfully, 'but then that was two year or more since. 'Twould be fifteen or twenty now, p'raps, having a new governor that don't want to dirty his snotter!'

He turned again to Joe with the same humorous grin. Beyond the ridge above them there was a long hollow booming sound.

'Warning gun,' said the fair-haired man philosophically. 'They knew 'e gone, then. They'd give twenty to 'ave 'e back. Least that.'

Joe stood with his back still pressed to the wooden planking of the door, the three guns held in a semi-circle before him.

'Twenty!' he said incredulously. 'You could have two hundred in a week more!' His eyes were anxiously upon the crest above them, fearing the first appearance of dark uniformed figures.

'Never mind a week more,' said the man with the shotgun. 'What's in 'ee pockets now?'

Joe shook his head.

' 'at's the problem, 'at is,' said the man thoughtfully. 'Two hundred what might come next week or never. And a good chance of being had for aiding an' abetting.'

'Twenty's safer,' said Will. 'Twenty's sure, an' no questions to answer either. If he could toss two hundred around as easy as tha', wha's he doin' on the hulks?'

'Wait!' said Joe urgently. 'Take me where it's safe, and let me send a message for the money. Keep me till it comes. If it don't, then ask your twenty guineas of the law.'

He watched them, looking for the glint of greed in their eyes. But they grinned back at him, unbelieving.

'You'm shy of the cat, my friend,' said the man with the shotgun jovially. 'They d' all get their backs skinned when they 'm fetched back. You'm shy o' that!'

'If I'm took back, my son,' said Joe bitterly, 'them that's got the two hundred sovs and more shall know why. And you shall hear from them in good time!'

The threat was lost upon them.

'Oh-ah?' said the man with the shotgun, as though the

matter hardly concerned him, 'S'posing they can find us, and s'posing they don't hear from us first.' He stepped back, while the two blunderbusses were trained on Stunning Joe, and pointed the shotgun at the blue summer sky. The blast of the first barrel rocked and reverberated from the cliffs, its echoes hardly dying before the explosion of the second barrel woke them again. From beyond the rising ground there was an answering howl of dogs and presently the black figures appeared in silhouette against the hot blue of the afternoon sky. In a long moment of stillness before they came to the little group at the Lower Light, Joe listened to the full swell of sea breaking on the rocks below. Now, surely, it was all over.

MacBride himself was with the men. Perhaps he had deliberately exaggerated the effect of Stunning Joe's attack upon him at the time. But why? Joe looked stupidly at the officer as the cuffs were locked upon his wrists and his legs were ironed. Why had MacBride been bought for an escape attempt which was doomed to fail? Then, for the first time, Joe O'Meara saw the matter in a new light. MacBride had not been bought. He had allowed the escape for his own cruel sport, the hunting down of the felon and the terrible vengeance which the rules of the hulks would exact from him once he was caught.

As at Wannock Hundred, Joe O'Meara had been trapped in the net of other men's schemes without knowing why. It puzzled him that he, the shrewdest and most agile spider-man in London, should so easily become the prey of their malevolence. The enigma ran through and through his mind as the uniformed warders half pushed and half dragged him across the rough turf, driving him onwards with blows of their boots. At last a kick behind his knee disabled him momentarily and they towed him by his manacled wrists, his heels bumping over the tufts of grass, the sun in its decline dazzling him with white fire.

He was vaguely aware of MacBride walking at the end of

the line, and of the smocked figure who almost ran to keep up with the senior officer. The coarse mouth was open again, but it was a grimace of genuine anxiety rather than a grin. And in Stunning Joe's mind the question echoed long after the peasant voice had ceased to ask it of MacBride.

'Wha's the bounty, mister? Wha's the bounty?'

They brought him on board the *Indomitable* in the centre of a phalanx of black-uniformed warders. As he was pushed towards the open hatchway the light glittered on the bayonets of the officers who lined the way. Since the moment of his capture neither MacBride nor any of the other officers had spoken a word to him, as though silence would multiply vengeance. On the lower deck the prison-cages were empty, still awaiting the return of the convicts from the quarries. At the head of the deck, in the very bows of the ship, was the tiny 'refractory cell', formed by the damp timbers of the ship itself and the iron door which closed the prisoner in darkness and stench. Immediately above the cell, the 'heads' of the ship formed an open sewer which ran down the outer surface of the cell timbers, the foul odour seeping through every gap.

The leg irons were unlocked and Stunning Joe was left alone and handcuffed in the darkness. Even for a man of his slight build the bare space of the cell was too small to allow him to lie down at full length. At night he would be given a single blanket, and in this he would huddle on the damp timber as best he could until the cramp and confinement woke him again. Men did not sleep much in the refractory cells but then it was part of their punishment that they should be put to discomfort in this manner.

Joe had no idea how long they left him like this. He judged that it was no more than half an hour before the iron grille in the door slid back and a bull's-eye lantern shone in upon him. Joe, blinking in the sudden glare, heard the voice of MacBride.

'Ten dozen with the governor's compliments, O'Meara!

And see if they don't cut yor focking backbon' through!'

The iron slat crashed shut again before Stunning Joe had time to say a word. He looked about him, blinking in the darkness. A man who was recaptured after an escape was invariably flogged just before sunset on the following day. The interval was allowed for the governor to judge sentence and for the medical officer to certify the man fit. Surgeon Doyle, even when sober, had never been known to spare a man the ordeal of the gratings. Several of those who underwent the punishment died afterwards, but it was never attributed to the effects of the flogging. 'General infirmity' and 'chronic venereal infection' were the official causes of death.

Joe O'Meara had known, without considering the matter specifically, that they would tie him to the gratings and take the skin from his back. To that extent he had been well prepared for MacBride's news. In the darkness he pondered MacBride's tone of voice. To judge by that, they were going to try and finish him. If he had known the choice, it would have been better to kill MacBride in the quarry. Then, at least, they would have had to try him for murder and he would have died like a man before the Newgate crowds.

Presently he was aware of the tramping of men returning to the prison-cages from their afternoon labour. They would not remain in their quarters longer than was necessary for them to wash in the buckets of water provided. After that they were marched to the chapel, a space formed on the two lower decks of the *Indomitable*'s stern, for an hour's religious instruction. When they had gone, MacBride and four armed officers came for Stunning Joe.

'Prisoner O'Meara to see the medical officer!'

The iron slat was opened first and then the main lock of the cell door. They no longer bothered to replace the leg-irons, judging the handcuffs alone to be sufficient for the short crossing to the hospital ship *Iphigenia*. Joe walked between them, past the barred corridor with its empty cages on either side and up the steps of the companionway at the far end. Through the wooden partition he could hear the low rumbling responses of the prisoners in the chapel to the prayers read by the chaplain. Then he stepped out into the redder glare of the summer evening.

Across the water, the hospital cutter was being rowed towards the *Indomitable*'s gangway. The warders held Joe where he could watch the rituals of justice being carried out amidships. A convict who was a stranger to Joe had been tied spreadeagled to the wide lattice-work of the gratings against the side of a hammock-house. Two senior warders stood to one side, where there was a bench with several pails of water upon it. Both the prisoner who was roped to the gratings and the officer who held the cat o' nine tails were stripped to the waist. From the distance of the gangway, however, the entire back of the victim seemed to be coated with an orange wash, where the water from the pails had just sluiced down his wounds. His head, which had been lolling forward as if he might have fainted, rose and then flopped forward again. The officer who held the cat held it high above him and then brought it down with all his strength. It made a sound like a butcher's cleaver going through soft flesh to the bone of a carcass. A cold sickness began to swell in Joe O'Meara's stomach.

The victim of the torment had not moved or responded. According to prison rules, the punishment would cease when he lost consciousness. But the cold shock of sea-water thrown over his back had caused a convulsive movement of the head. In the eyes of the warders he was therefore able to endure what remained. Among the lacerated flesh, Joe glimpsed a speck of white and knew instinctively that it was uncovered bone. As the cat was raised again, he averted his eyes. The savage vengeance of the underworld and the swell mob, he thought, was nothing compared with the justice of the hulks.

MacBride's voice spoke quietly beside him.

'There's places on a man's back, O'Meara, places where a good aim shall see he never climbs nor walks again. See if you don't find it so!'

But Stunning Joe felt terror no longer, only his numb disbelief at the horror which was about to envelop him. They bundled him down the gangway steps to the cutter below, placing him at its centre so that he was surrounded by the bayonets of the warders on every side. He knew that the rational course was to destroy himself now, quickly, before the threatened horror became a reality. The sharp little eyes darted from side to side, vainly seeking an opportunity. MacBride read his thoughts easily.

'Have no fear, Stunning Joe,' he said softly, 'you shall be fed and watched like a baby, until your turn comes at the gratings!'

The cutter bumped alongside the encrusted hull of the *Iphigenia*. At a glance, the hospital ship hardly differed from the other hulks of the prison fleet. The portholes, though somewhat larger, were as securely barred over. Two small boats rowed round and round the moored vessel, each containing its complement of red-coated riflemen, their carbines and fixed bayonets stacked in a grove of blades at the centre of the launches. Day and night, this military picket was provided by the regiment on guard-duty at Portland.

MacBride and the escort took Joe aboard and delivered him to two duty warders on the top deck. He was signed for and marched into the upper ward where the most gravely ill of the prisoners were kept. The ward was lined with beds, rather than hammocks, each occupied by a figure in a blue-grey nightshirt and a cap with the word 'Hospital' embroidered upon it. The *Iphigenia* had once been a 36-gun frigate and the barred gun-ports allowed more light and air into the ward than was permitted on the main hulks.

Joe looked furtively about him as he was marched down the length of the deck towards the surgeon's office and the surgery itself at the far end. Few of the patients here would recover from their sickness. Many were asleep, a few lay awake staring vacantly at the bulkheads or the decking above them. From the grey pallor of their skin, one or two might have been dead already.

If anything, he thought, escape from the *Iphigenia* was more difficult than from the main hulks. At the entrance to the ward the entire deck was railed off from the outside world by the familiar bars of a convict-cage. Two warders stood guard, one outside and one inside the locked gate. Because of the size of the gun-ports, they had been double-barred so that a man would have to cut through several thicknesses of steel before he could make a large enough gap to crawl through. Even then, he would have to work under the eyes of the warder.

But the arrangement of the far end of the deck made Stunning Joe's hope grow dimmer still. Beyond a further iron-barred grille was Surgeon-Major Doyle's own office, through which the prisoner and escorting warders passed to reach the surgery and examination room in the bows of the vessel. Here the portholes were smaller, too narrow for Stunning Joe to get through, even had he found the means of filing the bars. Coldly he counted up the barriers between himself and freedom. First he would have to pass back through the office, overpowering Doyle and anyone else in there. He must find Doyle's own key to unlock the grille beyond, which closed the way to the ward. Then he must either account for the two guards at the main gate to the ward, or else file through the steel bars of the gun-ports in full view of them. After that he had only to swim for freedom through a rain of bullets from the marksmen in the guard-boats. And all this was to be accomplished without a file or a weapon, and while wearing handcuffs. It hardly seemed a likely spec.

Doyle, a hulking brute of thirty or so, watched the new arrival sullenly as Joe O'Meara was led through the office to the surgery beyond. The Surgeon-Major's dark clothes were crumpled, his finger-nails showed half-moons of grime, and his breath carried an acid stench of brandy. Whatever decorum he had once possessed as he walked the wards as a student was now lost in the dull brown eyes and slack wet mouth.

'Take the brute through,' he said sluggishly. 'And leave his cuffs on, damn you!'

They bundled Joe O'Meara into the space beyond and slammed the door upon him. A plain wooden bunk had been fixed on either side of the surgery against the lime-washed timbers. At the far end of the room the area had been curtained off. Joe sat down on one of the bunks, looked about him, and detected a movement behind the long black curtain. He was about to get up and investigate when the door opened and Doyle came in. The Surgeon-Major ignored Stunning Joe. Instead he went to the curtain, lifted it at one side and dragged out the girl who had been concealed behind it. The reason for his ill-temper was now evident. Stunning Joe and his escort had arrived just as Doyle was about to enjoy a doxy, one of those brought aboard under the pretext of a compassionate visit to a dying felon.

The girl was eighteen or nineteen years old. She was tall and thin, her red hair cropped short as a boy's, suggesting that she might herself have undergone a recent sentence in a reformatory. The green eyes had a vicious slant and her high cheek-bones were carefully rouged. Stunning Joe had not so much as seen a girl for months but the excitement in his heart was one of recognition. The tall pale redhead was known in the Haymarket night-houses as French Claire. And Claire was one of a dozen girls run by Old Mole with the aid of his bully, Jack Strap.

The girl was stripped to her petticoats, giving a glimpse of the shape of her narrow hips and long white legs. Though she glanced at Stunning Joe, any hint of recognition in her green eyes was quenched at once. She followed Doyle into his room, the door closed, and Joe heard the key turned in its lock.

Having seen Claire, he knew that some plan still existed for his freedom. But unless he worked out its details for himself, it was unlikely that the girl would have any chance of telling him. A young whore like Claire would be skilful enough to keep the Surgeon-Major occupied for an hour or two, and he must make the best of his time.

Joe examined his temporary prison. There was no way out, except through Doyle's own room. But even if he had been able to get to the ward itself, he would have been seized at once by the guards. The timbers on all sides of him were stout and unyielding, broken only by two portholes, high up and heavily barred. Drawing a deep breath, he walked over to the curtain behind which Claire had been hidden, and pulled it back. A sudden exultation overcame his fright at the object which lay behind the black drape.

On a trestle-table a human shape lay stitched into an envelope of sail canvas. That space behind the curtain was all that served as a mortuary for the convict hulks. Rarely a day passed without one or two deaths among the felons. Their bodies were brought here for Doyle's cursory examination and a few hours of lying in state while the details of their deaths were entered in the record for the prison commissioners. Hardly was a corpse allowed to grow cold before the shrouded form was taken on board the burial cutter. No time was allowed for the contagion of the dead to contaminate the living in the confined space of the decks. A man who woke in the morning might be fifty feet deep by the evening, his weighted shroud carried clear of the convict fleet by the fierce currents of The Race, where two tides met beyond the tip of Portland Bill.

Still fearful of the sight, Joe stretched out his hands towards the shape within the tightly-sewn canvas, broad at the shoulders and narrower at the feet, like any coffin. At first he thought it was a dummy, but that would hardly do for the plan he was trying to envisage. His brow furrowed as he tried to read the thoughts of Mr Kite and Old Mole. He touched the canvas and his fingers read the shape of an arm and hand folded across the breast. The chest seemed absurdly thrust out, as if the dying man had drawn a great breath to hold for all eternity. And then Joe felt the faintest warmth, seeping through the canvas as though to answer his touch. Hope and horror mingled in his heart. As he stood there, still uncertain, the shape within the shroud gave a soft groan and the inflated chest seemed to fall a little.

Stunning Joe sprang back and let the curtain fall. He had heard of dead men's groans as the air left their bodies but the effect of it was no less appalling for that. He had no idea who the man was or why he had died. Something had been said about a convict dying in one of the quarries that morning, either by an accident or from a seizure. Composing himself, Joe lifted the curtain again.

He thought that Claire could occupy Surgeon Doyle's attention but there was no means by which she could smuggle a prisoner to freedom from the *Iphigenia*. That he must do for himself, using the only means that would be likely to occur. First he tried to lift the canvas shape and found it heavier than he had dared to imagine. Abandoning the task for a moment, he ran his fingers round it and with a sudden excitement touched something small and hard. While Doyle had hidden the half-dressed girl from the warders she had made use of the curtained space as her own place of concealment.

It was a tiny key, exactly of the pattern carried by every policeman and prison officer in the kingdom. To the uninitiated, handcuffs were a formidable means of restraint. But a villain who knew his trade also knew that the same key would open any handcuffs in police office or prison lodge. They were made in such quantities that it was out of the question to cut different keys or make variable locks. Moreover, the routines of the police and the prison service would have been hopelessly complicated if there was an infinite variety of keys and cuffs. Most magsmen and bullies professed a contempt for handcuffs, swearing that they would generally spring them open with a good hammer-blow. That was a trick Stunning Joe had never accomplished, but with a twist of one hand he had the little key in its lock. The cuffs opened at its first turn and he laid them on the floor, rubbing the red impress which they had left on his wrists.

As he turned to his task again, Joe's heart was beating high and fast with a new hope tempered by the knowledge that such means of escape from the hulks was very likely to be the means of his death as well. Yet his spirits rose for the first time since he had been brought to Portland. Had not Soapy Samuel promised him that he must die to live again?

Running his fingers under the edge of the canvas shroud again he searched out whatever objects Claire had left there. One was a small pearl-handled razor. The second, which he failed to find for a moment, was a stout needle with a length of wax thread passed through its eye.

Now he knew beyond question what it was that Mr Kite required of him. The escape at the quarry, with MacBride's apparent assistance, was still a mystery. Had they meant him to get clear? Or was it a mere device for bringing him to the *Iphigenia* and ensuring that he would never be sought again by the law? Perhaps Claire was present only to provide a second chance for him in case the escape at the quarry failed. If that were so, then Mr Kite and Old Mole must want him very badly indeed. He chuckled to himself with the elation of the idea.

The shroud had been stitched by one of the other prisoners, effectively but not with great neatness. Stunning Joe opened the little pearl-handled razor and cut the canvas thread where it secured the shroud above the corpse's head. Inch by inch he wrestled the canvas down, stripping it from the stiffening form.

The dead man's face was anonymous like all those of the Portland prisoners. Cropped hair and sallow features were almost universal among the convicts, making it harder to distinguish one man from another. In this, at least, the authorities had unwittingly aided Sealskin Kite's plan. For the first time, as he struggled with the weight of the corpse, it occurred to Joe that the man's death was no accident. Mr Kite had needed a body, and Mr Kite's power extended even into the brutal kingdom of the hulks and the labour gangs.

He drew the rough canvas shroud clear and dropped it on the floor. Then came the struggle to move the corpse from its trestle-table to one of the bunks by the green-washed timbers. Stunning Joe paused and listened. Through the closed door he heard the harsh drunken laugh of Surgeon Doyle and the exclamation of amused vindictiveness.

'Why, you young bitch! So you would, would you?'

There came sounds of an amorous tussle, enough in Joe's opinion to cover the noise of his own movements. He lugged the shoulders of the corpse from the table and dragged the body to the floor. Its limbs had not yet stiffened completely in death. As he towed it by the feet, slithering across the planking of the deck, the arms fell to either side. The dead man was still dressed in his prison garb, his number stitched to the brown jacket.

Before lifting the body on to the bunk, Joe took the pearl-handled razor and slit the brown jacket so that it came easily away. Then he peeled off his own jacket with his number upon it. For ten minutes he struggled to thrust the hardening arms through it, and at last pulled it down untidily over the man's torso. With a final effort, he dragged the body on to the bunk and turned it on one side, facing the timbers of the ship's side.

With any luck, he thought, Doyle would have been too dazed by drink to recognise him when he came in. And after Claire's attentions it might be next morning before the Surgeon-Major came in and found that the man brought from the *Indomitable* had died of 'general infirmity'. The trick was not foolproof but it was the only hope left. Stripped to the waist, he took the fragments of the dead man's jacket and went back behind the curtain.

It was easy enough to arrange the tapering shroud upon its trestle-table and to slide himself into its open end. While he was moving the corpse to the bunk, Joe had considered what must be done. He stuffed the mutilated jacket into the far end of the shroud, took the closed razor in one hand and the needle with its wax thread in the other. Then he slid face downwards into the faint creamy light of the sail-cloth. He would have to stitch the two flaps of canvas together from the inside, a labour which he guessed would be easier if he could work with the material below him rather than reaching overhead to do the job. Of course, close examination would show that the stitching had been done from inside, but burial parties were not likely to make close inspections of a shroud. Even if they did, it would be assumed that the prisoner who stitched the shroud had begun, clumsily, with that end of it.

Best of all, Joe thought, those who came for him would be only too glad to get the job over. Not one of them would risk opening the bladder of infection and disease which the shroud represented. If all was not as it should be, Surgeon Doyle would take the blame, not they.

The stitching took him a little while, not least because the light was so faint. At length he finished the work, squirmed himself over on his back, and lay still with the pearl-handled razor closed in his fist. If they should discover the trick now, he thought, he would try to cut his way through them with the blade rather than surrender. Better to die than to endure what was in store for him on the *Indomitable*.

He knew that a corpse would not be left overnight and that the burial party would do its work before sunset. With no means of calculating time, he guessed that it was about twenty minutes later when he heard voices beyond the Surgeon-Major's office and the door opened. Several men came into the narrow space of the bows. One of them made a sound of nausea and disgust in his throat at the faint sweet smell which had begun to seep from the corpse on the bunk. None of them doubted that its source was within the shroud.

There was a sudden movement as two of the men lifted the plank which formed the top of the trestle-table. As a further precaution against contamination, they were not even to touch the shroud. The dead man would lie upon this wooden bier in the cutter until the time came when he was tipped from it into the sea. Joe listened for the voices of Surgeon Doyle or Claire. He heard neither and he guessed that Doyle had taken her elsewhere for his enjoyment. Then he felt his heart beat in his throat with apprehension as one of the officers looked at the figure on the bunk and spoke.

'No use flaying his back, Master-at-Arms! The scum's dead!'

But there was only a grunt in reply and Joe felt the procession moving onward through the ward with its invalids in their two rows of beds. He was in a creamy twilight which filtered through the threads of the canvas, listening to the rattle of keys, the opening of the iron-barred gate at the far end of the deck. Then he heard the call of gulls and the whisper of the calm evening tide.

They kept him level as the funeral party descended the gangway steps. He had once seen it done, the bearers at the lower end of the board holding it high above their heads. Then he felt the movement of the cutter, the rocking of the trim little boat as the men of the party stepped into it and settled themselves. His mind was possessed by two conflicting thoughts. The first was that he would be dead in a few moments more, trapped fifty feet below the rippling waters of The Race or drowning on its surface beyond reach of land. The other was that he would be free, walking the Haymarket with its doxies in their merino gowns and the waving feathers in their pork-pie hats. He thought of the rustling silks, the soft voices, and then he prayed.

'Give way! Together!'

As the officer commanding the detail gave his order, the oars of the first-class convicts cut the waves with a rhythmic wash of spray. Joe felt the cutter emerge from the lee of the

Iphigenia into the bucking swell of open water. There was not another word spoken for several minutes while he lay and breathed as shallowly as he could manage. Sea wind whipped and snapped at a loose corner of the canvas. Someone touched it and he heard the solid impact of iron shot being set down as one of the men roped it to the shroud.

'Oars up!'

They had evidently reached the spot, and for an instant there was a great stillness. But as he listened Joe heard a sound, the purling of water close by and further off a long continuous roar. He thought of The Race, the great tidal swirl, and for the first time his fear was greater than his hope.

'Man that is born of a woman hath but a short time to live.' The officer in command was yapping out the burial service, the speed and the shudder of his voice testifying to a chill in the evening wind. 'He cometh up and is cut down like a flower. . .' The words were new to Stunning Joe, who had never heard anything like them in his life. But even to his uninformed mind there was no mistaking what came presently.

'We therefore commit his body to the waves, in sure hope. . .'

What it was that the officer hoped, Joe never discovered. The plank was upended and he felt himself going backward, head first. The shroud hit the water, with the force of an explosion in his ears. Desperately, he drew a deep last breath, filling his lungs until they ached. Then the creamy twilight was gone. There was darkness, sudden and bitter cold, the roaring and booming of unfathomable depths.

9

Like a madman in a strait-jacket, Stunning Joe fought against the heavy swathes of wet canvas. The thick cloth plastered itself over his face and round his arms as he sank deeper and more slowly into the dark tide. A noise of thunder filled his ears as the blood gathered in his head and he pressed the air frantically back into his lungs. In the moment of hitting the water he had somehow lost his grip on the smooth pearl handle of the razor. Now, in a convulsive frenzy, he scrabbled against the wet canvas to find it again.

His fingers touched the hard smoothness. To ease the pain in his lungs he released the first precious bubbles of air as he jacked the blade open. He stabbed at the canvas and found to his horror that the thin steel made no impact. The folds of sailcloth were so wet and slack that they presented no resistance to the edge of the razor. Vomiting air again, he clawed at the canvas stitching, found it, and then began to cut desperately at the waxed thread.

At length he managed to thrust his head clear of the open shroud, kicking and wriggling to free himself from it completely. The struggle had seemed to last for several minutes but it was a far shorter time. He was nowhere near the sea bed. Below him, the weighted cloth peeled away, sinking to its last resting place. Stunning Joe had always imagined the depths of the sea to be a wonderland of green and blue, like the water-show at the Britannia Theatre in Hoxton. Instead he found himself in the darkest night, choking as the first taste of brine entered his mouth and scorched his lungs. He struck upward to the surface.

Abruptly, he broke the waves and drew in the cold air, retching to clear the salt water from his windpipe. He had feared that the men in the cutter would be close enough to see him. But they had buried him almost in the last of the twilight, and in any case the drift of the sea had carried him from them as he sank. Joe could make out the shape of the cutter across the darkening water. It was fifty yards or more away, pulling for the gloomy sides of the hulks which rode against the dusk sky. The officers, sitting in the stern, had their backs to him. At their oars, the first-class convicts were too preoccupied by their labour to scan the surface of the flood tide. Had they done so, they would have seen nothing but a small dark shape bobbing among the waves as Joe's head appeared above the surface. In any case, the thought of a corpse released by the shroud and floating on the tide would have been enough to keep them rowing all the harder.

At the age of eight, Joe O'Meara had been a 'mud lark', scavenging the muddy shores of the Thames at low tide. His first companions were watermen and sailors. Before he was full grown, he had learnt to swim with the best of them. That alone might prove his salvation now.

For several minutes he trod water, taking care not to splash the surface until the cutter was well clear of him. At the same time, he tried to get his bearings.

At his back he could still hear the distant roaring of The Race. Yet with the shadows gathering and the wind growing chill, the burial party had dropped him short of it. Even in a cutter with a full crew they had no wish to be caught in the cross-tides after dark. Instead of taking him out beyond Portland Bill, they had gone to one side. He was just as far from the convict hulks but in the calmer water which was enclosed by the right angle of Portland with its isthmus and the main sweep of Weymouth eastward to Melcombe Regis.

Stunning Joe located the red lights of Portland quay and the new breakwater, measuring them against another blob of red which he judged to be the pier at Weymouth itself. Between them and beyond, the gaslights of the esplanade made golden paths over the crumpled water. He began to calculate his chances.

The Weymouth shore was further off, perhaps two miles away, but it was a secure landfall. By dawn he would have entered a house, helping himself to clothes and money as easily as if they had been laid out for his choice. The dark rock of Portland, which rose closer at hand, promised recapture and vengeance. Even if he could get safely ashore and find clothes or money, the guards across Chesil Bank stood between him and the mainland. The body in the bunk of the *Iphigenia* might be buried next day as his own. Or it might not. If Surgeon Doyle was sober enough to notice the deception, there would be no road out of Portland for Joe O'Meara.

Slowly, conserving his energy for a long ordeal, he struck out towards the further blob of red light, where the mainland esplanade of Weymouth and Melcombe Regis began. The distance was far beyond any which he had swum before. Paddling like a dog, he had learnt to stay afloat for half an hour at a time in the waters of the Thames. To cover so great a distance in a specific direction was another thing altogether.

Yet as he moved, Joe felt the tide bearing him on its flood into the great bay of Portland harbour and the Weymouth shore. For the time being it was running in his favour. He had no idea when it might turn, carrying him further out to his death in the churning currents of The Race. Even at the flood, it was not taking him in the precise direction he had chosen. The long channel swell broke across Portland Bill, its waves swept eastward, so that Stunning Joe found himself carried along the shoreline rather then towards it.

From time to time he stopped, easing his tired arms by treading water and letting the sea bear him unresistingly. At first it seemed that he was no closer to land than when he had begun, and then he saw that he was moving in, under the lee of Portland. The line of golden light along the esplanades had now fragmented into separate points of brilliance, like an embroidered pattern. Still it was too far, a distance beyond anything he could cover before the first menacing pull of the receding tide.

Earlier he had thought the summer sea was warmer than the evening air above it. Now, as he struck out wearily again, his arms were chilled and growing numb from cold and fatigue. He stopped to rest them, treading water again, much sooner than he had intended. But this would never get him safe on land. Grinding his teeth, prepared to weep with the frustration of it all, he thrashed forward with his arms again, thrusting their slow and aching discomfort from his thoughts.

It was no use. A few minutes later he had stopped again, his limbs in a shimmering dance just keeping him afloat. For all Stunning Joe's agility, his small wiry body was ill-suited to the long endurance of the sea. He was nearer, much nearer to land, than when he had begun. But there was a mile of dark and restless water between him and the pin-pricks of golden light, where men and women dined or took their ease. The reflections danced on the sleek shifting sur-faces of the waves, as though mocking his fatigue and terror.

With a roar that carried anger as well as desperation, Joe struck out again, clawing away the water in a last fury of physical effort. It carried him a hundred yards, perhaps more, before he could go no further. Then he knew he was done for. He had heard that the gentle slope of the Dorset sands enabled a man to get his footing quarter of a mile out to sea, and stand with the water no higher than his chin. However that might be, there was no ground under him now and none that he could ever reach. His head lay back on the water as his arms and legs paddled feebly.

'Help me!' he shrieked. 'Help me!'

But his voice sounded tiny, even to him, in the great vast-ness of the sea. He turned on his belly, clawing again but making no progress. And then a wave slapped against his face with enough force to drive the water into his mouth. He choked and spat, still snatching at the flood as though it would offer him support. Another wave broke over his head, and then another with greater force. He knew suddenly that the tide had changed and that, for all his struggling, it was carrying him further and further out to sea. If he could stay afloat long enough, he would hear presently the roaring cross-tides of The Race growing ever louder at his back. But he could hear nothing for the moment above his own screams which were draining him of strength and breath simultaneously.

'Help me! For the love of God! Help me-e-e!'

But the waves slapped harder across his face and he felt the first pull of the tide that would draw him backward and downward. He cried out again and listened for the roar of the currents crossing.

'I'll help you, Stunning Joe,' said a quiet voice. 'That's what I'm here for.'

10

He was dead then, he thought, hearing either the voices of heaven or the last flickering madness in his own brain. In a vision, it seemed that the arms of mercy were lifting him from the cold sea and laying him at last on something firm. And then the vision faded as he began to retch again, spewing out water where he lay. No one spoke again. There was a steady creaking, like a tavern sign being swung in the wind. The sea had gone and there was darkness everywhere. Stunning Joe felt himself sliding into unconsciousness and made no attempt to resist it.

When he opened his eyes, two men were lifting him by his arms and legs, carrying him across shingle which crunched under their boots. He could not see clearly enough to make out who they were or where they were taking him in the darkness. Indeed, it was only piece by piece that he recalled what had just happened to him — the shroud, the burial and the long ordeal of the tides. A gate opened, he smelt hollyhocks and wallflowers in the warmth of an enclosed garden.

Dazzled by lights, he felt himself carried upstairs and laid on warm linen. There was a scent of lavender and a girl's voice among the others. Soon it was dark again and he was alone. The warmth overcame him with the ease of chloroform. He could not have stirred a limb to save himself from being returned to the *Indomitable*. The weight of his eyelids seemed greater than all the power of the sea. He heard a tiny sound, the turning of a key in a lock, and then he slept deeply.

No one came to wake him. He opened his eyes the next morning in a sunlit room, still alone. There was little enough furniture. A china basin and pitcher stood on a plain table, and there was a small wooden chair beside the bed. It was a servant's attic, he guessed, the boards uncarpeted and the window small. He got to his feet and walked unsteadily across the floor. There were bars on the little window, quite as formidable as those on the portholes of the hulks. Not that Joe could have made his escape even if the window had opened. Either the trousers of his prison clothes had been lost in the sea, or else they had been taken from him by his rescuers. At all events, he was now completely naked.

He looked down at the scene below. The house was one of the Georgian villas which lined the shore beyond the regimented grandeur of the esplanade. There was the little garden, as he had remembered it, with a high wall and a wooden door leading to the pebble beach. At intervals, on either side, were similar detached houses, imitated from Regency designs with pilasters and wrought-iron balconies. To the west lay the grand front of Weymouth and Melcombe Regis, the bathing-machines drawn up by the water's edge and several striped tents along the top of the beach. The stone paving which edged the shore was now shimmering in the summer heat and the sea sparkled like tinsel.

Further out rose the great rock of Portland with the dark

prison hulks moored in its shelter. Joe turned away from the sight and went back to the bed. He sat down and thought that whatever lay in store for him here, it could hardly be worse than the obscenity of the convict transports.

His movements had evidently been heard. A key scraped in the lock of the door and the handle turned. The forehead of the man who entered the room was creased in a frown of bewilderment, though the yellowed mouth hung open in what might have been a smile of welcome. He scratched the close, dark crop of his head and grinned at the man who had been saved from the sea.

'Well now, Stunning Joe!' said Old Mole thoughtfully. 'What trouble you have caused your friends!'

He walked slowly towards the bed, tapping the back of one hand into the palm of the other. Stunning Joe stood up, his hands folded over his loins in an instinctive gesture of decency.

'I never peached, Mr Mole! They never had a word from me! And if they had stripped the skin from me, I'd a-bit off my tongue before I'd peach to bastards like them!'

Old Mole drew a deep breath into his burly lungs. He walked up to Joe and clapped a friendly hand on his shoulder.

'You're all right, Stunning Joseph. You're a safe cove. Ain't in your nature to peach on old pals, is it?'

Joe snatched a blanket as a girl with a deformed idiot face appeared in the doorway carrying a tray. She set it down and went meekly away again. Without waiting for an invitation, Stunning Joe took the tray on his knees and cut hungrily at the mutton chops in their dish.

'I know what was done for me,' he said through a mouthful of meat. 'You and Mr Kite himself. I mean to show myself grateful.'

Old Mole watched the knife cut vigorously across the dish.

'Oh yes,' he said gently. 'You'll show yourself grateful all right. That's what I'm here for.'

The last words woke a sudden memory in Joe's mind, the voice which had spoken when all hope was lost. He put down the knife and fork.

'It was you, Mr Mole! In the boat last night!'

Old Mole inclined his head, modestly.

'Me and Jack Strap. Mr Strap ain't even a swimmer. He can't abide the water. Even when he's had to send an awkward cove to his last long home, he won't do it by water. Turns him quite rummy. Even Strap got a bit of sensitive nature, ain't he?'

Old Mole's mouth extended in huge and silent appreciation of his own wit.

'I was let go by Mr MacBride,' said Joe insistently. 'I was saved by Miss Claire. And I was took from the water by you.'

Old Mole shrugged and watched Joe start his second chop.

'When Mr Kite wants a thing, he generally gets it. You was watched over like a child in its cradle, Stunning Joe. It was never sure you could get clean away from the quarries, what with bounty-hunters as well. But then there was the hospital to see you safe out again, if caught. When they came to bury you, it was me and Jack Strap had you safe in sight. Mind you, Joseph, I don't say we should have found you easy again without you calling for us. The tide that carried you was driving us back.'

Joe looked up from his food.

'You was watching? All the time?'

Old Mole shook his head solemnly.

'You've no idea, little Joseph, no idea whatsoever how you've been watched over these past months.'

'And you sweetened MacBride? A flint-hearted brute like him?'

Old Mole grinned again.

'Jimmy MacBride got weaknesses, Joe. Ain't we all? Likes

his helping of nancy.'

'MacBride?'

'What could be told might put him on the hulks for good. And he knows it. But let him act reasonable, and he can stiff all he wants, with Mr Kite's compliments.'

Stunning Joe blew out his cheeks.

'You must a-wanted me bad,' he said. 'You really must, Mr Mole.'

'True,' said Old Mole. 'And Mr Kite more so. You wouldn't believe how set Mr Kite was on having you sprung. The things have been done for you, Stunning Joseph!'

'And my young person, Mr Mole? What about her?'

'Millbank, Joseph, the penitentiary. She'll be there five years if she's there a day. Arranged the matter. Same block as where Missy Ludd is boss. Sad accidents can happen there, Joe. Vicki Hartle bathed in water boiling fresh from the copper. A good scrubbing or two with them wire brushes. Fed on piping gruel to get the beauty of it warm. Why, being locked alone in the dark on bread and water 'll be heaven on earth for your Miss Vicki. Scores is settled, Stunning Joe, have no fear.'

But Joe was on his feet, the quick dark eyes glinting with anger.

'I don't want none of that, Mr Mole! Just let her rot there five years and forget it. I seen enough cruel tricks these past few months and I don't wish 'em on a living soul. Let the law have her, Mr Mole, but Missy Ludd ain't to touch her!'

Old Mole nodded submissively and spread out his hands.

'As you want it, Joseph. Then Missy Ludd shan't raise a hand to her. I'd say them hulks had made you a changed man, my son. What they call humane. Mind you, there's times when a man can be too humane for his own good. But that's between you and the bitch that done you harm.'

Old Mole turned to the door, as if about to leave, and then swung back again.

'In course, you'll be seeing Mr Kite this afternoon. I'll

have some togs for you before that. Act sensible, Stunning Joe, and remember your pals and what they've done for you. That way you won't go far wrong.'

He moved towards the door again, but Joe called him, getting to his feet once more.

'Mr Mole! That heathen clasp was never there, never with them other jools in the safe. I had no chance to make away with it. You got to believe that.'

'I believe you, Stunning Joe,' said Old Mole reasonably. 'Who wouldn't?'

'I never so much as seen it, Mr Mole. And if I knew where it might be, I'd tell you and Mr Kite straight off.'

Old Mole's yellowed mouth hung open again but there was no longer any semblance of humour in its grin.

'Oh, you would, Stunning Joe,' he said reassuringly. 'Yes, you would. Not at first, p'raps. But you'd marvel at the things you might tell once your mind was put to it proper.'

The waves on the shingle were no more than a distant thunder as the afternoon sun caught the dark gloss of mahogany furniture in Sealskin Kite's parlour. There the old man sat, hunched in his chair. Kite's face was brown and wizened as a walnut, so that he seemed the twin rather than the husband of the old woman who now sat beside him. Mrs Kite squirmed in her seat as she adjusted her black bonnet and shawl.

Sealskin Kite had never seen a police office. His closest acquaintance with a constable was when he saw an officer standing protectively at the gate of his stockbroker villa near Hammersmith Mall, touching his hat as the master's carriage rolled in. Kite was the merchant banker of the swell mob, a man who could turn goods into gold, gold into notes of credit, notes of credit into goods, stocks or bonds. In a long life he had worked with great dexterity and complete impunity. His neighbours saw in him a benign and childless old man, who contributed to the relief of 'distressed trades', and dropped a gold sovereign into the collection plate of the chapel which he attended on Sunday mornings.

The turf and the whorehouses of the Haymarket were the basis of his wealth, though he had long passed beyond such obvious means of subsistence. He had not been on a race-course for a dozen years, and he knew no more of the Haymarket than could be seen from a closed carriage driving between Regent Street and Pall Mall.

At this stage of his life, he really had no idea how great his investments might be in this group of betting offices or that, in property whose tenants lived by prostituting themselves in the ill-lit streets near Piccadilly. From time to time he read of vengeance exacted on a rival bookmaker or a recalcitrant debtor. An iron stave might break a man's legs so that they would mend again and allow him to walk with a little difficulty. Or, if the crime warranted a second blow, he would do no more than sit out the rest of his days by a street wall, a tin cup collecting the coppers of those who were moved to pity his destruction before they hurried on their way.

Sealskin Kite could not have guessed, to save his life, which of these injuries were carried out in his own interests. The men who inflicted them were employed by others who themselves were strangers to Kite. When he read of a man crippled by his attackers, or a young woman disfigured, he folded his copy of *The Times* or the *Morning Post* and shook his head in dismay. Then he would turn to the old woman at his side and lament that he had no idea what the world was coming to.

All of which made it very odd that Kite should have involved himself personally in the plans for robbery at Wannock Hundred. In the normal way of business he would never have allowed himself to be seen with Old Mole, let alone Stunning Joe or a common bawdy-house bully like Jack Strap. Yet the prize of the Shah Jehan clasp had swept away all his sense of caution.

And still Joe himself could not understand it. Sealskin

Kite was not a man to covet the bauble for himself. He had little taste for beauty or splendour of that kind. Why, then, should he want it desperately enough to spring Joe O'Meara from the dark prison-hulks? Even if the clasp could be found and stolen, Kite would never find a buyer for it. It was too easily identified. Even its separate stones would hardly escape detection. And if the stones had to be cut and reset, losing much of their value in the process, why not steal a different treasure in the first place?

Such were the thoughts which had occupied Joe O'Meara in the hours preceding his audience with Sealskin Kite.

In the sunlit parlour, Kite and his wife snuggled in their adjoining chairs, their shrewd old faces peering up like two mice in a glove. Old Mole and Jack Strap stood either side of the door, like footmen. Jack Strap was a fat, grizzled bully, whose age might have been anywhere between thirty-five and fifty. His jowls hung in lines of sullen despondency but there was no mistaking the strength in his shoulders, broad and powerful as a coal-heaver on a Thames wharf.

'Come, my dear young sir!' said Kite, the little eyes twinkling in the old bulldog head. 'Be seated by me!' He beckoned Joe to the chair which was placed on the side opposite to Mrs Kite.

When Joe had perched himself uneasily in the place of honour, his host took O'Meara's hand between his own.

'Sealskin Kite keeps open house, sir. Always did and ever shall. You may call for what you choose, sir. Whatever you do not see here shall be sent up at once.' He turned to the old woman beside him who was rattling the plates on the table. 'A new-laid egg or two for the young gentleman, my sweetness. And a round of buttered toast.'

Mrs Kite nodded, taking her dismissal in good part. She got to her feet and the train of her black dress scurried over the carpet towards the door, which Old Mole held open for her.

'Now,' said Kite turning to Stunning Joe. 'And now

welcome, my dear sir! Welcome again to all your friends!'

Joe had determined to say his piece early.

'I shan't forget, sir!' he said quickly. 'I shan't forget what was done for me, Mr Kite, nor what I owe to them that did it. Try me and see.'

Sealskin Kite smiled, shaking his head gently from side to side, as if such gratitude was beyond all expectation.

'Mr Mole,' he said, without turning his face from Joe. 'What is the news today from Portland?'

'Buried him, Mr Kite. Buried him just on noon in the name of Joseph O'Meara. Seems that Surgeon Doyle was quite poorly after last night's frolic. His assistant had to do the business. Surprised to find Joe dead in his sleep, of course. But no question of it. Thought he might have been smothered to death, yet who'd want to do that?'

They had murdered for him then, Joe thought. A man smothered, a body without mark upon it. Kite looked at him, took his hand again and smiled. In the intervals of speech, the old man's breath came in a faint buzzing sound as if he was always framing words even though he might not utter them.

'Only tell me what you want, Mr Kite,' he pleaded. 'Only tell me and I'll do it for you.'

Kite patted the hand and then released it.

'My dear young sir, ain't I a man of business? And what's a man of business to do unless it's to protect his investment?'

'If I knew where that heathen clasp was, I'd tell you, Mr Kite,' said Joe earnestly. 'And I'd fetch it for you this minute.'

Kite clicked his tongue and shook his head again, as if speechless with admiration of Joe's loyalty.

'But I don't know where it is, Mr Kite. May I be shot if I do.'

'Course you don't,' said Kite amiably. 'But Sealskin Kite knows.'

They were interrupted by the opening of the door. The

girl with the deformed head of imbecility brought in a plate of poached eggs on buttered toast. She placed it before Stunning Joe, bobbed to Sealskin Kite, and then withdrew.

'Eat your vittels and listen,' said Kite more sharply. 'That jewel can be took now and never a word said. A lot's happened since they put you away, Stunning Joe.'

'Such as?' Joe inquired.

'Such as the poor Baron Lansing taking sick and dying, with never a word or sight of the Shah Jehan clasp. All that he left went to his children, but never the clasp. Not sight nor smell of it again.'

'Then who had it?'

'Not my place to call Banker Lansing a rogue,' said Kite reasonably, 'but sure as I sit here that clasp was never in the safe for you to steal. After your bitch sung the whole caper to the law, Baron Lansing saw how he might improve himself. If that jewel weren't in the safe, but if it was thought to be, he might make his fortune from the London Indemnity insurers and ne'er lose a stone of the clasp. What he could make on it later would double his luck. Course, *you* might swear it was never in the safe, but who'd believe a thief that was caught by the law?'

'He never took it to the grave with him?' said Joe.

'No,' said Kite, 'he never did. Nor it didn't go to his family either. What else he had was theirs by right and they took it. But the Shah Jehan clasp went another way from the first. It never, never was at Wannock Hundred. Lansing's doxy had it.'

'Doxy?' said Joe uncertainly.

'A real young beauty,' breathed Kite, 'no more 'n eighteen years old. Cosima Bremer. Set her up in a house in Brunswick Square in Brighton, easy to visit from London or Wannock Hundred. Old Lansing pleasured her till one day he gave himself a seizure at the game. Died in the saddle!'

For the first time Joe heard Sealskin Kite laugh.

'So Miss Cosima kept the jewel he gave her for safety?'

Kite nodded.

'Safe and sound in the big house in Brunswick Square. And there she sits all alone, poor little mouse, with a great heathen jewel as her inheritance. She can't sell it and she can't eat it. What's she to do? Why, my dear young sir, the man that relieves her of such a burden does her a kindness.'

'Stop a bit,' said Joe cautiously, 'you can't *know* she's got it, Mr Kite. Not know it for a fact, that is.'

Kite chuckled again.

'The London Indemnity insurers know it, Mr Joe. That's enough for me. There's a watch on that house, day and night. Sometimes their own men and always the police. When old Lansing snuffed it, his banking business was in very poor health. He'd been putting aside a few little trinkets to be made off with in the event of a smash. The Shah Jehan clasp was best of all. A little bit of fortune when he and his doxy did their bunk. Now the law knows it and the insurers know it. Course, they ain't got proof strong enough for a justice to sign a warrant. But there they sit, front and back of Brunswick Square, like two cats outside of a poor little mouse-hole.'

'And you mean to have the jool, Mr Kite!' said Joe excitedly.

'I do, Stunning Joseph. I do indeed. And here's the beauty of it all. I may take that heathen treasure without fear of raising a shout. For when a jewel is supposed to have been stole already, only kept back by the owner for purposes of fraud, why there can hardly be a complaint when the party loses it in earnest. He can't go to the police office and complain of being robbed of a treasure that he's not supposed to have in the first place. Rich, ain't it?'

'Rich,' said Joe, nodding eagerly.

'And that ain't the best of it!' Kite allowed the breath to buzz humorously through his teeth for a moment. 'The best is that I have a spiderman to steal it for me. The best spiderman of all the trade. And he won't be looked for, nor suspected, nor even recognised. For all the world knows him dead and buried off Portland a few hours since. You was worth springing, my dear young sir.'

'It'll have to be slippy,' said Joe thoughtfully, 'what with jacks and insurers all about it.'

'Why,' said Kite humorously, 'we thought of that too. There's a tame jack among 'em. A jack that was tamed special for you.'

'You bent him?'

'No,' said Kite, 'but we tamed him. Mr Mole got him on a string. Verity. A big fat jack to be led by a ring through his nose. And the best of it is that he never knows he's being led. He's been through every hoop that Mr Mole held for him.'

'Then you mean to have that jewel from under their eyes, Mr Kite?'

'Oh, I do, Stunning Joseph. I do. If you can count so high, there's one hundred thousand pounds to be had for it.'

Joe looked startled.

'Never!' he said. 'The law and the insurers never said above ten thousand when I was put up at Old Bailey.'

'Ten thousand to you or them,' said Kite softly, 'ten thousand to the rest of the human race. But to me, one hundred thousand straight. And I ain't told a living soul why. And I shan't start now.'

Joe looked up at the impassive faces of Old Mole and Jack Strap as the two men guarded the door. He glanced back at his host.

'I'll do my best, Mr Kite,' he said at last. 'I swear I will. I mean to show myself grateful to you.'

'Course you do,' said Kite. 'And don't we trust you to? After all, where's your other friends? You might throw yourself on the mercy of the law, but that would be ingratitude. And they'd take you to the hulks, strip the hide from your back, and cut your backbone almost in two. Then you'd be shipped to do your time, walking like a cripple and crying like a baby. So you ain't the sort to peach on us.'

'You know that!' said Joe insistently.

'Course we do,' said Kite. 'Even if we didn't, a man that's dead and buried won't be looked for. Supposing he should be killed a second time, no man will look for him and no man will hang for him.'

'I swear, Mr Kite!' said Joe, suddenly frightened. But Sealskin Kite calmed him by a gesture.

'Course you do, Stunning Joseph. But a man like you is the only man for the job. A right, tight friend. Why, Stunning Joe, I don't know that you aren't the only sort of friend that a man of business ought to have! You being dead already!'

And Sealskin Kite laughed a second time, louder than before.

SEALSKIN KITE'S LITTLE TICKLE

11

The mid-morning sun burnt with a silver fire above the delicate ironwork of the Chain Pier. On the placid surface of the water it was reflected like polished metal, slanting a colourless glare down the busy little streets beyond the promenades. By July the fresh white paint of shop-fronts and taverns had been raised and blistered in the heat.

Beyond the huddled little streets stood Folthorp's Royal Library and Reading Rooms. Its Grecian elegance contrasted oddly with the oriental domes of the Queen's pavilion which it flanked. Twice a day, in the middle of the morning and the afternoon, Folthorp's became briefly the meeting place for visitors of rank and fashion in Brighton. An elegant advertisement in brass letters on black glass promised: 'Tables with newspapers and magazines, railway records, share lists, army and navy lists. A newspaper room is set apart exclusively for ladies.' A uniformed constable stood conspicuously near the glass door to deter youthful beggars or 'happyjacks', as they were known to Brightonians.

The reason for Folthorp's brief popularity was easily explained. At eleven in the morning and three in the afternoon, the latest share prices and financial news were received by telegraph from London and posted up for the benefit of subscribers. A man of business could take a house in Brighton for the summer, yet still be as well informed as if he had remained in his villa in Highgate or Hammersmith.

At about quarter past eleven, the subscribers began to leave. Gravely-bearded men in silk hats, the gold chains of hunter watches looped across their waistcoats, stood in little groups outside and paused to pass the time of day. Their dress and manner was quite as formal as if they had met on the floor of the Exchange itself. A few men were unable to join their colleagues who now wandered away, arm-in-arm, to the Turkish Baths of the Old Steine or to take Brighton Seltzer at the German Spa in Queen's Park. These were the invalids whose tapestried carriages or Bath chairs, each with its attendant, stood in a row outside the reading rooms. Elderly and retired brokers, their morning and afternoon visits preserved an illusion of continued vitality.

The last of the old men hobbled out into the sunlight, the walnut colour and complexion of his face just visible in the surrounding bandage which bound his jaw and skull, as if he had been a martyr to toothache. His attendant, a dark young man with a finely-trimmed beard and a tall hat stood behind the invalid carriage as his master climbed in. It was the most elegant of all the Bath chairs, built with the serpentine grace of a Park Phaeton, except that the seat itself was a solid padded chair, covered with a rose and leaf tapestry. To balance the two large wheels at the rear, there was a single small wheel at the front with a long curving handle by which the occupant could direct the carriage as he wished.

With a sigh of contentment, the old man settled back in his padded chair and felt the pressure of his attendant's arms on the handle behind him.

'Push away then, my dear young sir,' said Sealskin Kite genially. 'Push away!'

Stunning Joe leant forward and the carriage moved, slowly at first and then gliding more easily as it picked up speed. Down East Street, towards the sea, the arbiters of summer fashion displayed their dresses and bonnets as elegantly as in Regent Circus. Joe looked briefly at Pocock's Family and Complimentary Mourning, wondering for the first time if anyone was in mourning for him. The Jupon Imperial and the Corsage Venus for Equestriennes were discreetly advertised by Madame Virginie Dawney, 'Artiste en Corsets,

Modes et Robes'.

'Why, Joseph,' said Sealskin Kite with a chuckle, 'a man might almost think himself nearer to Paris than London in this sort of a place. Eh?'

Joseph agreed, and Kite chuckled again, as if to reassure him. Mr Kite had laughed and smiled since the moment of their first meeting. Whenever Kite turned his face to Joe, the smile was always there, impassable, impregnable. Once, Joe had come into the room at the end of a conversation. Kite was reminiscing to Old Mole on the subject of a welsher.

'And he *don't* walk straight again, Mr Mole,' the old man was saying. 'Not *quite* straight.'

And when Kite turned to Joe he wore the same frozen geniality on his face as when he had given Old Mole his confidence.

They came into view of the sea just where the fishing-smacks had been pulled up on the shingle. The tight, strained rigging ran in indigo relief against blue sky. Men with baskets of turbot on their shoulders walked in groups towards the Market Street stalls. Smells of fresh mackerel, pitch and tar lay heavy in the warm air. Sealskin Kite shifted in his chair, drawing a rug over his knees and lighting one of Milo's best cigars.

'Don't pay no notice to the Bedford Hotel this time, young sir,' said Kite pleasantly. 'We ain't going home there yet. Just push on a little more. You never seen the beauties of Brunswick Square as yet. Mr Mole never took you, did he?'

'No, Mr Kite,' said Joe, a little breathless as the invalid chair bumped over the uneven paving of the promenade. 'Never did.'

The sun caught the waves with a tinsel glitter and Sealskin Kite chuckled again.

'You'll like Brunswick Square, Joseph. Ain't it where you're to make your fortune? And ain't a man to love the place that makes him rich?'

'How rich shall I be, Mr Kite? How rich, if I was to find

that clasp for you?'

Kite began a teasing, humming sound, like a good-natured uncle who knows that his gift will be far greater than anyone expected.

'What would you say, Joseph? What would you say if I was to tell you this? Fetch me what I ask for and you shall have the entire value of that Shah Jehan clasp. What d'ye say to that? Eh?'

Joe looked westward into the light, where the sea became a deeper blue.

'I'd say I didn't understand it, Mr Kite. I don't see why a man went to so much trouble over me for me to steal him a jewel, and then to give me all the value of it. Where's the sense?'

The old man chuckled.

'Did you ever know, did you ever know, my dear young sir, Sealskin Kite to cheat himself? Eh? That sort of man? Eh? Eh?'

'No,' said Stunning Joe doubtfully.

'Then, Joseph, rest easy. If I give you the value of that clasp, 'tis only because I shall make ten or twenty times what it's worth.'

Joe had heard all this before, and it left him uneasy. To be offered a hundred pounds for stealing the clasp was one thing, but to be offered the full value of the item stolen was against all the rules. Perhaps they meant him harm, as soon as he should have got the jewel for them. He thought at first of setting down all the details, including Kite's name, and leaving the confession in a place where it would be found if he were killed. But the absurdity of the idea was evident. So far as the law was concerned, he was dead already. Dead and buried off Portland. There was no protection for him now, save in the good nature of Sealskin Kite. Joe looked at the back of the old man's head and pictured again the implacable smile.

Presently they passed the little toll-booth, where fees were

levied on coals being brought into Brighton. The massive
Georgian façade of Brunswick Terrace faced the sea from
the far side of the road.

'Attention, then, my dear young sir,' whispered Kite. 'See
what it is that must be done.'

On Kite's instructions they avoided Brunswick Square for
the time being, turning into Brunswick Street West, which
formed a mews running along the backs of the houses in the
square. One side of the little street was given up to stables
for the houses themselves, the far side to a miscellaneous collection of cottages, livery stables and a tavern. Kite glanced
at the upper floor of the tavern as they passed it.

'Jacks,' he said quietly. 'Watching night and day.'

Stunning Joe hardly spared the building a glance. It was
one of a dozen such public houses in the area. In the little
yard a woman was boiling whelks in a wicker basket. Inside,
it was one of the ratting, dog-showing, horse-racing and general sporting houses. Somewhere on the first floor, or in one
of the attic rooms, the officers of the law sat patiently, day
and night, watching the rear of the big houses in Brunswick
Square. Joe could see no way in from that direction.

They came to the top of the narrow street and turned
towards Brunswick Place, which ran down into the square
itself. Outside the house of the Right Honourable Henry
Layard stood a plump self-important man, his red face contracted in a scowl under the tall chimney-pot hat. He was at
ease, hands clasped lightly behind his back, like a sentry. If
he paid any attention to the elderly invalid and the attendant, his eyes showed no sign of it. As they passed out of ear-
shot, Sealskin Kite began a muttered commentary on the
situation for Joe's benefit.

'There's your jack for you, all right? Stood outside that
doorway. Day and night likewise. Clear view of the Lansing
house. They had two of 'em on duty at one time. Seems they
think one's enough now. There's another stood by, though,
to follow her wherever she goes.'

Joe's quick little eyes flicked over the Baron Lansing's house in its corner of the square. He took in the front door with its black-railed steps, the way down to the basement, the ledges and window balconies which would carry his nimble feet swiftly to the elegant windows of the upper drawing-room. But the eye of the private-clothes jack was upon them all.

As they were approaching the corner, his attention was taken by the adjoining house. A tall imperious woman, veiled and dressed in black, walked slowly up its steps. Her movements suggested age and authority.

'Madame Rosa,' said Kite. 'Look.'

And Joe caught sight of the printed card which Kite was holding.

Madame Rosa Woolston receives a number of young ladies for board and education at the Brunswick Academy, Brunswick Square. Great attention is paid to the health and comfort of all the pupils. Terms twenty-four guineas per annum. Laundress two guineas. Each young lady is requested to bring a fork and spoon, and six towels, to be returned on removal.

References are kindly permitted to the Reverend J. S. Masham, 18 Norfolk Square.

As though reading Joe's thoughts, Kite said, 'Drop it, young sir. There's nothing there for us.'

'She can't have young ladies there now, being the vacation time.'

'There's her and a maid,' said Kite softly. 'The old girl can't be bent or bought. No, Joseph, it's through the front door for you.'

Kite had just finished speaking as they came to the corner of the square. At that moment, from the steps leading down to the basement, a figure darted out on to the pavement. It flashed a quick glare from almond eyes, swung its pink skirts, and set off down the pavement with a tight, purposeful little swagger.

'Law,' said Kite. 'Even the servant girl's a nark. They got their eyes on the front and their eyes on the back. They got their nark in the house itself. And even if you could get in the next house and chloroform Madame Rosa and her servant and break the wall down to get through, it wouldn't do. Them that knows Sealskin Kite knows he's not a man for noise and inconvenience. This whole business got to be quiet as oil and sweet as a nut. No bother and no noise about it. Why, my dear young sir, it's not even you pushing my chair just now. Quite a different party. I don't even know of your existence. Savvy? You and Sealskin Kite have never met.'

Stunning Joe was hardly listening. All his attention was given to the house and its surroundings. His ears were alert for every sound, the tiniest noise of lock or handle turning. His nose drew the air deeply into his lungs, tasting fresh paint, the odours of cooking unattended, soft putty of a window newly sealed. His eyes mapped a dozen ways up the walls of the Georgian mansion. His feet traced every unevenness in the York stone of the pavement. Joe had to admit that the jacks had sealed the crib up tight. A mouse could not enter front or back. There was no hope of smuggling a crowbar into Brunswick Academy and knocking out the bricks of the partition wall. As for the front door, it would be opened to him by the pretty nark in the pink skirts. But Joe looked once more at the tall windows and the white-painted Georgian masonry. He hummed a little tune to himself. Sealskin Kite heard him and chuckled.

'Tell me, then, Joseph, can you fetch my little jewel for me?'

Stunning Joe, with all the arrogance of his youth, leant forward over the old man's shoulder.

'Tonight be soon enough, will it, Mr Kite?'

It was going to be an easy turn. Verity knew that. Indeed,

all Brighton knew it. He had come on duty at two in the afternoon and would stand guard outside the Honourable Mr Layard's until midnight. There would be a ten-minute relief at six. A long watch, he thought, but an easy one. It was the evening of the grand summer ball at the Royal Pavilion, given by the regiment stationed in Brighton, the 18th Hussars. Of course Cosima Bremer had been invited and, of course, she would take her maid to attend upon her.

At first Verity had been disgruntled to find that Cosima never allowed Jolly to be in the house alone. Indeed, the sullen little maid was rarely allowed above stairs and had no hope of being able to search her mistress's apartments. On second thoughts, Verity was reassured. Cosima's behaviour was clear evidence that the Shah Jehan clasp remained in her possession, somewhere in the house.

During the fortnight of his surveillance, Verity had found a great sense of tranquillity in the sunlit peace of the square. In the early summer mornings a hazy sun lit the distant sea, which lay calm as a lake under the rising mists. By midmorning he could feel the heat of the sky on his back, the waves catching its tinsel glitter until they darkened in a horizon strip of azure. At noon, the blue surface deepened until it was bottle-green by the decline of day.

The routine of the square, particularly the Baron Lansing's house, varied little. There was the seven o'clock bread, the eleven o'clock milk, the one o'clock leg of lamb. From time to time the cat's meat cart or a vintner's wagon made deliveries.

This afternoon it was the turn of the vintner, the canvas awning of his cart painted in stark red lettering which promised 'Wines at the Reduced Duty'. Jolly's head appeared briefly above the basement railings as the crate was unloaded. Presently, Piccirillo of St James's Street made his delivery. The van this time was smartly painted in olive green with a pair of black horses. 'Naples and Genoa Macaroni. Brunswick and Westphalia Hams. . .' Verity's mouth watered uncontrollably and his stomach groaned at the unfulfilled promise.

The peace which settled on the warm empty square was ended half an hour later by a shrill warbling. Verity remained almost motionless, only his eyes seeking the cause of the disturbance. It came from a young man who had entered the top of Brunswick Place and was walking slowly down to the square, dragging his feet listlessly. Verity recognised him, a whistling-man, as such beggars now called themselves. His face was long and thin, his cheeks appeared hollowed by hunger and by being habitually drawn in to whistle before the houses where he begged. His thick lips were parted, giving him the look of the simple-minded, until he pursed them to try snatches of a tune. He glanced nervously at Verity but then plucked up his courage again. Standing before one of the upper houses, the ragged man cocked his head at the first floor windows and began to whistle 'The Little House under the Hill' in a plaintive, insinuating manner.

There was no response from the occupants of the building. The little man's shoulders moved in a visible sigh as he turned away and walked further towards the square. Outside Henry Layard's house, he stepped off the pavement to avoid the man who stood guard there. This time, Verity's eyes stared ahead of him, indignant but immobile. It was his lips which moved.

' 'ere! You! 'ook it! Sharp!'

'Pardon?' said the whistling-man.

'Hook it! Hop the wag! Clear out! While you got the chance!'

'Why?' said the little man peevishly. 'What was I doing wrong then?'

'Breaching the peace!' said Verity furiously. 'It been peaceful here all day till you come by. Peace is what parliamentary gentlemen come here for, and they ain't special about having to listen to your noise!'

The little man's thin face reddened, as if to offer defiance. Then it seemed he thought better of it and shuffled away again up Brunswick Place. He turned the corner into Western Road and was seen no more.

Verity chuckled to himself. A whistling-man! It was just the dodge to draw a police officer's attention away from his surveillance. Twenty or thirty seconds spent in seeing off the whistler. Long enough, he thought, for Miss Cosima or her fancy-man to be out and away with a pocketful of heathen clasps.

'Not if I know it, miss!' he said firmly.

During the encounter with the whistling vagrant, Verity's stern gaze had never wavered from its object. He chortled again with self-satisfaction. They must think him green as a leek and soft as new cheese to fall for such a trick.

'Why, miss,' he said to his unseen adversary, 'all the time I could a-seen a fly land on your window and counted his legs for him before he took off again!'

The long afternoon silence continued almost uninterrupted. Where Brunswick Square opened to the sea, Constable Meiklejohn now sat in a plain carriage waiting to take up surveillance of Cosima and her servant when they left for the regimental ball. In their little room above the ratting-pit and the sawdust tavern, Inspector Croaker and Mr Bunker watched the rear of the grand houses, the drab yellow of the London brick. The fashionable grace of the square itself was Verity's alone.

A collier's dray drawn by a lumbering horse came down Brunswick Place, turned into the square and stopped outside Madame Rosa's academy. Verity's eyes narrowed with suspicion. He watched the round iron covers of the coal chutes in the pavement as though they were his personal property. The two draymen clambered down, their hair bound in blackened cloths, their eyes flashing white in the grime of their faces. Half a dozen sacks were lowered to the pavement beside the iron chute-cover. Verity satisfied himself that it was indeed Madame Rosa's which had been opened, not Cosima's. He heard the rattle of coals from the emptied sacks as they slithered down the chute into the little cellar which extended under the pavement. He watched each sack opened and saw that nothing but loose coal was shot from it. Presently one of the draymen went down the steps and then came up again, holding out his hand to prevent the other man from opening the next sack. The cellar was full. The two remaining sacks were loaded back on to the cart, still bulging with their contents, and the wagon clattered away.

Just before eight o'clock a hansom cab drew up outside the corner house. Cosima Bremer, with Jolly in attendance, came out and entered it. As the cab moved off, Meiklejohn's closed carriage pulled out and followed it at a little distance. Verity took a dozen steps down the pavement and resumed his watch on the corner of Brunswick Place and the square itself. He rocked a little on his heels and surveyed the scene with a sense of ownership.

12

Stunning Joe was not in darkness for long. Old Mole and Jack Strap had brought the coal wagon to rest conveniently outside Madame Rosa's academy in Brunswick Square. After that it was simple. The greenest stickman would never have attempted to open the round iron cover of the Baron Lansing's coal chute, while a private-clothes jack watched from Brunswick Place. But this was quite different. At the worst, Madame Rosa would merely find that she had received an unexpected delivery of coal, when the trick was pulled.

Old Mole and Jack Strap were rendered completely anonymous by their disguise, the grimed faces and the soot-blackened headscarves. Strap had undertaken most of the coal-heaving until half a dozen hundredweight sacks stood in a huddle on the pavement, where Madame Rosa's cellar chute had been opened. Stunning Joe's light-boned, childish body was crouched in the last of these, which Jack Strap lowered carefully so that it stood upon the iron chute-cover of the Baron Lansing's cellar.

Thin, strong wire, of the sort used for wiring moss and flowers into a wreath, had given Joe's sack a plausible, bulging outline. When his two accomplices had gone through their pantomime of filling Madame Rosa's cellar and loading the two unwanted sacks of coal on to the wagon again, the shape of this one would remain unaltered.

Joe worked quickly at the first and easiest part of his task. Slipping a razor from the pocket of his dark clothes, he cut open the bottom of the sack which concealed him and stuffed the piece of sacking out of sight. His fingers ran on the smooth iron of the coal-hole lid where it was set in the pavement. He jacked it up easily with a short chisel and began to lower himself carefully into the darkness. It was just large enough to accommodate a man of Joe's build with the head and shoulders of a skinny urchin-boy. From the day that he was full grown it was assumed that nature had formed him to be a thief.

There was no chute inside the cellar, but Joe hung deftly by one hand, easing the iron cover back into place with his other. Then he dropped, light as a squirrel, on to the loose coal beneath. It was no more than a minute or two later when he heard the rumble of the cartwheels, iron rims on stone, and knew that Old Mole and Jack Strap were on their way back to Mr Kite.

Of course, he thought, the worst part of the whole thing was that he must wait in the gloom of the coal cellar for several hours, until Cosima Bremer and the pretty nark had left for the regimental ball. The fires of the house would be kept banked up whatever the season and there was a risk that the servant would open the door to fill the coal scuttle. But Stunning Joe doubted that she would do more than put her head into the cellar and he was confident of concealing himself in that case.

He tried the latch gently and found, as he expected, that the cellar was unlocked. After all, the occupants of the tall houses were hardly in danger from thieves walking down the basement steps in full view to steal a few lumps of coal. No servant girl would want the bother of locking and unlocking the cellar every time that she came out of the house to fetch a scuttleful.

Joe's consolation was that he knew his patience must be rewarded. Like the officers of the surveillance detail, he was fully informed about Cosima Bremer. What chance was there for a German governess to make off with the riches of the Shah Jehan clasp? Now that the man who had kept her was dead, she had no friends and no refuge except her own country. But Joe knew, as well as any police officer, that she would be stripped and close-searched at the first attempt to make a bolt abroad.

He took out a little pocket-watch and saw that it was nearly eight. Presently he heard the lighter wheels of a hansom cab above him, the sound of voices, one belonging to Cosima Bremer, the other to her maid, Jolly. That Jolly had been planted by the law was obvious enough, even to Cosima herself, Joe supposed. He listened and heard the cab door slam. Then the light wheels rolled forward and there was a profound silence. He reached for the latch of the cellar door.

Joe edged out into the twilight of the basement area, the steps to the pavement at one end and the kitchen door at the other. As a precaution, he raised himself slightly and peered quickly an inch or so above the pavement level. The fat figure of a private-clothes jack stood in tall hat and frock-coat on the far side of the square. But the basement itself, including the kitchen door, was concealed from watching eyes, at least for the time being. Joe took a thin strip of steel from his pocket. As he suspected, the lock on the kitchen door was of the simplest kind, three levers each of which could be operated in turn to open the bolt. When the great houses had been built, the servants' basement was constantly occupied and so there was no fear of a break-in. The owners of the houses were far more concerned about robbery by dishonest servants themselves.

With the lock open, the door was held on the inside by two ordinary bolts. Joe produced a 'teaser', scissor-shaped blades of metal thin enough to pass through the crack between the door and jamb. The strong slim blades began to close on the bolt and edge it back, little by little. Five minutes later, Joe opened the door of the kitchen gently and stepped inside. Then, as a final precaution, he bolted himself in.

There was no question of lighting the gas, but fortunately the summer evening was still bright enough to show him the interior of the rooms. In case he should have to explore darker areas with no external windows, he helped himself to an oil-lamp from the kitchen and then began to climb the basement stairs.

At the top his progress was ended by another door, securely locked. Of course Cosima Bremer would not let her servant girl run all over the house. Except when called, Jolly was evidently banished from the upper floors. Joe smiled as he worked on the lock. At least he was sure that the Shah Jehan clasp was not concealed anywhere to which Jolly might have access.

There were two rooms on the ground floor. Joe entered the first, overlooking the square and its gardens. The walls were covered with a dark-red paper, thick with a pattern of honeysuckle flowers which shaded from salmon into cream. Two little display-cabinets, their shelves covered by blue velvet, stood either side of the window, set out with ornamental china. Joe swept the china to the floor and found nothing. The deep crimson window-curtains were edged with gold cord and crowned with pelmets of similar design. Taking care not to show any movement outside he examined them gently. An ornate moderator-lamp, deeply fringed with red silk, hung from the centre of the ceiling. He inspected it by standing on a padded stool. But it was still warm from use and only a fool would have hidden the clasp among its intense flames.

The rest of the furniture yielded nothing, but Joe had felt from the first that this was not the room in which the clasp would be hidden. He made a final tour of inspection, throwing over the little occasional tables, upending the padded chairs and sofa, smashing to the floor the two jardinières and seeing the fern-pots break apart. There was nothing.

The room at the back was even less promising. It was a housekeeper's parlour, barely furnished, a curtain on a brass rod behind the door to match those at the windows. Joe shook his head. It was all too neat and clean. Instinct and experience told him that even Cosima Bremer would not choose to hide the clasp in a room swept and tidied by a copper's nark.

He went up the stairs to the first-floor drawing-room. This was the grandest of all the rooms in the house, the scene of summer dances and evening parties. The partition doors were folded back and the room extended the full depth of the house. Joe looked about him. The drawing-room was furnished in Louis Philippe style with ormolu tables and buhl cabinets upon which statuettes and other ornaments stood under glass cases. Filigreed gas-brackets and groups of water-colours cluttered the yellow walls. Gilded tables, cabinets, glass-shades, and heavy picture-frames gave a gloomy richness to the interior. Joe looked fretfully at it all. He took down the pictures one by one and examined their backs. He made a careful inspection of each cabinet and table. Where there were drawers in the tables, he drew them out and turned their contents on to the floor. Paper and trinkets were scattered from the front drawing-room to the back, but there was no sign of anything which might lead to the clasp.

Finally, Joe looked at the walnut canterbury which held the albums of piano music, and at the piano itself. The instrument was a fine Erard upright in a flame-pattern case of polished rosewood. He knew at once that he had found Cosima's secret. Not in the mechanism, among the strings and dampers, but in the place where such pianos offered the facilities of a good-sized family safe. The very place that a governess would choose!

He looked into the dark and narrow space which separated the back of the piano from the wall. At a glance it appeared solid enough. Only on closer inspection was it evident that the back of the instrument had been covered by a fine wire mesh held lightly in place by corner screws. Joe lugged out one end of the piano from the wall and detached two of the screws. A considerable recess now appeared in one end of the rosewood case. This was where the shorter treble strings were housed and where, in consequence, the inner case which covered them tapered away towards the top corner.

Joe slid his hand under the mesh and felt something move beneath his touch. It was the hard polished leather of jewel cases. He grinned at his own expertise. He brought them out, one by one, until he was quite sure the space was empty. Seven of them lay on the floor beside him. Sitting there he broke them open in quick succession.

Two were empty. The other five contained baubles which even to Joe's casual glance were nothing more than glass and paste. Of the Shah Jehan clasp there was no sign.

In his frustration he threw the last case across the room, with such power that it shattered the glass door of a cabinet. Despite his fury, his mind continued to weigh chances and probabilities. If she had not chosen the best hiding-place on this floor, then the clasp must be elsewhere. He headed for the stairs again and, to his relief, found another locked door at the top where the upper floor of bedrooms began. If

Cosima Bremer had left him a trail of messages she could not have been more informative as to which floor contained the greatest treasure.

He had the door open in a minute and was ransacking the three rooms. Only one appeared to have been used. The servant girl was evidently made to sleep by the kitchen fire. Better than a nark deserved, Joe thought.

The room which claimed his attention was Cosima's own. Its centrepiece was the bed, upon which she had given such pleasure to her elderly master that he had died of it. The polished brass rose from the corners of the bedrails to join in a crown, high in the air above the bed's centre. On this framework a 'tent' of delicate blue silk was hung, creating an effect which Joe had never seen before except in one of the most expensive bawdy houses off Panton Street. Like vines on a trellis, brass fruit ornamented the bedframe and the air was musty with stale feminine perfumes.

Joe was startled suddenly by a chirrup from the space before the window. Turning he saw a pet canary in its cage. The tall brass stand from which the cage hung, and indeed the cage itself, had been made to match the bed. In its elegant bell-shape, the bird-cage seemed a work of industrial art. The canary cocked its head, regarding him with its small black pupil.

'Pretty bird!' said Joe encouragingly, and then he began to look about him. The room was in a good deal of disorder. Gowns and petticoats hung from the posts of the bed. Undergarments lay scattered on a black horsehair divan. The matching chairs were a litter of stockings and slips. It was a room where the servant was never admitted, Joe guessed. Somewhere within it lay the great Shah Jehan heirloom.

Jacking open his razor again he slit the mattress and bolster of the bed, filling the air with a blizzard of tiny feathers. The custard-yellow canary hopped excitedly between its perches and sang with renewed enthusiasm. But neither the folds of the bedclothes, nor the gutted mattress and bolster yielded any sign of the clasp. Joe hacked open the horsehair divan and chairs. He scattered the drawers of the dressing-table and overturned the furniture. Neither the pockets of the clothes nor the velvet window-curtains contained a single jewel. Finally he pushed back the bed and began heaving up the carpet. But the polished wood of the floor with its black lacquered surround showed no trace of interference, not even the scratch of a knife-blade where a board had been levered up to make a hiding-place. The boards were tongue-and-groove, impossible for a girl like Cosima to open without leaving obvious marks.

Joe scratched the dark scrub of his head. The canary warbled and trilled its wordless oratorio.

'Daresay *you* might tell where it's put, if you only could,' he said. The canary stopped singing, cocked its head on one side again and looked at him as though it understood. Joe stared at the cage, the fine brasswork of its bars and ornaments, the solid base from which Cosima drew the seed-tray, since she alone must tend the bird.

'*Course* you could!' said Joe suddenly. He sprang across the room and looked into the cage. The canary shifted about nervously. But now Joe could see the whole dodge. The round circular bottom of the ornamental cage was like a drawer, two inches deep if one chose to make it so by raising the floor upon which the sand and seed were scattered. Joe pulled and the bottom of the cage came out. In it there lay a fine leather box, highly polished, red with a gilt design. It opened easily, and even Joe gasped at the sight within. In the twilit room the Shah Jehan clasp glowed and shimmered in all its purple and emerald glory. Swallowing excitedly, he thrust the box and its contents in the breast of his coat, then slid the bottom of the tray into place. The canary cheeped reproachfully.

'You ain't a bad little fellow, you ain't,' said Joe consolingly.

He ran down the stairs in his excitement and stepped out

into the darkened basement area. He left the kitchen door unbolted. No harm in throwing suspicion on to the pretty young nark. Then he waited in the dark for the return of the cab. When it came, the jack who had been shadowing it left. Only the fat one watching the house remained. Really, Joe thought, it was like taking pennies from a blind beggar's cup. Cosima Bremer entered the front door, followed by the servant girl. Joe counted twenty and then the screams began as the lights went up on the scene of theft and destruction. The fat policeman at the corner of Brunswick Place came pounding over, the boots of his plain-clothes quite as heavy as those of his uniform. Joe heard him thump up the steps to the front door, heard it opened by the hysterical little nark, and gave him ten seconds to get inside. Then Joe walked unobtrusive as a shadow up the basement steps, vaulted the railings to the pavement, and strolled casually away in the direction of the moonlit waves. Brunswick Square would see him no more.

Against the grey wash of the office wall, Inspector Henry Croaker's yellowed face seemed more sickly than ever. As he swallowed, the leather stock appeared to cut cruelly just below his adam's apple. His mouth hung open a full inch, as though the immensity of the disaster was still registering in his brain. Behind him stood Mr Bunker of the London Indemnity, his features immobile with a visible embarrassment on behalf of his constabulary colleagues.

Sergeant Verity stood smartly at attention, perspiring lightly, his tall hat clamped under one arm as he faced the inspector's desk.

'No sir,' he said, in response to a previous question. 'No one. No one come and no one went. Had me eye on the house-front every second, sir. Had a full view from the corner of Brunswick Place every minute from the time they left till the time they got back.'

Croaker looked keenly at the fat sergeant. The inspector's

customary pleasure in the downfall of his subordinate was tempered this time by the sense of his own predicament. Whatever blame might be put on Verity, it was Croaker as the officer in charge of the operation who would incur the displeasure of the commissioners and the Home Office.

'Let me have this plain, sergeant,' he said softly, swallowing rapidly between his words. 'Let me have this plain as day from you. No person entered or left the front of the house during your surveillance, while the mistress and her maid were absent?'

'Yessir!' snapped Verity smartly. ' 'a's it, sir!'

'And you know that both Mr Bunker and I, as well as two uniformed men, had a constant watch on the rear of the premises?'

' 'ave been so informed, sir.'

'And that you alone were at the front of the building, unsupervised and with no other person in sight of you for considerable periods?'

'Sir?' said Verity, his eyes shifting uneasily.

'Sir!' echoed Croaker derisively, the relish beginning to creep back into his voice. 'The matter stands very plainly, sergeant, does it not? How will the board of inquiry see it? There are two entrances to the dwelling. The word of four officers is proof that no attempt was made at the rear. For the rest we have your own uncorroborated statement.

'My *word,* sir, same as yours!'

'Silence!' said Croaker sharply. 'Moreover, the thief made his entry via the basement kitchen. The door conveniently left unbolted and unlocked. By whom, sergeant? By the very girl who was put in as servant upon your suggestion!'

'No sir!' said Verity desperately. 'Any case it don't make odds if she left it open or not. *No one* got in!'

Croaker appeared to be savouring something on his tongue. Then the little movements in his mouth grew still.

'No one,' he said gently, 'except you, sergeant. That is it, is it not?'

Verity shook his head, unable to find words.

'Stand still!' yapped Croaker.

'I never, sir!' he gasped. 'And she never! She got too much to lose, sir! Back to the first day of her sentence! She'd be mad, sir.'

Croaker dismissed the subject.

'Three years ago, sergeant, was it not? Suspended from duty for suspected complicity in theft? That was the board's decision then. Hmmmm?'

'I was exonerated, sir!'

'To be sure.' The inspector sat back, a compulsive grin twitching at the corners of his mouth. Verity searched his mind frantically for some explanation which might stave off disaster.

'Sir, I think I got it! I think I know who done it! That beggar! That whistling-man! It must 've been 'im!'

Before Croaker could reply Mr Bunker stepped forward.

'What whistling-man?'

'The one that been whistling outside houses. Disturbing the peace. I seen him off once.'

'One moment,' said Bunker. He left the room, while Verity stared over Croaker's head and heard the inspector's breath quicken with the excitement of conflict. Bunker returned with a companion.

'Is this your whistling-man, sergeant?'

'Thank goodness you got 'im, sir!'

'Got him, sergeant?' said Bunker quizzically. 'We have had Mr Foxfane for several years. One of our best men at surveillance.'

Verity blinked. Dressed like an assistant clerk, the dapper little figure was still unmistakeably the whistling-man of the previous day.

'And is this your man, Mr Foxfane?' asked Bunker quietly.

Foxfane nodded.

'All afternoon and evening. I left as the cab came back into the square last night. Never heard the screams. But all the time until then he'd never left his spot.'

'All evening?' shrilled Croaker. Foxfane ignored him and directed his explanation to Bunker.

'All the time that Constable Meiklejohn was away, following the two suspects to the ball and back, I kept my watch. Only one officer at the front, so the danger of complicity or assault must be greater there. Mr Verity, though never knowing it, was in my observation from the minute the cab moved off until it drew up again at the door.' Foxfane consulted a little notebook. 'He discharged his duty in normal fashion and never once left his post. As to the young person Jolly, she may have left the basement door unbolted and may have done so deliberately. Being now a suspect for this, she must be withdrawn from her duties in the house. However, no robbery was undertaken by the front of the house that I could see. With all respect to the officers watching the rear, I conclude the thief may have entered that way during a temporary lapse on their part. I left Brunswick Square at a quarter past midnight as the Misses Bremer and Jolly were walking up the steps from the cab. Mr Verity had never moved, let alone attempted the building, sir.'

A silence followed. It was ended by a deep digestive howl which rose, plaintive and agonised, from Inspector Croaker's martyred entrails.

13

Old Mole and Jack Strap had cared for him like a brother. On the evening of Stunning Joe's entry to the house in Brunswick Square, Sealskin Kite had been in London, on public view at a Mansion House dinner for the distressed weavers of Spitalfields. It was a customary precaution. Until their master's return on the next day, Mole and Strap treated Joe like 'a schoolbook 'ero', as he kept telling them. A lesser man than Kite would have hesitated to entrust the stolen treasure to his underlings. But they knew what a man might expect who cheated the old Sealskin. In any case, neither Old Mole nor a mere bully like Jack Strap could have got the Shah Jehan clasp further than the next pawnbroker.

On the evening of Kite's return, Stunning Joe was under the protection of Jack Strap at a Swell Mob ordinary near the Race Hill. The large open saloon was brilliantly lit by gasoliers, its walls covered by mirrors and gilding. A bar ran the full length of the saloon, the coloured bottles glowing beyond the sweep of polished mahogany. The room was divided by a wooden partition, four feet high with a gate at its centre. On one side were the unaccompanied women, on the other those who had found male escorts. Waiters with small trays of drinks, sandwiches and cigars served the tables scattered about the areas. There was a constant scraping of chairs and popping of corks. Several unaccompanied men were making assignations with the girls across the partition by the traditional gesture of raising a glass. Stunning Joe's ears rang with the din and the infrequent, bellowed conversation of Jack Strap. His eyes smarted from the acrid fog of cigar smoke.

The attention of the men and women in this section was drawn to a further room which opened out of the saloon and where the 'entertainers' appeared from time to time. These were generally young street-girls who performed dances to earn the coppers thrown to them by the men. The floor of this further room was bare, the benches round the walls suggesting that it was used for the communal dancing with which the race-week evenings ended. A band of four bearded and dark-skinned men, their clothes shabby and their hair unkempt, sat in one corner of this room. They provided an accompaniment with fiddle, cornet and a pair of flutes.

Joe O'Meara started as Jack Strap slapped one hand into the other with an ear-splitting impact.

'Jane Midge!' bellowed the bully appreciatively. 'Lookee there!'

Stunning Joe glanced up at the girl who had appeared on the deserted floor. She was about fourteen years old, a pretty girl dancing in an eastern costume as an excuse for showing her arms, legs and belly. Jane Midge was not particularly tall, but she was quite well developed and her skin was clear, suggesting that she had only recently been orphaned or turned on to the streets for some reason. Her straight brown hair was worn loose, though cut short above her shoulders, and a brief appealing fringe slanted on her forehead. There was a cautious playfulness in her brown eyes, which illuminated a firm young face with clear, strong lines in her nose and chin. Her finely-set lips opened in a smile which displayed the most perfect teeth Joe had ever seen in a girl's mouth.

The eastern costume was simple enough. A cardboard diadem was the headpiece which fitted over her hair. A green silk halter sloped from her shoulder, enclosing her breasts. Beneath the leather waist-belt with its glass 'jewels', she wore tight fleshings from waist to knee, in the same translucent green.

In her dancing she was anything but professional, though this made no odds to Jack Strap who growled and guffawed his approval. As the flutes and fiddle struck up, the girl made sinuous motions with her bare arms, as if to suggest the allure of a harem dancer before her master. Standing sideways to the spectators, she began to sway her trim adolescent thighs and hips in time to the music. Joe glanced at Jack Strap. The bully's mouth was open, his eyes glistening, his breath coming harshly like a faint and distant murmur of delight.

The girl tilted her chin coquettishly at her admirers, pressing her upper teeth on her lower lip in a teasing and provocative grimace. Still she sheltered her loins from their view. Joe could see why. The thin green silk of the fleshings was tight enough and transparent enough to show the firm pearly texture of the limbs beneath. It was clear that the girl had not been brought up to this life and, for all the merriment in her eyes, her natural timidity had not been subdued. A single coin rang derisively on the floor near her feet, and Joe felt his anger begin to rise.

The men grew bored and turned to their cigars or shrub. Their women, dyed and painted as marionettes, caught Jane Midge's gaze and smiled vindictively at her. The youngster had thought herself clever enough to be their rival and now she was learning a bitter lesson.

Stunning Joe cursed them all, their amusement at the young dancing-girl's predicament, caught between modesty and necessity. All the cocksureness had gone from her eyes now. In an attempt to hold their interest she turned her back and swayed the firm young hips again, watching the men and women over her shoulder. Jack Strap grinned as the taut transparent silk gathered in a little sheaf of creases between the rear opening of her legs and pulled, smooth as drumskin, over the cheeks of Jane Midge's bottom. But Stunning Joe had had enough. Several more copper coins rattled on the floor. Joe got up, brushing aside two spectators who stood in his way, and seized the girl in the middle of her dance.

He took her bare arm and led her to the door where he knew the staircase began. The customs of such houses were simple. Among hoots of encouragement from the crowd and a grin from Jack Strap, Joe put his money on the bar, and dragged the unwilling girl up the stairs.

It distressed him that she was too frightened to listen to his protests. In the shabby little room with its linoleum, plain mattress and china ewer, he turned his back on her and drew the curtains. The gas was already lit and when he looked round again he was dismayed at what she had done. The

153

halter and headpiece lay on the mattress. She was just step-
ping out of the silk fleshings. Joe looked at the firm elasticity
of the young body, the small formed breasts, the flat belly,
the incurve of bone-pattern at the base of her spine, the taut,
smooth buttocks.

'No!' he said, exasperated. 'Yer don't 'ave to!'

In the mirror he caught sight of them, Jane Midge with
her firm young figure nude and pale, he with his stunted
growth. They looked like a pair of children playing a game.
Jane caught the weariness in his eyes.

'You don't like me!' she wailed. 'After all that, you don't!'

Joe touched her shoulder.

'Course I do,' he said gently. 'Who wouldn't? But you're to
do as I say. Stay here. Room's paid for. All night and tomorrow too. 'ungry, are you?'

She shook her head, sitting on the stained mattress. Joe
squatted down and looked into her face. He saw the same
hopelessness now as he had seen in the eyes of the men on
the hulks. All the grinning merriment which pretty Jane
Midge assumed for her dance was now gone. She might as
well have been on the hulks, he told himself. But there was
no need. For her, as well as for him, the whole bloody world
was a hulk.

'I gotta go and see someone,' he said gently, brushing the
youngster's brown hair back from her face. 'I'll be back as
soon as I can. Then it'll be all right. Wait here. See?'

'Yes,' she said, her voice sounding tearful though the dark
eyes were dry. Joe comforted her a moment longer. Then a
boot crashed against the door.

'C'mon Joseph!' bellowed Strap from the passageway.
'Your friends is missing you.'

Joe kissed the girl clumsily on the cheek and stepped to the
door.

'Get dressed,' he said. 'I'll be back. That's a promise.'

Jack Strap was in great humour.

'Mr Kite sent for you,' he said. ' 'ad yer greens all right? I

154

could fancy chasing pretty Jane's arse for her meself if there was time! 'ere, Joseph! You never let her go? You silly little bugger! What they do to you on that hulk then? Or did you hook it in such a hurry that yer whatsits got left behind?'

And Strap grinned hugely at his silent companion.

Stunning Joe followed Jack Strap up the thickly carpeted stairs of the Bedford Hotel. Sealskin Kite's suite of rooms opened off the first-floor landing. Strap was dressed with unaccustomed elegance, russet suiting and silk hat disguising the crudity of his muscular figure. The interior of this, the most exclusive of the Brighton hotels, was designed like a temple of the ancient world. Doric columns and a balustrade turned the first-floor landing into the atrium verandah of Greece or Rome, looking down into the well of the vestibule below.

Jack Strap tapped once at the main door of the suite and the two men were admitted. Sealskin Kite, the old woman beside him, and the sallow figure of Old Mole, were like figures in a family bereavement. Everything in the room exuded a sense of luxury and extravagance, from the Italian sideboard and the Venetian mirror-frames to trefoil grates with their ormolu of burnished steel.

Sealskin Kite and his wife were snuggled together on a settee of fringed velvet. They stared at Stunning Joe simultaneously. In the shrewd old faces there was now a common look of accusation and the indignity of betrayal. Joe, who had been about to smile at them in recognition of a mutual triumph, suddenly let his jaw go slack. Something, it seemed was badly out of place. Mrs Kite turned her gaze aside from Joe, as if unable to bear the sight of him, and scuttled from the room. After a long pause, during which Mole and Strap took up position behind their master, Kite spoke. In one hand he held the red leather jewel case, from the other he dangled the glory of the Shah Jehan clasp as though it had been a soiled rag. For the first time, in Joe's experience, the old man was not smiling.

'Now then,' said Kite at last, 'now then, my young friend! What d'ye call this? Eh?'

Joe swallowed, suddenly and compulsively nervous.

' 's the clasp, Mr Kite. I meant to show meself grateful. And I did.'

Kite waggled the clasp which still dangled from his right hand.

' 'Course it's the clasp, little Joseph! Don't I see it? Sealskin Kite ain't blind, though you may wish him so! Sealskin Kite may take his ease in an invalid carriage, his legs ain't what they once were. But he ain't *blind*! And by God he ain't blind, least of all, when a trick's put up against 'im!'

The panic began to rise in Joe's gullet until it almost stopped his breath. He wanted only to throw himself before Mr Kite, to make the old man see that he had been nothing but brave, loyal and true to every promise.

'God's my witness, Mr Kite, I never had so much as a thought of tricking you!' In his terror Joe could not produce a voice louder than a whisper. He watched the cruel satisfaction kindling in the eyes of Old Mole and Jack Strap. With a rag to stop his mouth, they could practise pain and death upon a victim even here, in the most famous hotel in Brighton. Perhaps it was only a joke, Mr Kite pretending anger to amuse his friends by Joe's discomfiture. 'I owe you everything, Mr Kite. Me and any that come after me shall bless your name for what you done. I couldn't trick you! How?'

The fury of the little old man had mottled his face and flecks of saliva spun from his lips as he talked.

'Then Sealskin Kite is blind, sir? You call him blind? An old loon? This is the present you bring him, after all he does for you?'

The last words rang in Joe's ears like a scream.

'Ain't it the clasp?' Joe whined. 'Ain't it, Mr Kite?'

'The devil take the heathen rubbish, and you with it!'

Joe started as the old man caught up the Shah Jehan clasp

and flung it petulantly on the carpet, like a sulky child with a
toy. The other hand wagged in the air.

'This!' squealed Kite. 'What d'ye take this for? Eh?'

'Case,' mumbled Joe. 'Case as belongs to the jool.'

Kite leant forward, his mouth twitching as he sought for
words to convey the force of his displeasure.

'That's just what it ain't, sir! Just what it ain't!'

'May I be struck dead, Mr Kite,' said Joe softly, 'if that
ain't the case the jool was in.'

Kite hissed back at him.

'If it ain't, little Joseph, things shall be done to you as shall
make you wish yourself back on the hulks under the drum-
mer's lash! This was never the case that Banker Lansing had
made for his clasp.'

'It's the only one I ever saw, Mr Kite. There was nothing
at Wannock Hundred that time. Neither jool nor case.'

He was calmer, now that he understood the cause of Kite's
anger. There was only one thing to be done, tell the truth as
he knew it. If that would not save him, then there was no
safety to be found at all.

'There was other cases, Mr Kite, hid in the back of the
drawing-room piano. But they was full of nothing, just glass
and trumpery.'

Kite had ceased to listen. His head lolled forward on his
chest and he appeared to be talking to himself.

'You lost Sealskin Kite a fortune,' he murmured. 'Sealskin
Kite had a fortune almost in his hands, and you let it slip
from him.'

'Listen, Mr Kite,' said Joe gently, 'I'll go back. Only tell
me what it is and I'll go back to that house and get it for you.
And if I'm caught, I'll take me chance. 'fact, I'll make such a
fight that I won't be took alive, not to be sent back to the
hulks. Only say the word, Mr Kite.'

But Kite's energy seemed spent by his anger and he made
no acknowledgement of having heard the offer. It was Old
Mole who stepped round the settee and took the little spider-

man by his arm.

'Seems you'd best be put in your quarters, Stunning Joseph. What's to be done in your case must need a little sleeping on.'

The room in which he was confined was the smallest of the suite. Visitors to the Bedford Hotel were accustomed to bring at least one of their own servants with them, a maid or valet who slept in a cupboard-sized room off the master's quarters. It was here that Joe had been kept since their arrival in Brighton, cast in the role of Sealskin Kite's attendant. During the night which followed he slept little, puzzling in his mind why Mr Kite should make such a bother over a leather jewel case when he held the splendours of the Shah Jehan clasp safely in his hands.

When they came for him the next morning Joe followed Jack Strap and Old Mole apprehensively into Sealskin Kite's drawing-room. The Shah Jehan clasp lay on a scrap of black velvet on the table. By the light of day, the emerald green and the maroon rubies had an almost funereal pomp about them. Joe looked and thought that every stone seemed either a green eye of evil or a red eye of bloody death.

He turned and, to his astonishment, saw Sealskin Kite on the sofa, the old man's eyes twinkling merrily as he smiled up at Joe once again.

'Well, my dear young sir,' said Kite amiably, 'you have more friends than you ever knew, it seems. Mr Mole is your friend. And is there anything Mr Mole could ask that Sealskin Kite would refuse? Eh?'

Kite looked about him, but no one spoke.

'Mr Mole has convinced me, Joseph,' the old man continued, 'that you did all a man could have done. Why, after all, should you know the actual complexion of a jewel case, never having seen the same? No, Joseph, you was good as your word. True, Mr Mole?'

'Yes, Mr Kite,' said the scrub-haired man impassively.

'Very well,' said Kite, the breath whistling between his

teeth, 'and what's Sealskin Kite if he ain't a man o' his word.
I ask you, sir? What is he, eh? The jewel case ain't to be had.
Well, so it ain't, and there an end on 't. But all the world
knows that Kite keeps his bargains, and so he shall. Mr
Mole! See the young gentleman paid!'

Mole stepped round the settee again. He folded the black
velvet over the rich green and purple shimmer of the clasp.
Then he handed it to Stunning Joe.

'Understand,' said Kite more sharply, 'that you and the
old Sealskin have never met. You was never here, my dear
young sir.' He snuffled at his own wit. 'Indeed, you ain't
anywhere now, being dead. The party that attended me was
quite a different man, who shall be brought to testify if
necessary. I never so much as saw that heathen gee-gaw. But
I *did* make you a promise, little Joseph, that you should have
the value of that item for your labour. And so you shall.
Take it, depart hence, and let us meet no more.'

For a moment Joe could hardly believe what he had
heard.

'You never mean to have the clasp, sir? All them jewels
that you went to such bother to come by?'

Kite's eyes crinkled with elderly benevolence.

'Indeed, Joseph, I never do. Why, a man of business can't
bestow the value of an item more exactly than by giving that
item in its own proper person, can he?'

'But what am I to do with it, Mr Kite?'

'As you will, Joseph.'

The dismay in the little spiderman's face was now visible
to the other three men in the room.

'Mr Kite! How'm I to go on if all I got is this? I can't sell it,
not for months at least. And I can't eat it, Mr Kite! I'll take a
hundred pounds instead.'

But Kite wagged a finger and gave a wicked little smile.

'A bargain is a bargain, little Joseph. And after saying so
often how much you meant to show yourself grateful, you
could hardly do otherwise now, could you? Why, my dear

young sir, a man in your position had best cut his throat before he turned against his pals and peached to the law. Only think, Joseph, only think what waits for you when they take you to Portland again. You can't harm a living soul but yourself. Take Sealskin's advice, my young friend. Don't he speak to you friendly, like a true man o' business?'

His mind numbed by the sudden reversal of Kite's mood and his own position, Stunning Joe allowed himself to be led to the door of the suite. Jack Strap thrust him out on to the landing and slammed the door again. For a moment Joe hesitated. Then from beyond the closed door he heard a shrill, skinny clamour. It rose piping and vibrant like a childish tantrum. Rising and falling, it continued for a full minute and longer. It was at once vindictive and witty, triumphant and plangent. It was the sound of Sealskin Kite laughing with genuine amusement.

Along King's Road the clouds stretched ash-grey to the eastern horizon. The shifting tide was a dull steel colour except where patches of faint sun turned it pale lavender green. The scarlet and blue of a regimental band was just visible among the shrubs of Brunswick Lawns, where it played for a morning party.

Joe clutched the velvet shape of the clasp and hurried onward. He was alone now, alone despite the pretty bonnets and swinging crinolines along the rails of the promenade, despite the men in their shallow straw hats, primrose gloves and clay pipes. Last night, on an impulse, he had become the protector of the little dancing-girl, Jane Midge. Now it was she who offered the sole hope of protection to him.

Outside the Ship and the other hostelries of the old town the carriage steps were being let down as the first visitors of the day arrived. An elderly gentleman in high humour chortled to his companion, 'Come on, my old Ten-and-a-half-per-cent! Out with the tin!'

Other voices called for devilled kidneys or hock and soda

in coffee rooms, the dark interiors stocked with Gorgona anchovies, old bottled sherry, French mustard, plovers' eggs, Bombay mangoes and Emmenthaler cheeses. Joe walked through the sunshine, among the good humour and rich smells of food, like a leper tainted by his disease. Two men got down from a smart Queen's coloured brougham, outside the Royal Albion. Their velvet and silk, chains, lockets and puffy, pink-tinted shirts were a match for their easy, fatuous conversation.

'Stay long?'

'Don't know.'

'Long as it's agreeable, p'raps?'

'Just so.'

'Nice place.'

'That it is.'

Joe in his misery cursed the world. He came at last to the tavern near the foot of the Race Hill, quite expecting that the girl would have gone. But she sat on the bed in the dusty little room, as if she had never moved. Now, instead of the dancing costume, she wore a drab brown dress and there was a little pork-pie bonnet beside her.

'See?' said Joe, more cheerful than he felt. 'Told you I'd come back, didn't I?'

She nodded and he went to call for an ink and dip.

While Jane Midge sat silent on the bed behind him, Joe perched at the little wooden table and wrote in his scrawling laboured hand. By the end of an hour he had covered two sheets and reached the limit of endurance. Then he folded them together and put them in an envelope. He turned to the girl, studying the firm features, the last fading liveliness of her brown eyes which had once animated her face in easier times.

'From now on,' he said softly, 'neither of us is going to be alone. We'll be together, you and me. Understand?'

She nodded doubtfully.

'Anyone asks, you got a protector. I can't say how we shall

manage things but we shall somehow. Do what you can with your dancing and I'll see you don't go hungry nor cold. Where d'yer live?'

'Lodging kens mostly,' said Jane softly. ' 's twopence a night in the public ward. Not in summer, though. Waste of tin, ain't it? Just as soon sleep in the parks or on the pebbles. And there's the viaduct arches, come to that, where the railway goes out to Clayton tunnel on the London line.'

Joe nodded impatiently.

'You got any sort of hiding-place?'

'Only in me clothes.'

'That'll do,' he said quickly, holding out to her the envelope with the two sheets of writing. 'Take this and keep it. I'll ask for it back if I need it. But if ever I'm missing and I ain't said why, if ever you can't find me, you go to the police office and you tell 'em it's a letter from Stunning Joe. All right?'

She slipped the envelope into the bosom of her dress.

'Stunning Joe,' she said thoughtfully. 'That's a funny sort of a name.' And then Jane Midge put her arms about him and leant her head against his breast.

'Dancer,' said Jack Strap, his jowls taut with disapproval. 'Goes as Jane Midge.'

Old Mole nodded as the two men stood at the promenade rails and watched the little yachts bucking in a sunlit swell.

'There's work to be done, Strap. Work to be done by you and me. Mr Kite ain't in it. Fact is, Strap, you never met Mr Kite. See?'

' 'oo's Mr Kite?' asked Strap, and grinned horribly at his own facetiousness.

Old Mole nodded again and took out a paper packet. He counted out fifty sovereigns, fresh and yellow from the mint.

'That's for now, Mr Strap. There's five hundred more up for auction. Savvy?'

'Five *hundred*?' The contortion of Jack Strap's heavy face

reduced the eyes to pig-like points of brightness in the pouched flesh.

'One hundred when Jane Midge is took to safe-keeping. One hundred likewise for Cosima Bremer. Two hundred when Stunning Joseph is sent to his last long home. Got it?'

' 's only four hundred,' said Strap suddenly.

'Yes,' said Mole, 'and there's one hundred more for a little piece of business involving another young person. You'll be told.'

Strap chuckled at his own good fortune. Old Mole interrupted him.

'Commissions to be executed when and where you're told. See?'

The bully slapped his hands together and rubbed them eagerly.

'Name 'em, Mr Mole. Name 'em!'

' 'nother thing,' said Mole. 'If all this comes safe through and Mr Kite's fancy should canter home in Brighton races for the Bristol Plate, that five hundred guineas doubles itself. One thousand guineas for yer trouble, Jack Strap!'

Strap pocketed the sovereigns. Then, for all his stupidity, he rose to the occasion.

'Why, Mr Mole, and 'oo might that gentleman be? I never had the pleasure o' meeting a party called Mr Kite. Never did!'

He nudged his companion and let loose across the shingle a great whinnying guffaw. Old Mole nodded again and turned away from him, walking in the direction of the Bedford Hotel. Jack Strap rested his back against the promenade rails and watched the passing armada of crinolines. His mouth opened again, huge in its merriment. Then, in his anticipation of the jollity to come, he slapped one hand into the other with an impact which carried clear across the promenade.

14

From the depths of his tapestried chair, Sealskin Kite twinkled at Old Mole like an indulgent bachelor uncle. In the lines of the shrewd, mousy little face the old man's excitement teased the sallow, scrub-haired mobsman who watched him across the table. He tossed a scrap of paper in Mole's direction.

'What's this?' Mole's yellowed mouth hung vacantly as he read it.

'List of cheques, Mr Mole. Banker's cheques written by persons of great consequence upon their accounts with Baron Lansing. Look at the names, Mr Mole! Old Sir Aylmer Byrd. Young Lord Stephen with his racing stables! Mr Thomas Crawley Esquire what keeps that fat doxy they calls the Female Hussar! All clients of the Lansing bank! Why, Mr Mole, who could bother himself with that heathen Shah Jehaney caper when he might have such clients as this?'

Old Mole put down the paper.

'Then, Mr Kite, we'd best have the truth of things before they go further.'

Sealskin Kite sniggered like a schoolboy, beating his little fists up and down on his knees with excitement and triumph.

'So we shall, my dear sir. Mr Mole asks the truth! And is there anything Mr Mole could ask which his friend Sealskin Kite might deny him? Why, the truth is that Banker Lansing — rest his cunning soul — was a bigger rogue than you or I! I knew 'im, Mr Mole! And I knew the damned old reprobate for what he was!'

'Rogue?' said Mole cautiously. 'Over the Shah Jehan, you mean?'

'Shah Jehaney-haney!' shrilled Kite impatiently. 'No, Mr Mole! Lord Lansing was banker to some of the greatest in the land. Specially he was banker to men who didn't want 'quite all their private doings made public. Nothing against the law, o' course. But Mr Crawley Esquire might choose to keep that Janet Bond, the Female Hussar for a few months. No need for Mrs Crawley to twig it. A nice discreet account with Baron Lansing and the whole affair goes smooth as oil. And I tell you, Mr Mole, if you never met Banker Lansing, you don't know what discreet was!'

Mole looked blankly at Kite, still not catching the old man's drift.

'You mean to blackmail 'em, Mr Kite, with your little list?'

Kite shook his head in wondering disappointment at his crony.

'Mr Mole! Do I look the poor wretch as must stoop to blackmailey? No, Mr Mole! 's their money as old Kite wants! Every penny.

And then Kite explained the neatest caper that Mole had ever heard of.

Banker Lansing had seemed to die rich but Kite, who knew him better than most, knew also how precarious were the affairs of the business in Pall Mall East. Lansing had seen the crash coming but his trick with the Shah Jehan clasp was the least of his misdemeanours. It had always been assumed that a banker could be trusted beyond all question. But suppose he could not? Men like Lord Stephen and Sir Aylmer Byrd wrote promissory notes, sometimes for as much as £5,000 or even £10,000. These notes changed hands, endorsed by each holder, with almost as much ease as Bank of England notes. Those who accepted them might take a small commission for their risk, but they knew that risk was tiny. The names signed to the bills were proof of their dependability.

Eventually the notes would come home to the bank upon which the client had first drawn them. There they were cancelled and the account was settled.

But suppose the banker failed to cancel them? Suppose

that he kept a dozen of these notes of the largest denomination as his own investment against hard times to come? He was the one man who could use them a second time, passing them fraudulently and then withdrawing abroad, taking the proceeds with him. A dozen carefully selected scraps of paper would yield him more than £100,000. The victims of the fraud would know nothing until the bills were presented for payment a second time. By then the dishonest banker would be far beyond their reach. If he was lucky, it might be a month or more before his dupes discovered the extent of their loss.

'Now, Mr Mole!' sniggered Kite. 'Now then! Banker Lansing knew he'd have to do a bunk soon enough. The dear old reprobate meant to bolt from his creditors taking with him the Shah Jehaney nonsense and that young German naughtiness, Cosima. But, Mr Mole, what was confessed to me was this. In the velvet lining of the old blue box as held the clasp there was a slit made. And in that slit was tucked a dozen slips of paper. See?'

'Yes!' said Mole, the yellow mouth in a rictus of glee, the dark little eyes gleaming. 'Why, Mr Kite, there ain't a word for it but genius! What a stroke you might pull!'

'In good time, Mr Mole,' said the old man, the breath humming in his mouth. 'First the notes must be got, being held by that little vixen Cosima in the old jewel case. Then the names of various parties must be put to 'em, making it seem they changed hands all the time since Banker Lansing's death. Then, a week from now, the stroke is pulled, Mr Mole. The racing and the Bristol Plate. See?'

'Not exactly, Mr Kite,' said Mole doubtfully.

'Suppose,' said Kite wistfully, 'suppose there was heavy backing of the six runners in the Bristol Plate. A man like Lord Stephen might wager £10,000 on his fancy. The notes go to back four of the horses at best prices, in shops all over London. Just before the race the two other favourite horses is scratched, leaving only the four backed by the notes.'

'What if they shouldn't be scratched, Mr Kite?'

Sealskin Kite looked up with a sharp displeasure at Mole's obtuseness.

'But they will be, Mr Mole. Arrangements is made. You never thought the old Sealskin went this far without knowing he could have the two nags scratched? Orders is given, Mr Mole! Whichever of our four fancies should win, that's where the dibs is collected. Nice odds too. Monday after, Tattersalls and the settling of bills. The firms who took ours pass them easy. A week or two more and several men of importance must find that they were robbed by Banker Lansing who put their notes of promise out a second time.'

Old Mole chortled.

'But we'll be far away by then, Mr Kite! Eh?'

Kite looked shocked.

'Away, Mr Mole? You won't catch Sealskin Kite going away, my young sir! Don't you get the beauty of it? There's no man can cast a glance at us. No man can put our names to the caper. Why, suspect us! You might as soon suspect the Prince Consort! No, sir. When the truth is out, who shall carry the blame for it? Banker Lansing, the rogue! Only Banker Lansing, being dead, may bear the load a bit more convenient than you and me!'

The pouchy old face crinkled and the shrewd little eyes shone with the neatness of it all.

'How's them notes to be got, Mr Kite?'

For a long interval the buhl clock ticked time away while Kite's jaws moved in a slight chewing motion, as if he hesitated to commit himself at last. Then he spoke.

'You and me, Mr Mole. And Jack Strap. The three of us must visit the little chit at Brunswick Square and come away with the notes. You do comprehendey, Mr Mole? You do comprehendey?'

Mole nodded, though he was uncertain and uneasy as to just what the old man intended. But if Sealskin Kite was prepared to take part personally in one of his crimes, Mole reckoned that there was every bit of the £100,000 at stake, and probably a good deal more.

'Now,' said Kite, 'as one man o' business to another, see what must be done. There's a jack still on the door of the house. He must be sweetened. There's one or two young persons must be put where they won't come to harm. It ain't a lot to ask, is it, Mole?'

Mole shook his head.

'And that squeak, Stunning Joseph, and his little whore Jane Mitch or Midge, or whatever she calls herself?'

'Leave 'em to Strap,' said Kite soothingly. 'See to the German girl yourself. Miss Cosima. Lime your bird, Mr Mole. When we come to her door it must open for us. Make her willing, my dear sir. Lime your bird!'

After his conversation with Sealskin Kite, Old Mole sat by himself for half an hour and considered the scheme. He was not sure that it was not the most perfect fraud he had ever heard of. The crime of concealing the promissory notes for use a second time had been committed by Baron Lansing before his death. Even if it was discovered that Kite and his friends had passed them through betting offices during Brighton races, it would be assumed that they were as much victims of Lansing's fraud as anyone else. True, if Cosima Bremer were to confess or complain, the scheme might be in danger. But Old Mole knew that such confession or complaint would never be permitted.

First of all he set out to follow Kite's instructions. This time, they must go through the front door of Brunswick Square, opened to them by the German girl who now lived there alone. To ensure admittance, Mole must appear as an acquaintance, even as a friend. Liming the bird was not always easy, and now it had to be done fast.

By watching her movements, Mole knew that every afternoon Cosima went down to the beach, where the little caravans of the bathing-machines were drawn up at the water's edge. It was an area of the shingle reserved exclusively for women, as the stretch east of the Chain Pier was kept for men. Between two of the wooden groins which ran down from the promenade wall to the sea, canvas screens protected the girls from observation as they bathed. A stalwart bathing attendant, once a fish-wife in Market Street, presided over the arrangements.

Old Mole smiled as he looked at the candy-stripes of the canvas screen. He had not been in Brighton two days before discovering what half a crown in the palm of the attendant would buy for any well-dressed gentleman. The woman was easily persuaded to turn her back while the telescopes and cameras of admirers focussed on the pretty bathers from convenient points around the wooden groins. Sometimes the bribes came from girls who wished for an opportunity to meet secretly with lovers where the wooden partition marked the limit of the beach.

Old Mole was short of time. He decided that a camera, rather than a spy-glass, was the best means of gaining the young woman's acquaintance. By the time that he sauntered down to the shingle beach at the end of the afternoon, he was carrying the varnished wooden box of a Scott-Archer self-developing camera, and a neat little stand. Despite the lines of his sallow face and the look of decay about his mouth, Mole had tricked himself out with yellow kid-gloves, suiting in duck-egg blue and a silk hat to match. At a distance he might pass for a gentleman of fashion.

It was still warm, the heat shimmering from the pebbles and the wavelets rippling ashore with the glitter of broken glass. But to his satisfaction he saw that Cosima was alone on the stretch of beach. Perhaps the fish-wife, well-paid for her trouble, had hurried her other customers on their way. At his leisure, Old Mole studied his prey.

Now that he had time to watch her carefully, Cosima appeared to be no more than about seventeen years old. She was pretty enough with firm regular features and blue eyes crinkling against the sun. Her fair hair, brushed from its central parting, waved loosely down either side of her face but was trimmed just above her shoulders.

Her bathing costume seemed to belong to different outfits. The top was a red singlet which showed the twin weight of her breasts. The pants below were of a white cotton web which fitted with suggestive tightness over her hips and thighs. The long agile legs were lightly suntanned, as she walked acrobatically along the narrow top of a groin. Jumping down, Cosima began to draw with her toe in a patch of wet sand. Mole saw that she was writing her own name. Then she kicked up her feet and began to walk nimbly on her hands. Mole waited his chance. Two small boys bounced a ball across the groin and clambered over to retrieve it, earning the pretext to view the ladies' bathing beach. Cosima joined them energetically, pushing her way to the ball and kicking it with as much vigour as they.

Mole stepped on to the deserted beach and set up the camera. He aimed it here and there. Once Cosima ducked her head, as though fearing she had interrupted his view. He thought at first that she had performed her antics for his benefit, but she was moving far too quickly for the camera to capture them. Then he saw, or rather heard, that there was a boy of her own age beyond the further groin, to whom she had been talking casually. The boy stood, his chin level with the top of the groin, and admired her across the partition.

Cosima posed herself with all the nonchalance of an artist's model. Perhaps, Mole thought, she had once done so professionally. In her bathing costume the girl sat along the top of the groin, leaning back on one arm, the agile suntanned legs drawn up, her profile turned slightly away, as if inviting the camera's attention. Old Mole began to uncap the lens with a genuine enthusiasm.

Presently the girl slipped down on to the sand and stood facing the afternoon sun. She shook back the fair hair where it had strayed across her forehead and then she leant back against the wooden structure behind her. Mole, pretending to take his views of the sea, saw her image in the aperture of the lens. The firm features were clear and the shape of her breasts was perfectly mapped by the tightened singlet. He uncapped the lens again. After all, he told himself, it was necessary to his plan that there should be several photographs of her available.

She turned aside, not noticing him, and jumped on to the wooden groin. Like a diver, she bent forward, swung her arms back behind her and sprang nimbly down on to the far side where the boy was standing. She repeated the exercise a dozen times. On each occasion she paused in the diving position, all the curves of her body accentuated. Her knees were bent, her thighs taut, the white webbed cotton drawn skintight across her broadened seat as her head went down. Old Mole grinned, thinking that this set of plates might sell for a few pounds as stereoscopic views.

To draw her attention, he moved closer, no longer concealing the fact that he was photographing her in these poses. He was alarmed to hear the boy calling her 'Cosie', as if they were known to one another. But then he saw that the youth had merely read her name where she had traced it in the sand. She bent to dive again. As Mole worked the shutter he heard the boy call out.

'Look, Cosie! He's been taking pictures of you!'

Cosima straightened up from her posture, looked over her shoulder, and saw Old Mole with his camera. Her mouth opened in a smile of astonished amusement at his impudence. But then she went forward again, holding the pose quite long enough for him to take a final view.

Of course, he thought, she had been posing for him all the time! A kept girl looking for a new protector! Accustomed as he was to his dingy appearance, Mole had quite forgotten the impression he must have made with his new duck-egg blue suiting, silk hat and expensive camera. Indeed, the camera was of more value to her than to him. It recorded her stripped to what were virtually the last fragments of her underwear. In this state she had deliberately cavorted in front of the lens, posing to show the sculptural beauty of face and breasts, the agile suntanned legs flashing, Cosima bending cheekily as she dived. She must have known that her admirer would contemplate a score of such portraits in the privacy of his own room. By the next day, their effect would be to bring him back to the beach in earnest.

'Why,' said Old Mole delightedly, 'you damned little bitch!'

There was no more to be done while she was in the company of the boy, but Mole was gratified to see that she kept looking back at him from time to time across the groin. He waited on the promenade until she had dressed again and was making her way back to Brunswick Square. He raised his hat politely as she passed and followed at a little distance. Cosima kept ahead of him, laughing once or twice over her shoulder. He doubted that she felt much in a laughing mood. It was part of her professional training, as a young courtesan. When she turned into Brunswick Square, he guessed that she might expect him to accompany her. But that was too risky. Mole contented himself with watching her across the trees and shrubs of the private gardens in the centre of the square.

He knew better than to enter the square itself. After Stunning Joe's burglary and Jolly's departure as servant, the local constabulary had insisted upon providing some protection for the lonely young woman until the danger of another such intrusion was past. In consequence, a private-clothes jack now stood directly outside the steps of the corner house. The law might conclude that the Shah Jehan clasp had gone, but its interest in Cosima Bremer was by no means extinguished. From the distance of the promenade Old Mole made his survey. Mr Kite would be grateful for the information. Late afternoon sunlight shone like fire in the opposite windows of the Georgian houses. Cosima went up the curve of the stone steps to her black-painted door. Old Mole saw the man outside touch his hat respectfully to the young mistress. Then the private-clothes jack drew a deep breath into his barrel-chest and rocked to and fro upon his heels as if he had not a care in the world.

Groups of young women with their escorts emerged from the streets converging on to the sea. Like clouds of butterflies the dainty parasols opened against the sun, white, lilac and lavender. By the middle of the morning the promenades from Hove to Kemp Town seemed afloat with crinolines, light bonnets, airy dresses, organdies and brilliantés. Languid young men, their hands thrust into the pockets of peg-top trousers, eyed the expanse of water where the breeze was chopping the wavelets into white spray. A silver band played Rossini on the enclosed lawns.

Here and there, the groups of less affluent trippers thrust themselves forward, men in shallow-crowned straw hats and fat women eating prawns. They gazed at the two buoys, each carrying a small Union Jack, which marked the start and finish of the regatta. A dozen urchins pushed and struggled against one another on the shingle below, urging the spectators above them to throw coins to be fought over.

'Make a scramble, gents! Gi' us a scramble!'

Just then there was a boom from the starting-gun on the lugger-yacht and the little white-sailed boats bucked forward into the waves. Telescopes, single and double Dollands, appeared from the cases of several expensively-suited gentlemen who watched the progress of the *Sarah Ann*, *Prince Consort* and *Lord of the Isles*.

Bella tugged little Billy Verity's leading reins to check the boy's insistent progress towards the promenade rails. She glanced quickly at her companion. Ruth held the younger child, Vicky, in her arms. Solemn-eyed and wondering, she watched the marine pageant before her.

Bella glanced again, her mind going back to Verity's stern

warnings over Stringfellow's behaviour to the young maid-servant. Bella had tried to raise the subject gently with Ruth herself. 'You sure Mr Stringfellow ain't no inconvenience to you, Ruthie?' But sixteen-year-old Ruth had looked back with such pretty solemnity and such an air of innocence under her cropped fair curls that it had been impossible to pursue the conversation. No inconvenience whatsoever, it seemed. After that, Bella was certain Mr Verity was wrong. Having so much to do with the criminal class, she thought, it must give his mind a bit of a turn that way.

'Ruthie,' she said presently, wearying of Billy's efforts, ' 'itch his reins on your arm for a minute, do.'

And then, relieved of maternal duties for the time being, she opened an elegant new turquoise parasol and luxuriated in a sense of sunlit indolence.

She had drifted into a reverie, almost forgetting where she was, when someone touched her arm and there was a voice behind her.

'Mrs Verity, ma'am?'

It was a stranger, a sombre-looking man in black with a tall hat and frock-coat. He seemed to her like an undertaker.

'Yes?' she said, frightened a little by his appearance.

'Mr Inspector Croaker's compliments, ma'am, and he begs your attendance at his office most urgently.'

The sunlit afternoon around her was frozen by a sudden chill which struck her heart with the force of a blow.

'Mr Verity?' she gasped, and then her voice strengthened to a cry. 'Is it Mr Verity?'

The man inclined his head a little.

'Best you should come now, ma'am,' he said gently. 'You'll be with Mr Croaker in two minutes. He sent his own cab special-to find you, when you wasn't at home.'

By now she was terrified at the thoughts which rushed through her mind. The man indicated the dark official-looking cab which stood by the kerb. Bella turned a wild, distraught face to her young servant.

'Take them home, Ruthie!' she cried. 'Take them home and care for them!'

And then she blundered through the crowd towards the cab, where the grave-looking man held open the door for her.

15

Tranquillity had passed into tedium. Each morning Verity watched the early mist rising from the placid sea like the gauze curtain in the transformation scene of *Sinbad the Sailor* at the Suffolk Music Hall. Then there was the noon glitter, the bottle-green surges of the afternoon tide, and the crimson ripples before twilight. He was stationed in the corner of the square now, immediately outside the Baron Lansing's house with the curve of stone steps to its front door. They were watching an empty nest, every man of the detail knew as much. Even the girl's own behaviour confirmed that the Shah Jehan clasp had flown of its own mysterious accord on the night of the curious burglary. Now she smiled and inclined her head at the men on duty as she entered or left the building. Verity acknowledged this each time, touching his hat as a matter of formality.

Mr Croaker was bored as well. No one imagined that Cosima could doubt the true purpose of the guard upon her. Yet the surveillance was to be maintained until orders to the contrary were received from London. The inspector relieved the monotony of his own watch on the rear of the house by reverting to his literal duty of inspecting. The primary task of a uniformed inspector was to tour the beats of his men to catch malingerers or those who associated too freely with the criminal class.

Two or three times a day, a plain black cab which was as nondescript as one hired from a stand drove slowly down the far side of the square, travelling from Brunswick Place towards the sea. Verity was aware of the thin sour face of Inspector Croaker gazing balefully in his direction. The plump sergeant's jowls lengthened in a slow grimace as he yawned behind closed lips.

Once, as a diversion, he formed a little sentry-go for himself, marched smartly from the corner railings as far as the other end of the next house, Madame Rosa's academy, stamped about, and marched back again with a rolling military gait. To pass the time he counted out to himself the steps and the turns that he made. Presently he was aware of a door opening and, stamping round, saw Madame Rosa coming down the steps, tall and imperious, one hand gathering the black skirts of her dress to hold it from the ground.

She stood above him, her voice quivering slightly with indignation but her tones those of a woman born to command. 'Stand off!' she said angrily. 'Stand off these premises!'

Verity, quite taken aback, made the mistake of hesitation. 'Beg pardon, milady?'

There was something so innately aristocratic in Madame Rosa's bearing that he responded at once in the manner used when he was a footman at Lady Lineacre's in the Royal Crescent at Bath. Madame Rosa came down the steps in a fury. Standing before him she lifted the black net of her veil and revealed a face crazed by the wrinkles of age and dusty with powder. Her voice was quiet and close but no less angry.

'Trespass once more,' she hissed, 'and your superiors shall hear of this impudence!'

Verity's brow furrowed. So far as he knew the law of trespass, it had never applied to a man who walked in front of a house. He sought for conciliatory words, but the old woman turned her back, gathered up her skirts again, and sailed up the steps where the double oak door stood open for her.

Denied even this modest exercise, Verity drew out a red spotted handkerchief and patted his cheeks with it. Once or twice when Madame Rosa appeared he touched his hat in an attempt to make amends. She ignored him on every occasion. After that he stood forlornly in his corner of the elegant square of houses, fat, embarrassed and warm.

He had lost count of the hours of duty spent on the surveillance, and there seemed to be no end of it. Then, in the middle of one of the afternoons of bottle-green waves and summer sun, another cab entered the square. Verity looked at it and frowned. The bilious yellow of its paintwork, the driver's emblem on the door in the form of what looked like a dissected bat were familiar enough to him. Stringfellow, in the driving-seat, was belabouring the aged horse, Lightning, and cursing like a lunatic. The ramshackle hackney coach lumbered towards the corner of the square and then Stringfellow dragged desperately on the reins. Verity was vaguely aware that Bella had promised the children that they should one day be driven past to see their father performing his constabulary duty, but this hardly seemed to be the occasion. Indeed, as he glanced into the cab he heard the frightened whimpering of Ruth as the servant-maid clutched to her the bawling figures of the two Verity children. Stringfellow clambered down from his box.

' 'ere!' said Verity suddenly perturbed. ' 'ere, Stringfellow! Draw it mild! You mustn't speak to me now. I ain't allowed! Not on duty! S'posing Mr Croaker comes by?'

But the old cabman stood lopsidedly on his wooden leg, his mouth stretched open in a howl of toothless consternation.

' 's Miss Bella!' he wailed. 'She's gone!'

'Gone?' said Verity stupidly. 'Whatcher mean gone?'

'Lil Ruwfie!' sobbed Stringfellow, indicating the pretty servant. 'They was on the front! Miss Bella commends the children to her care, sends her home, and goes off with a man in 'ansom cab!'

Verity shook his head, as if he were recovering from a punch.

'She can't a-done, Stringfellow! 'ave some sense! Must be a reason.'

Stringfellow held out a hand. A slip of paper trembled between his fingers. The old man's voice broke again as he urged it upon his son-in-law.

'This come,' he gasped. 'Slipped in the door while I was round the stables in Station Street getting the 'orse. It's yours.'

'What's it say?'

But even in his misery Stringfellow spared a look of pity for a man who thought learning to read could possibly be of equal importance to the cabman's art.

Mrs Verity presents her respects to Mr Verity and begs him to believe that she has taken this step as the only means to end her insupportable agony of mind. What Mr Verity has told her of the robbery in Brunswick Square is too much for conscience to bear. Henceforward their destinies must therefore part.

Verity read it through twice to ensure that he had missed no part of its meaning.

'This ain't from Miss Bella,' he said quietly. 'Nasty-minded joke is all it is. There's nothing I could a-told her about the robbery here, Stringfellow, a-cos I don't know nothing to tell.'

Stringfellow paused in his lamentation. Then he remembered the other cause of his grief.

'Went off in 'ansom cab!' he bawled. 'Commending the future care of her infants to the servant's tender heart!'

Verity was thoroughly alarmed. From the hackney coach he could hear young Ruth's adolescent fear and misery rising siren-like in a prolonged 'Hoo-hoo-hoo!' It was overlaid by the screams of the two children.

'Stringfellow,' he said gently, 'take 'em home and stay

there. We don't know what Mrs Verity had in her mind. Ten-to-one she'll be back in Tidy Street presently, if she ain't there already. You'll see.'

'The note!' bawled the old cabman. 'Read the note!'

'Now, now,' said Verity kindly. 'That's just a piece of nastiness. 'fact I can tell you what it is. Someone wants me flayed and salted by Mr Croaker over that burglary. 'spect he's had a copy hisself. Go 'ome, Stringfellow. If Miss Bella comes back, drive here and tell me. It'll be all right. You'll see.'

But despite his assurances to the old cabman, Verity's heart was pounding and his stomach had tightened. The summer afternoon was cold as Christmas and the air seemed darker. After much persuasion Stringfellow mounted the box again and the lurching coach with its howling occupants disappeared round the corner of Brunswick Place.

The truth was that Verity needed time to think. Every word of the note appeared to be in Bella's hand. Her italic dame-school script would be easy enough to imitate. But to what purpose? As for the man with the hansom cab, there must be an innocent explanation. She would not suddenly drive off with a stranger, abandoning the children to Ruth's care. The notion of a secret lover was even more preposterous. The routine of Paddington Green and Tidy Street left her little opportunity for such rendezvous, even if she had been so inclined.

There was no reason whatever for alarm, he thought, as a sick terror began to engulf him. It was only the slow impact of the shock which prevented him from taking to his heels, deserting his post, and running all the way to Tidy Street to see if she had not come back after all.

His attention was recalled to his surroundings by the clatter of hooves. A black cab passed slowly down the far side of the square. Like a thin, waning moon the face of Inspector Croaker peered through the glass panel of its window. Further along the line of houses the cab stopped. Mr Croaker dismounted and stood gazing across the central gardens of the square. He watched Verity, the swagger stick tapping against his boot with a mixture of impatience and menace.

In his growing terror over Bella's fate, Verity felt an urge to run to the inspector, tell him the entire story, and beg his assistance. He braced himself to burst across the square, through the gardens, to where Mr Croaker stood. But as he gathered the breath into his lungs, Croaker turned smartly about, mounted the foot-board, and the cab moved off with a rattle of harness.

Verity stared after the swaying vehicle. In his torment he would willingly have deserted his duty to save Bella. But from what was he to save her? Where was he to look? At the back of his mind lingered the knowledge that he must not do the very thing which would deliver him into the hands of his enemies. To remain calm, to move only when he had a certain destination. That must be his path.

Deliberately he tried to compile a list of the places where Bella might have gone. There was nowhere in Brighton that he could think of, except perhaps the chapel or one of the shops. Would she have returned to London? It was easy enough for her to be there this evening by train. Paddington Green, Stringfellow's little house? There was no reason that he could think of. In her behaviour she had been the same to him on that morning as always.

Verity was urgently considering these possibilities when the black cab returned to the square again. He pulled himself up to attention for Mr Croaker's benefit. This time, he decided, if the cab should stop he would dash forward and beg the inspector's assistance in finding Bella. The black cab had turned now and was coming towards him, down his own side of the square. For the first time Mr Croaker was going to pay him a visit. Verity stepped smartly forward, ready to open the door, but the cab did not even slow down. In a panic he ran along beside it, shouting,

'Sir! Sir! Mr Croaker, sir!'

But the cab was gaining speed and the face which he glimpsed inside was not Inspector Croaker's, nor anyone else that he recognised. Verity dropped back, knowing in his misery that it was not the same cab but one of hundreds of black hansoms which were almost identical in appearance. As if to mock the fat, shouting policeman, the occupant of the cab lowered the window on its strap and threw back a crumpled sheet of paper which fell near Verity's feet. At the same time, the cabman slashed with his whip at the clumsy figure who had been trying to keep pace with the coach. Verity swerved to avoid the razor cut of the whip, lost his footing and fell. The cab turned at speed into the seaside traffic of King's Road.

Verity got up, his lungs aching with the exertion, and reached for the scrap of paper. Its message was printed in bold capitals.

THE LAST ACT OF MISS BELLA'S TRAGEDY WILL BE PERFORMED ON THE SANDS BEFORE THE OLD BATTERY THIS EVENING, AT SEVEN O'CLOCK PROMPTLY.

There was no further doubt. The one thing he had feared most and expected least had happened. Whoever had set him up had abducted Bella as well. In his dismay, he tugged out his watch to check the time. It was a battered timepiece, so thinly plated with silver that constant handling had already worn it to the brass in several places. But he kept it right, and its hands now pointed to ten minutes past seven. 'They never told me soon enough!' he howled. Then it occurred to him that they would hardly have delivered the message if it were too late. Lunging forward he ran down the length of Brunswick Square towards the evening sea, turned east, and began pounding along the promenade to the astonishment of its sedate strollers. Men and women turned to stare at the gasping, floundering figure as he struggled onward. His tall hat came off, rolling away, but he never paused to pick it up. A wag shouted, 'Stop thief!' Several of the urchin happyjacks began running along beside him and then gave up the sport after a little way. Before him Verity saw the web of the Chain Pier stretching out to the dark blob of its landing-stage. Closer than that was the little crescent, Artillery Place, where the battery of guns had once stood. A grassy slope with a little pathway led down from the promenade to the beach at that point. He stumbled down it, saw the shingle and, beyond it the wet patch of sand which would presently be covered by the evening tide. Then he looked about him.

The beach was deserted, not another figure anywhere between the stretch marked off by the wooden groins before the Old Battery. On the promenade, the strollers had ceased to interest themselves in him and had resumed their walks. In his anguish, he roared above the gentle thunder of the incoming waves.

'Bella! Mrs Verity! Where yer gone? Bella!'

Mingled with his fear for her there was now a fury at the taunting cruelty which his persecutors displayed.

'Sons of whores!' he bellowed. 'Where is she?'

There was no answer beyond the light breeze and the ripple of the tide at his back. He turned to the flat, shining sand which separated him from the water. And then he saw.

The first salty tide-mark had almost reached the letters which were cut into the sand. They were several inches tall, appearing from the promenade only as the ruffling of the sand by a child's stick. At close quarters their message was clear to read, though meaningless to a casual reader.

THE HEALTH OF MRS BELLA V. CONTINUES EXCELLENT. IT MAY REMAIN SO WHILE HER HUSBAND IS ATTENTIVE TO INSTRUCTIONS. THE ISSUE TO BE AT HIS DECIDING.

Verity looked round the empty beach with a wail of despair. He turned to the promenade above, but not a single face was watching him. He had no doubt that Bella's kidnappers had satisfied themselves that he had read the message, but even while he was doing so the watcher would have turned away. Taken with the other two messages, the writing in the sand left no doubt as to what had happened. The words traced by the stick showed the motive precisely. Mr Croaker must see them! But the first wave had already swept smoothly over the message, leaving the words perceptibly fainter as it drained back into the sea.

Racing up the beach, Verity burst upon the promenaders, clutching men by the arms, dancing into the path of oncoming couples.

' 'elp me! Quick! I gotta have a witness! There's writing on the sand! Young person's life depends upon it! Someone gotta read it too before the tide wipes it away!'

They walked in a careful circle about him, the women drawing their skirts in a little, the men glaring at the plump, hatless drunk who struggled to molest them.

'Lissen!' Verity howled. 'Lissen! All of you!'

But he was like a bull in an arena, formed by the moving procession of men and women on either side. Suddenly, his despair was pierced by the realisation of his own powers. Of course! His eye sought out a slightly-built man, inoffensive in appearance, who was walking on his own.

'You!' shouted Verity, plunging through the crowd and seizing the man's arm. 'Yer under arrest!'

In the mêlée, a woman screamed and there was a mutter of anger. But the men regarded the ferocity of the drunken bully and kept clear of him. Verity twisted the little man's arm and propelled him, squealing in terror, down the path to the beach.

' 's all right!' he gasped reassuringly as they ran. 'You only got to read some words!'

They came to the patch of sand below the shingle. From a distance Verity could see that the marks were still there. But his acquaintance with tides was slight enough. By the time that they stood over the inscription the wash of the rippling waves had reduced it to a pattern that was as obscure as hieroglyphics. Verity let the man's arm go and swung around with a sob to the spectators on the promenade. In a gap between the figures he saw that a black cab had pulled up. From its window stared the haggard face of Inspector Croaker.

Old Mole smiled. He was not a greatly pleasing sight, but then it was not the girl's role to be pleased. Cosima smiled back, eyes taking in the expensive suiting and the silk hat. Mole removed the hat and executed an odd genuflection. He handed her a neat parcel tied by a bow. Cosima pulled the bow and emitted pleasantly shocked laughter, lightly stifled by one hand, as she saw the photographic cards of herself within.

'Allow me,' said Mole in a voice which was almost a sneer. He put one foot over the threshold of the double door. At that moment the surly figure in tall hat who stood waiting at the foot of the steps turned about. He strode rapidly up to the door, bundled Mole and Cosima inside, and followed them. Then the double doors closed and there was the click of a key being turned.

Within the hooded shade of his olive-green Pilentum, Sealskin Kite watched the closed door on the far side of Brunswick Square. Then he craned round to catch a view of the distant promenade, where old Mrs Kite would open her blue parasol at once upon the return of the private-clothes jack. But a long time passed and the parasol remained shut. Sealskin Kite whinnied with merriment at the neatness of the whole thing.

Inspector Croaker had himself well under control. He had chosen to give the impression of a man struggling to be fair. His words might almost have been those of an officer acting as prisoner's friend in a court-martial.

'Assault, false arrest, desertion of duty,' he said pleasantly. 'Enough to be going on with. Eh, sergeant?'

'Yessir,' said Verity glumly. Though at attention before the inspector's desk, he moved sufficiently to ease his fleshy neck away from the cutting torment of a tight collar-edge. Mr Croaker did not even reprimand him for the movement.

'Try to see, sergeant, how it will look to the board of inquiry.' Croaker's voice had the distant quality of a man who has attained the perfect equilibrium of bliss. 'Assault upon a member of the public, admitted. False arrest, admitted. Absence from duty, admitted. Causing an affray upon the promenade, admitted.'

'Mitigation, sir!' said Verity firmly. Croaker looked at him dreamily.

'Ah yes, sergeant. I was forgetting the mitigation. Three messages about Mrs Verity's departure. One written upon the sand and read only by yourself. One written in block capitals on paper. You see, sergeant, do you not, that the board will be inclined to regard both such writings as your own work? Which leaves us with one note, written by Mrs Verity perhaps. It announces her intention of leaving you.'

'She never, sir!'

'No, sergeant? Lastly there is the servant's evidence. Mrs Verity going off with another man, having commended her children to the girl's care.'

'No, sir!'

'No?' said Croaker. 'Evidence to the contrary, sergeant?'

'Mrs Verity, sir. Her character and her *dooty*!'

Croaker sighed.

'Neither I nor the gentleman of the board, sergeant, have the advantage of the lady's acquaintance. She is not evidence.'

'She ain't run off, sir! It's villains as means to sweeten me by taking her! She gotta be found!'

'I see, sergeant,' said Croaker tolerantly. 'Mrs Verity has been kidnapped in order that you will have to obey instructions from these villains. Is that it?'

'Yessir!'

'And have you received such instructions?'

'No, sir!'

Croaker shook his head.

'How very unfortunate, sergeant. In the absence of such demands, I fear the board must simply decide that Mrs Verity has — how shall we say it? — bolted.'

Verity's face was suffused by a blush of fury. But Croaker had not done.

'Moreover, sergeant, it seems that during your absence from duty Cosima Bremer also took the opportunity to bolt. Not a movement, not a light in the house since then! The board must consider that as well.'

'Search-warrant, sir!'

'On what grounds, sergeant? A young person is entitled to travel if she chooses. There is no crime against her name, no suspicion to be proved. However, sergeant, the whole sad story of the Shah Jehan clasp now lies at your own door does it not?'

'Mrs Verity, sir! Let her be found!'

'You shall have leisure for that yourself,' said Croaker happily. 'Pending the hearing of dismissal proceedings by the board, it is my duty to suspend you from employment. The young person Jolly, being only casually engaged by the police authority, may now offer her services elsewhere. Remain at your present lodging until otherwise commanded.'

'Then there won't be a search for Mrs Verity, sir?'

Croaker clicked his tongue.

'Every wife who leaves her husband mayn't be *searched* for, sergeant! Our force was not constituted for such interference! Seek her out for yourself if you choose. For the present, a man suspended without his pay might be glad of one less mouth to feed.'

Croaker grinned humourlessly at his plump victim.

'Then I'm suspended without me pay, sir?' Verity inquired.

'Oh yes,' said Croaker reassuringly. 'Why, sergeant, a man that sits at home in idleness must not expect reward for it, must he?'

Verity looked hopelessly at his commander.

'No, sir.'

'Very well!' snapped Croaker brightly. 'Dismiss!'

16

To his surprise, in the days following Bella's disappearance, Verity felt neither the desperate anguish nor the frantic distraction which victims in stage melodrama displayed. The torment of her absence filled him instead with a dull, cold sickness of heart. The Tidy Street lodgings resembled a house of bereavement. Stringfellow hobbled about, speaking little, apparently in the same state of numbed inertia. The old cabman and his son-in-law were like battle casualties after some amputation or mortal wound, the nerves deadened by an atrocious blow and the pain not yet registering.

Even the children, in Ruth's care, were silent for the most part. The tearful young servant nursed and coddled them but they were thoughtful and indifferent. Verity's pretty nark was housed in one of the attics, from which she now rarely emerged. There, almost in solitude, Jolly pursued her strange existence.

On the first day, Stringfellow had gone to London on the train. But the house in the shabby little street at Paddington Green was still empty. Of Bella there was no sign and no news. Then the two men searched the streets of Brighton, the missions and lodging houses, hospital wards and refuges. Verity sought out Constable Meiklejohn to see if any clue as to Bella's whereabouts might have come the way of the Private-Clothes Detail. Meiklejohn shook his head, a guilty movement in his eyes as though he had compromised himself by associating with the disgraced sergeant in this manner.

Each morning Stringfellow would assume a courage he did not feel as he fetched the cab and the old horse Lightning from the hired stable in Station Street. 'C'mon Verity, me old sojer!' And the two men continued their useless search. For the first time in his life, Verity felt like a beggar, entreating the charity of strangers. With the little daguerreotype of Bella, done the day before their wedding, he accosted the keepers of lodgings and charity houses, even the strollers on the promenade. They shook their heads, avoiding his gaze as if embarrassed by his misery. Not one of them, in his view, showed the smallest human feeling for his plight.

On the third evening he sat opposite Stringfellow across the rough scrubbed wood of the kitchen table. The dark ale in his glass was an inch or two lower than it had been half an hour earlier, but the bread and cheese was untouched.

' 's no good, Stringfellow,' he said at last. 'Someone got 'er. They must 'ave. Mr Croaker was right, too. We've not had a word from 'em in three days. There ain't no instructions to be give me. It's done for spite. Some villain I must have crossed done it for revenge. She ain't never coming back. They don't mean her to.'

Then, for the first time during his wretchedness, a single manly tear brimmed in his dark eyes and spread glistening down the flushed portly cheeks. Stringfellow looked thoroughly alarmed.

' 'ere!' he said. 'Never say die! Even if it was true, which it ain't, a man gotta stand to his guns. You know that, Verity! You been a sojer, same as me! You got the Alma and Inkerman clasps to prove it! You never turned your back on them Rhoosians at Sebastypul, did yer? An' our lads rode straight and true against them heathen cannon at Bhurtpore.'

Verity nodded, unable to speak, as though conceding the argument.

'Well, then!' said Stringfellow triumphantly. 'What d'you think your Queen 'd say to you if she could hear you treating for terms now?'

The crisis was over. Verity heaved himself up presently and made his way to bed up the winding stairs behind the latch door. Stringfellow gave a sigh, as though catastrophe had been averted. But now that he was alone he sat in his wooden chair and stared into the embers of the kitchen fire, his old face ravaged by lines of despair.

Since Bella's disappearance, Verity had slept little. When he left Stringfellow, he was thoroughly exhausted. He snuffed out the candle and pulled open the curtains to reveal the starlight glistening on Brighton's slates as though the roofs had been the sea itself. He turned to the straw mattress on the iron bedframe, an alien and cheerless place now that its emptiness served only to remind him of Bella's absence. But in his exhaustion he lay down and fell quickly into a profound sleep.

It seemed to him that he had slept long and deeply. He came slowly and with an effort to the surface of consciousness. Even before he could recall the details of his bereavement, he guessed that Bella had come back to him. It was still the dead of night, and distant chimes of a church clock carried above sea and rooftops in the starlit air.

The sharp profile on the pillow beside him was no illusion. Then he felt the warm smooth pressure of her naked body, stirring his loins insistently. Verity floated between dream and reality, fearing that the vision might melt into shadow if he were to speak. Starlight glistened on smooth gold, the bare skin of her trim shoulders. Her breasts were smaller and harder than he had remembered. Rediscovering her as she lay against him, he touched the tip of a vertebra forming a slight eminence at the slim nape of the neck.

His face touched the sleek bell of hair and he was puzzled that it should be dark and scented. Later he reproached himself with knowing already who she was. The faint light from the uncurtained window was surely enough to identify Miss Jolly's dark questioning eyes, the hair brushed back clear of her proud forehead. In his wretchedness there was relief merely in pressing against the body of another creature with no intention of committing the ultimate offence against his marriage vows.

As she squirmed herself against him, he allowed his hand to map the oriental delicacy of her shoulders, the fine bone-pattern of her spine curving inward to the waist, the swell of her hips. He stroked the silky firmness of her thighs and allowed the softer twin curves of Miss Jolly's bottom to fill his hands. She arched a leg over him, her hand pressing his own to delve between her hind cheeks to the opening of her thighs. Her lips were so close that he saw only part of her face, new to him and strange. She arched her hips back, opening herself to his hand behind her, her other fingers seeking his loins. When he put his free hand to her mouth gently to prevent her kiss, Jolly licked the fingers coaxingly.

Now he was fully awake. Sitting up suddenly he reached for the matches and lit the candle. Jolly lay nude and golden-skinned in the flame-light, dark eyes slanting the first quick anger of rejection.

'No!' said Verity vigorously. 'Ain't you got the least sense of. . .'

The anger in her eyes became apprehension, as though he might strike her for what she had done. Verity looked at her and his sternness melted away. Of all the men and women who owed him nothing, Jolly was the only one who had offered him all that she had to give. He touched the side of her face gently with his hand.

' 's all right,' he said softly. 'I shan't be cross. You're a good girl, 'course you are. Only you must go back to your room and stay there, just as if Mrs Verity was here.'

Jolly gave him a quick feline glance and her voice was a soprano wail.

'What's the matter with me, then?'

'Nothing,' said Verity hastily. 'Nothing's the matter. You're a good girl and you got nothing to fear. If you don't understand about me and Mrs Verity, 's not your fault. You can't be expected to know what you was never told.'

He guided her to the door with a hand on her arm. The candlelight threw a warm flickering gold on her nude shape, the slim young figure and the tight little swagger of her hips. Verity ached with unappeased longing, tempered by a corroding remorse at the thought of Bella. Just before the door he allowed himself to administer one or two affectionate little pats. Jolly responded by exaggerating her swagger. Then she was gone and the door was closed.

Verity lay on the straw mattress in a fit of self-reproach. He knew that when he recognised his companion as Jolly rather than Bella he had allowed himself to go on caressing and fondling her. Such crimes against chastity, he had been taught to believe, constituted a harm that could never be made up for. In the solitude of the starlit room his self-disgust mastered him completely. He thought that if Bella had indeed left him of her own accord, it was the justice he deserved.

The next day was no more fruitful than its predecessors. From time to time, Verity thought that Stringfellow looked at him rather oddly and he prayed that the events of the previous night had not somehow come to the cabman's notice. Ordinarily, Stringfellow's enthusiastic appreciation of young Ruth would have left him in no position to complain. But since his daughter's disappearance, Stringfellow had avoided the young servant girl's company with uncharacteristic fastidiousness.

It was two days after Jolly's offer of consolation that Verity received his final instructions from his tormentors. By the time that a muddy-faced little happyjack slipped the note through the door at Tidy Street, Verity had given up all thought that Bella's kidnappers meant to contact him again.

The final note was in block capitals with no pretence that it had been written by Bella herself. Indeed, it was neatly printed on a square of card, as though it had been a formal invitation.

MRS BELLA VERITY BEGS TO ANNOUNCE THAT SHE WILL TAKE LEAVE OF FRIENDS AND FORMER ACQUAINTANCES SATURDAY THE 27TH OF JULY AT THREE IN THE AFTER-NOON PROMPT. SHE WILL RECEIVE FOR THIS PURPOSE AT NUMBER 33, BRUNSWICK SQUARE, FROM WHICH ADDRESS SHE WILL DEPART AT HALF-PAST THREE EXACTLY.

Despite his fears for Bella, Verity's heart rose with a new hope and he could almost have loved the man who had sent the message. But the hope was quickly checked.

'It can't be right, Stringfellow!' His plump hand slapped the scrubbed wood of the kitchen table. 'Not Brunswick Square! There's still a guard on it! Meiklejohn was outside when I spoke to him day before yesterday!'

'Well,' said Stringfellow glumly, 'it ain't nowhere else, 's the only place mentioned. And the time's four hours from now. Better do something quick. Show this paper to Mr Croaker.'

Verity shook his head.

'Waste o' time. They got a man back and front. They won't do more 'n that, will they? They see who comes and goes.'

'Verity,' said Stringfellow thoughtfully, 'you never thought this means just what it says? Miss Bella there of her own free will? Then leaving of her own free will?'

Verity slapped the table harder.

'You know your own daughter better 'n that, String-fellow!'

'Yes,' said Stringfellow meaningfully. 'Only I was disturbed the other night. P'raps Miss Bella felt something the same.'

Jolly was sitting in a low nursing-chair darning a smock. Verity felt his cheeks burn.

'Don't judge, Stringfellow!' he said warningly. 'What you hear of me at nights and I hear of you is a bit different. See?'

The old man shrugged, as if the matter were no longer his concern.

'What's to do then, me old sojer?'

Verity thought for a moment. Then he looked at the card again.

'First off, we probably been set up. They 'spect us to go there at three o'clock and just put our heads in the noose.'

'Ain't much else to be done,' said Stringfellow morosely.

'Yes there is, Mr Stringfellow. They expect us then. But what if we was in there already, before 'em, waiting for 'em to show up? Then it's our noose and their necks. See?'

'How d'yer get in with law back and front?'

'I'll do it, Mr Stringfellow. There's a window down the basement you could put a child through to open the bolts from inside.'

'You ain't got a child,' said Stringfellow reasonably, 'and you ain't got time to find one.'

But the glint of combat was in Verity's eyes. He nodded in the direction of the nursing-chair.

'What's wrong with 'er?'

Without looking up, Jolly said, 'I wasn't servant there for nothing. There's not just bolts, you'd need keys as well.'

She stood up and came towards him.

'Keys?' said Verity uncertainly.

The beautiful odalisque eyes regarded him with the quiet disdain of a pedigree cat.

'Yes!' she said insistently. 'These!'

They jangled on the table, three of them on a small iron ring.

'Where the 'ell d'you get these?' snapped Verity.

'Took them, didn't I?' cooed Jolly. 'Spare ones from the kitchen shelf. Only present I ever got there.'

Verity's face contorted, astounded and disapproving. But Stringfellow reached out, seeking a little fold of flesh on Jolly's hip and pinching it knowingly.

'There's a clever little 'orse!' he said encouragingly.

17

Concealed by the laurel shrubs of the Brunswick Square gardens, Jolly drew a deep breath and sang a long shrill soprano note. She paused and peeped over the bush in the direction of the house at the corner of the square. The private-clothes man looked about him uncertaintly. She sang another note at the top of her range, frantic and despairing. Then she put words to this cadenza of terror.

'Oh no-o-o-o! Oh please! N-o-o-o! AHHHHHH!'

He was crossing the square now, coming towards the private gardens at its centre, moving towards the source of the disturbance. Jolly let out a final scream, less piercing but with a suggestion of a throttled windpipe. The policeman broke into a run, though still looking to right and left as if he could not decide precisely where the cries had come from. Jolly, in a snug-fitting vest and riding trousers in the familiar tight blue genoa cotton, moved quietly away. Her hair was gathered into a black woollen helmet which covered her head so that, at a distance, it was hard to distinguish her sex, let alone her appearance.

As the private-clothes man floundered into the shrubbery, threshing among the laurel bushes, the girl walked briskly over to the corner house. Another figure was already

disappearing through the little gate in the black-painted railings which led to the steps going down to the basement area
of the building. Its burly outline seemed emphasised by tight
black trousers and vest, as well as a black woollen helmet
identical in style to that worn by the girl. At the top of the
basement steps this stouter of the two paused and pulled
down the helmet so that it covered the face, leaving only two
holes for the eyes and a slit for the mouth. Jolly imitated the
same gesture and followed quickly through the little gate in
the railings, shutting it after her. They met at the foot of the
steps and the burly figure turned upon her at once.

'Right, miss!' it said. 'Sharp's the word and quick's the
motion. That little performance of yours won't hold him for
more 'n a minute or two!'

They found the little window to one side of the kitchen
door. It had been built to ventilate the pantry and, at first
glance, Verity feared that it was too small even to admit a
girl of slender figure. But this also meant that it was ill-
protected. Bunching his gloved hand into an impressive fist,
he punched out a little square of glass between the glazing-
bars, slid an arm through and moved the catch. The lower
half of the tiny sash-window moved up easily. Stretching her
arms out before her, Jolly appeared to dive through the narrow space until her shoulders were inside and her hips outside. Then she seemed to be held fast. Verity guessed that
she had found nothing to grip on the far side.

There was a bizarre pause. With mounting anxiety Verity
looked about him. At any moment the private-clothes guard
would return. In the meantime he was confronted by the
grotesque view of the girl kneeling through the window. As
though in a suggestive work of art, the window acted as a
frame round the spectacle of Jolly's stretched trouser-seat,
the taut round buttocks distinctly separated and marked by
the suggestive seam between them.

'Push the-e-n!' she wailed.

Verity's face grew hot as a furnace as he watched his

hands cupping the cheeks of Miss Jolly's bottom. He tried not to look as she wriggled with apparent eagerness against his palms. The absurd but necessary vulgarity renewed his earlier remorse. With relief he felt her move suddenly and then she vanished through the space. A few seconds later the bolts of the kitchen door rattled, the lock snapped back, and he stepped into the darkened basement after her.

The kitchen was deserted. He led the way softly to the top of the servants' stairs, where she had warned him that the door might have to be forced. Verity tried it and found that it was open. Perhaps, he thought, his tormentors were here already. He swung it open and moved cautiously through, keeping his back to the wall as he looked from the hall into the rooms of the ground floor.

After the warmth of the summer afternoon, the elegant house was cool, dark and still. There was a mustiness of closed rooms which suggested that it had not been opened since the day of Cosima's departure. Just before Jolly began her cries of alarm among the shrubs, Verity had checked the time. It was then half past one. He guessed from the state of the house that those who had lured him to it had not yet arrived themselves.

Convinced of this, he relaxed and moved away from the wall. Then he motioned Jolly from the darkness of the stairs where she was crouching apprehensively.

' 's all right, miss,' he whispered. 'We stole our march on 'em. Now, you keep out o' harm's way and leave this to me.'

He went into the housekeeper's room at the back where the door curtain still hung on its brass rail. The room was cold and smelt of damp. He was quite sure that it had not been entered in the past few days. Had his adversaries brought him here merely for their own pleasure in seeing him rise to any bait they offered? Verity shrugged and went across to the window of the room. He slid the catch open and made sure that the frame moved easily on its sash-cords. They thought him a fool, of course. But he was not such a fool as to leave himself without some easy means of escape.

In the double drawing-room of the first floor the sunlight from the square fell in beams that were heavy with dust particles. Verity stood back and stared with experienced eyes at the furniture. The arms of the chairs, the surfaces of the inlaid tables and cabinets were all covered by an immaculate powdering of dust. It lay evenly and undisturbed, no finger-trail of brightness marking it. From the state of the room, Verity guessed that no one had entered it since Cosima had slipped away from the house.

He frowned. For the first time he had no idea as to why he had been brought to Brunswick Square at such a time. All his expectations of villains lying in wait or devices to trap him had come to nothing. Jolly hovered apprehensively in the doorway as he turned and walked through into the back drawing-room of the first floor. In front of him was a pol-ished table of mahogany inlaid with a walnut leaf pattern. The table was empty, except for a small gold ring which lay exactly at its centre. Verity's heart beat faster as he stooped forward and examined it. The dust on the table was undisturbed and the ring had evidently lain there for several days. He picked it up, knowing even before he examined it more closely that it was Bella's wedding ring. When he looked at the inner surface of the little gold band, he saw their initials which he had had engraved there as a symbol of their mar-riage for eternity.

He stood quite still, listening for any movement in the rooms above or below him. There was none. Then he glanced ahead of him towards the windows of the rear drawing-room which looked out across the backs of Bruns-wick Street West. Between him and the window was a green velvet day-bed, its carved back facing him and its cushions angled towards the window. The surface upon which its occupant would recline was hidden from him by the raised back. But looking more closely he saw something protruding just beyond the end of that. It was a woman's shoe, and the shoe encased a dainty foot.

Sick with the apprehension of what he was about to find, Verity crept forward and looked falteringly over the back of the day-bed. The young face stared up at him, the fair hair neatly arranged, the blue eyes opened and untroubled, the lips parted, the features cold and immobile in death like a marble effigy. Despite all his preparedness and his courageous resolve, he let out a little cry of fear. Cosima Bremer's body, when he touched her cheek, was still faintly warm. Her composure and stillness was unmistakeably that of the dead.

Verity turned and raced up the stairs to the remaining floor. After his tortured longing to see Bella again, he could almost have cried with relief at finding that she was not here. His mind sifted a confusion of thoughts. Cosima had died somewhen that day. He guessed that she had been smothered by a pillow or cushion to judge from the state of her body. Either she had been killed by a man who entered the house, or she had been killed elsewhere and her body brought here. In either case, the murderers had been able to find their way past the private-clothes guard. A suspicion which had lurked in Verity's mind now began to take a precise form. All that had happened was explicable only if his tormentors had a tame jack working in the Brighton police office. Surely that was the answer.

Then all his suspicions were submerged in an agony of terror at the thought of Bella's fate. The men who held her would kill without compunction. He had thought at first that she was merely taken in order to make him obey such orders as were given. Now he knew that he had embarked upon a blind and frantic race to find her before she was put to the same death as Cosima.

He raced down the stairs to where Jolly was waiting, still with no clear idea in his mind of what he was about to do. Perhaps the best thing would be to hide and wait for his adversaries to appear at three o'clock. But he was no longer sure that they meant to appear. A cruel message had been delivered by allowing him to discover the body of Cosima and Bella's wedding ring. The ring was a token of assurance that one young woman would go the way of the other once her purpose had been served.

At the foot of the stairs he faced Jolly, the agony of his face reflected in the dismay of her own expression. He stood there, trying to find the words which would convey his helplessness. From the other world of the sunlit square he heard voices and footsteps. There was a thundering on the wooden panels of the front door, not the sound of a man knocking for admission but the splintering of staves and the thud of axes as the door was broken down.

Verity dashed to the window of the upstairs drawing-room. He almost expected to see the body of the private-clothes guard lying on the pavement as Cosima's murderers forced their way in to seize him. But the murderers would surely find an easier way, as they had already done. The carriage outside was unmistakeable. So was a dark police van parked several yards down the road. Among the voices he could now hear Inspector Croaker's impatient braying.

The confusion in his mind vanished. Of course, he thought. Sergeant Verity in burglar's clothes, discovered in the act of ransacking a house and, indeed, standing over the dead body of its recently-murdered tenant. There was only one thing to be done.

Jolly's dark almond eyes were a study in simple fear.

'Move!' roared Verity at her. 'Downstairs and out the back window, 'fore they get a man on the mews gate! Run! And don't stop till yer see Mr Stringfellow's cab up Western Road!'

She scuttled like a frightened mouse down the stairs and into the housekeeper's room at the back. Verity threw up the window, pushed her out, saw her scamper across the lawn at the back and disappear into the narrow mews of Brunswick Street West. He had given her a start but he knew that Jolly

would never out-distance Inspector Croaker's men to Western Road once they took up the pursuit. There was a bolt on
the inside of the door in the housekeeper's room. He ran
back, grateful to his own foresight in providing the Balaclava
helmets with their woollen masks which concealed the face.
As he reached the hall, the private-clothes men burst
through the shattered panels of the front door, Inspector
Croaker at their head, followed by a dozen powerful shapes,
each with its truncheon drawn and held out at the approved
angle.

'Stand where you are!' Croaker shrieked, bearing down on
the masked figure.

They would overwhelm him in a minute, Verity knew
that. But in the doorway of the housekeeper's room they
could only get at him singly. With improbable speed and
agility, he delivered a resonant blow with his fist, which took
Mr Croaker full on the mouth, and drove his knee into the
inspector's belly. Croaker doubled up with a scream of
nausea and fell back into the arms of the constable behind
him. For a precious moment the way was blocked. Verity
slammed the door, shot the bolt across, and sprinted for the
open window.

As he dived through it, he heard the first splintering of the
door under the axes of the private-clothes detail. By the time
that it gave way, Verity had reached the wall beyond the
grass, scaled it and raced away up Brunswick Street West.
Croaker's men watching the back of the house would, of
course, see the two fugitives from their attic room above the
little tavern, but they would be in no position to give chase.
He turned into Western Road and saw Jolly ahead of him,
close to Stringfellow's yellow hackney coach. Verity had
snatched off his mask as he emerged from Brunswick Street
West, relying on his speed to keep him clear of the pursuit.
He scrambled after Jolly, through the open door of the
coach, and heard Stringfellow yelp at the old horse. Then

the wheels moved and the cab turned sedately into the stream of carriages rolling toward Hove. It was well on its way by the time that Verity pressed his face to the little rear window. He was just quick enough to catch the first sight of men pelting out of Brunswick Street West, pausing and looking to right and to left, before they slowed down with abrupt indecision.

Far away from him now, as they approached the sunlit streets of Hove and the sea glittering at the far end, Old Mole sauntered down Brunswick Place towards the square and the promenade. Mole made his way beyond Brunswick Lawns where an old invalid man took his ease under the canopy of a swan-neck carriage. The scrub-haired mobsman spoke half a dozen words to the frail gentleman. Whereupon, Sealskin Kite's genial old smile faded. His lips drew back on his teeth in a sharp little snarl of displeasure.

' 'ave some sense, Stringfellow!' said Verity for the seventh or eighth time that evening. 'What else could I a-done? Stood there over the poor dead person with a mask on me face, having broke into the house, 'n just shook Mr Croaker by the hand? It's my neck they'd bloody stretch for it, me being suspended already!'

Stringfellow wiped his whiskers on the back of his hand.

'All I'm saying, Verity old sojer, is that you ain't made things easier for finding Bella. Even with that mask on, Mr Inspector Croaker might a-known you. Them villains has got you on a short string, my son. You don't know who they are, you can't go to Mr Croaker no more. They lures you to Brunswick Square then tips the nod to the law that there's a burglar in there, and you and Jolly gets out by a whisker. And where's that leave Miss Bella?'

Tears of self-pity were starting in the old cabman's eyes.

'All right, Stringfellow,' said Verity consolingly, 'all right.'

'As for Miss Bella,' moaned Stringfellow, 'we ain't no nearer seeing her now than the day she was took. . .'

'*All right!*'

There was a silence of mutual reproach. Jolly, in the nursing chair, picked unenthusiastically with her needle at a half-mended petticoat. Ruth sat in a wooden chair by the grate. In her hand was a printed tract which she appeared to study with frowning concentration as she held it upside down.

'They killed 'er, that young Cosima person,' said Verity, trying to make peace. ' 'eaven knows how many others they done for as well. After Miss Bella was took they sent me that message, knowing I'd leave me post to run to the sands. And while I was away they must a-got in easy. They snuffed Cosima later, somehow. P'raps she knew where their heathen clasp was. If they was prepared to take Miss Bella just to have me out of the way like that, they must want something pretty bad. Still, now they got all they want in that way, no reason they shouldn't send her home.'

'No reason they shouldn't do something else either,' said Stringfellow darkly.

Verity felt that sudden coldness along his spine which he had been brought up to believe was caused by someone walking on the patch of ground under which he would one day lie in death. Against the worst that the Swell Mob and Mr Croaker could do, his little army numbered old Stringfellow, Ruth and Miss Jolly. To divert himself, as much as the others, he changed the subject of conversation.

'What a man'll do for a few heathen baubles,' he said philosophically. 'Now I suppose they got it, the beastly thing. Whoever Shah Jehan was, he'd best have kept it and all the bad fortune what it seems to bring.'

Stringfellow shook his head.

'If your Mr Croaker and his insurance chums wanted it that bad,' he said, 'couldn't they a-had its picture done to put on all the walls? Same as they do with faces o' friends in 'uman form as coopers young girls and so on?'

Verity snorted.

'Old Croaker 'ad its likeness done. Photographic engraving

handed out to all of us in the detail. Much bloody use it is if you're never to see the original. Eh?'

He reached into his capacious frock-coat and drew several frayed scraps of paper from an inner pocket. Sifting through them he found a piece of thin card, about four inches square. Even in the coloured engraving there was an aura of malignancy and brooding evil in the funereal purple of the rubies and the sick green of the emerald leaves. Stringfellow pondered it, holding the card this way and that in his hand. Then he looked up at Verity with a grimace of toothless incomprehension.

'Is 'er only one of these heathen clasps, then?'

'Course there is,' said Verity irritably.

'And all the jacks from London has been looking for it and not finding it?'

'Yes.' A deep unease began to stir in Verity's mind.

'And you can't find it?' The old man's face was lined with incredulity.

Verity's head thrust forward like a fighting-cock.

'If I'd a-found it, Stringfellow, I wouldn't be sitting here like this now with Mrs Verity gone and me pay stopped! Would I?'

The old cabman shook his head wonderingly.

'Then you don't none of you know where 'tis?'

' 'ow should we know?' Verity bellowed in his exasperation.

Stringfellow looked at the coloured engraving.

' 'Cos,' he said, ' 'alf of bloody Brighton knows where this is!'

There was a profound silence. Verity felt as if someone had just punched him very hard in the pit of the stomach.

'You never said it was this jewel,' gabbled Stringfellow defensively. 'I never so much as seen this card before. You never said. . .'

'Where?'

'Eh?'

'Where does half of Brighton know it is?'

'Oh!' said Stringfellow, relieved and anxious to be helpful. 'Lots of places, 'ccording to the time o' day.'

'The time of day!'

'Yes,' said the old man impatiently, 'as it might be the Dog and Duck at noon, the old Union tavern bit later on. Always in the public eye.'

'How?'

Stringfellow's voice dropped to a stage whisper as if to keep the words from Ruth and Jolly. Their two heads moved perceptibly in his direction as he spoke.

'Young tavern dancer, Jane Midge. Street-girl what dances for coins to be thrown. 'bout fourteen years old with fair skin and dark brown hair.'

'Yes?'

'Well,' said Stringfellow, as if fearing his son-in-law's wrath, 'she do wear it pinned to her knickers when she dances. Gives her a certain class.'

'The Shah Jehan clasp? The clasp of the Mogul emperors?'

' 'f that's what you say it is,' said Stringfellow obligingly. ' 'f that's what's in your picture. Same thing whatever the name.'

Verity thumped the kitchen table.

'Act sensible, Stringfellow! What's a fourteen-year-old street-girl called Jane Midge doing with a jewel that might buy the whole of Brunswick Square? No one murdered and thieved to get it just so's it could be worn by a dancing orphan!'

'See for yourself then,' said Stringfellow sulkily.

'Yes, Mr Stringfellow, that's exactly what I mean to do!'

On the eve of race week the Swell Mob ordinary in the tavern room was crowded by men and women on either side of the wooden partition dividing the bar. The half of the room reserved for unaccompanied women was exceptionally full now that a hundred or more London street-walkers had arrived in Brighton for the festivities. It was the room which Stunning Joe had seen in company with Jack Strap. There was the same mahogany gloom, the coloured bottles, an acrid fog of cigar smoke, a perfume of cheap champagne. The space at one end, where street-girls had performed casual dances, was now reserved for a 'select party' of race-week entertainers, with a master of ceremonies in a battered silk hat.

The programme opened with a London favourite, Janet, the plump Female Hussar. She was about twenty years old, her pale face soft and lightly freckled, her brown eyes coyly timid, the dark hair cut in a helmet-shape round her head and its length built into a little topknot with a tortoiseshell comb. Her dark brown tights and short coatee showed off her stocky thighs and the plumpness of her hips, confirming that she lately 'dropped a cub' on her keeper.

The pantomime of the girl and a country clown shocked Stunning Joe on Jane Midge's behalf. Janet was presented pushing a scarecrow in an invalid carriage. Behind her saun-tered the country clown with his spyglass, crowing with delight over the vision. As she leant harder and harder over her labour the seat of Janet's brown tights became a pair of vulgarly fattened globes which threatened to split the brown cotton under their pressure. The clown's fingers fiddled bus-ily in the air, an inch or so from her. Janet turned her face to the audience, miming simultaneous fear and eagerness. Then the clown performed an unambiguous phallic comedy with his spyglass, opening and closing it rhythmically.

These performances alternated with turns by comic singers, most of whose offerings were well known 'flash dit-ties'. Standing just off-stage, holding Jane Midge's hand, Stunning Joe had only to hear the first lines and he could have recited the rest faultlessly. In the tap-room the spec-tators roared their appreciation loudly enough to match the raucous chanting of the singer.

> *Of all the blowens on the town,*
> *There's none like my flash Sally;*
> *By prigs and whores she is well known,*
> *And she lives in Pisspot Alley. . .*

This particular song had been going the rounds of such 'select parties' for many years, even when Joe's father was young. All the same, with a sense of indignation, he placed his hands gently over Jane Midge's ears, as much to protect the frightened young dancing-girl from the roaring of the crowd as to shield her from the lewdness of the song. He kissed the crown of her head lightly.

' 's all right,' he said, quiet and reassuring as he could be, ' 's all right.'

> *Her father he was lagged for life,*
> *An out-and-out highwayman,*
> *Her mother she's a lushington*
> *And stone blind drunk all day man.*
> *But blow me if I care a damn. . .*

Another roar from the bar-rooms drowned his words. Clamped in his fist Joe held the eight coppers which represented Jane's earnings for the day and night, indeed all that remained of the money they had acquired. Presently the comic singer stormed off in an exchange of good-natured insults with his friends in the crowd. The master of ceremonies was speaking, begging attention for Pretty Jane, the dancing-girl.

The crowd fell silent, in expectation of seeing the youngster. Jane walked demurely on to the stage in her harem diadem of gilded card, her silk breast-halter and the green silk fleshings from waist to knee. Like a cheap glass gee-gaw, the Shah Jehan clasp was pinned to the front of her pants at the waist, so that it rose against the flat satin texture of her bare belly. With her chin tilted pertly, her upper teeth touching her lower lip in brazen teasing of her admirers, she began her dance.

In the hot smoky rooms the silence grew deeper. Each member of the audience sat alone in contemplation of the bare young arms and midriff, the agile knees and firm calves. She moved sinuously, and it seemed that the swaying of Jane's hips and bottom was performed for every man, individually, in the room. They stared intently, imprisoning the youngster in the harem of their own fantasies. The irony was never lost on Joe. Before them glowed the dark riches of the famous clasp. Yet not one of them spared it a glance. It was worth nothing to them beside the real treasures on display: the firm young face; the slight swell of breasts in the silk halter; the light-sinewed belly; the taut elasticity of Jane's hind cheeks; the unflawed smoothness of her young thighs and legs. Men would kill one another for the clasp, he thought. An entire heathen kingdom had bowed down before it. But a pretty child like Jane could starve in the streets for all that the world cared. Stunning Joe had never before thought much about beauty and its value. Now it seemed to him that he had the leisure to learn.

The dance came to its end. Jane had to go down among the tables to collect the coppers from those who held them up. Their patting and stroking was the price which these benefactors demanded. Then she turned and ran back across the floor of the room where she had danced, pressing the coins into Joe's hand, unpinning the clasp and slipping that to him as well.

Jane Midge had hardly disappeared up the stairs to the dusty little room in which she changed, when two men appeared at the far end of the bar. The old man who hobbled on a wooden leg was a complete stranger to Joe, but Sergeant Verity was not. Joe told himself that there was nothing to fear. The law itself had pronounced him dead. If they seized him now, he had only to give another name. So far as they were concerned, he was dead and buried with a coroner's certificate. They might prove him to be anyone else in the Queen's dominions, but he could never be Joe O'Meara.

All the same, he stepped back a little into the shadows of a passageway behind him where the overflow of men from the bar lounged against the walls with their pots of ale. Verity and Stringfellow came on, but Joe knew he was safe. Then he saw that they were making for the stairs and he guessed that they must be looking for Jane. Like a cold swelling in his breast he remembered that though he had the clasp, Jane Midge had his affidavit, as he called it. The roughly scrawled testimony of all that had happened to him since the night at Wannock Hundred was set down on that document. He had intended it to be seen in the event of his death or disappearance on the orders of Sealskin Kite. If it were seen now, the result might be his death in real earnest.

Joe slipped out of the passageway and moved after them, silent as a shadow up the stairs, keeping just out of sight of the two men. He heard their feet on the worn linoleum of the landing, the boards creaking under their tread as they moved towards the door of the shabby little room. There was a pause and then one of the men hammered with his fist.

'Open this door, if you please, miss. I'm a police officer. There's no harm intended to you, I'm here for your own safety.'

Joe heard no reply and no movement. He edged another step or two up the stairway.

'At once, miss!' said the voice. 'Else it'll be broke open!'

Still there was no sound. Then one of the men muttered to the other, something which Joe was unable to make out. There was the thud of a boot against a flimsy panel of wood. From experience Joe knew that a jack would never break the door down. It was enough to kick out one of its panels, reach through and undo the fastening.

They were in the room now, and still Jane had not uttered a sound. Then Joe heard the policeman's voice.

'Got through the window. Down over the outhouse roof.'

'Still,' said the other man, 'she never had time to put on her outdoor things, they'm still here! She done a bunk in her dancing clothes! Won't get far like that!'

They were coming back now, Verity in the lead. Joe slipped downstairs into the crowded passageway where the mass of bodies and the shadows of the oil-light concealed him. He pushed his way through until he came out into the clear air of the pavement doorway. His first instinct was to run, one way or another, in search of Jane. But there was no way of deciding where she might have gone. With every step he might be running away from her. Her only skirt and blouse were here. She knew that he was here. Surely her first instinct would be to return as soon as she safely could. Cautiously, Joe drew back into the shadows of the street and watched the noisy, brightly-lit building.

Jane was running already. The road was dark beyond the tavern, only the glimmering oil-lamps of carriages shining at intervals along it. She crossed to the far side, looking for the first place of concealment, and saw the tombs and tall grass of St Peter's churchyard. Clambering over the railings, the girl dropped down and felt the dew soak her feet. She crouched there and listened as the frantic beating of her heart subsided. In one hand she clutched the sheets of paper with Joe's writing on them. For safety's sake she pushed them into the tight silk of the halter, safe against her bare breasts. Then she waited. Joe would save her, she thought. It was the only truth that she any longer had the courage to maintain.

Time passed in the darkness as she crouched with her back to the tombs, her eyes watching the road through the railings. Jane had no idea how long she had been there, but the lights in the houses were going out and hardly a carriage wheel rattled on the road which ran into Brighton from Lewes. The wind stirred lightly among the grass. When she heard the voice it was so faint and gentle that it might almost have been the stirring of the long heads upon their stalks.

'Jane! Jane Midge! 's all right! 's me! Stunning Joe! Jane! Jane Midge! Where yer gone?'

The man who thundered at the door, the man who said he was a policeman! No, she thought, it could not be him. How would he know enough to call himself Stunning Joe? She rose without speaking, her pale shoulders and belly ghostly in the darkness. There was a sound just behind her and she turned straight into the arms of a giant. It was her sudden fright at his size which made her draw breath to cry out. The towering figure must have heard the intake of air. His hand slashed down, knocking her almost senseless on the ground and cutting short the cry even before she could utter its first gasp.

Then Jack Strap stooped down, slung the limp body of the young dancing-girl over his shoulder, and moved stealthily towards the dark closed carriage which stood in the shadows of the church tower.

Wrists and ankles strapped, a gag in her mouth and a blind-fold over her eyes, Jane Midge might have been anywhere in the world. There was a moment on the way when an odd-smelling bottle was held to her nostrils and she drifted into a strange trance. Once, it seemed, she was in the open air, being led like a cripple with sympathetic voices all about her. Then she came to her senses in an attic room with bare boards and two iron beds. She struggled to sit upright and saw that there was a cold steel cuff round one ankle. A continuous loop of iron chain ran through the cuff and round a waterpipe on the far wall. The effect was that she could reach the bed and the little closet, but the door and the window were beyond the range allowed her.

The fat pallor of Jack Strap's pouched face loomed above her. He looked at her dispassionately, his eye noticing the paper through the thin green silk of her breast-halter. He extended his fingers and the girl instinctively crossed her arms over her chest. Strap drew his hand back, raising it and turning his body slightly to put more force into the blow. He spoke as if it were a matter of supreme indifference to him.

'Fancy a hiding already, do you?'

Forlornly, Jane Midge uncrossed her arms and the bully lowered his hand. Strap thrust his fingers under the silk and drew out the folded sheets of paper. He glanced at them and sneered.

'So he would, would he? The dirty little squeak!'

He turned out the oil-lamp, picked up his own lantern and made for the door. A heavy key turned in the lock. Jane Midge, in her fear and stupor, had hardly realised that she was not alone. The springs of the other bed moved. A second chain stirred on the boards.

'Don't cry!' said a voice in the darkness. 'You gotta be a good brave girl and not cry.'

'I'm not crying,' said Jane dully.

'What's your name?' said the voice.

'Jane Midge.'

'I'm Bella. Bella Verity. Before you and me has finished with them bullies, they're the ones as'll have something to cry about!'

18

In the marine sunlight and morning breeze the flags streamed out above the buildings of the town for the first day of the races. The streets were almost blocked by carriages and drays, the din from the taverns overlaid by the sound of an Irish fiddle being played in a taproom. The hucksters who

followed the meetings of the flat season had descended on
Brighton in their hundreds. There were vendors of 'hokey-
pokey', the Neapolitan ice sold for a penny in silver paper;
purveyors of sherbet and lemonade, wheeling about a huge
block of ice surrounded by lemons; the man with his basket
of lobsters crying, 'Champions a bob!'

On the downland high above the sea and the town, where
the stand and the enclosure were set, the gypsy encampment
of racecourse and fairground prepared for the afternoon's
entertainment. Stakes were being driven into the ground
and tents erected by barefoot men and women. Tired children were cradled on straw under the wheels of the station-
ary carts, shaded from the hot sun. Donkeys and thin horses
had been turned loose to graze hungrily upon the turf.
Everywhere there was a litter of pots and kettles. Candles
which had lighted the workers through the night now lay
wasted and cold.

To add to the traffic in the streets of the town, processions
of horsemen in tawdry tinsel set off down the Race Hill to
advertise their entertainments. There were medieval knights
and squires, Circassians and Tartars in armour, coarse-
looking women parading as the damsels of legend. The
cavalcade was preceded by the din of a small brass band,
huddled in a gilt cart and drawn by two piebald horses. On a
painted cart behind, advertising Newsome's Equestrian
Novelties, stood the fifteen-year-old figure of Elaine. Toss-
ing her fair hair, she looked contemptuously round at the
spectators. In order to lure the dupes she wore a short
pleated ballet-skirt which left bare the greater part of her
sturdy young thighs. From time to time the breeze lifted its
hem, revealing to the expectant followers only the tight
webbed cotton of the pants which covered Elaine's broad
hips.

During the morning the appearance of the racecourse
changed as the first of a long line of carriages rolled softly on
to the turf. Men with spyglasses, ladies with parasols, and

servants carrying wicker baskets began the long ceremony of luncheon. There were silk waistcoats and chains, Tom and Jerry hats from the prize-ring, white top hats, fawn waistcoats and trousers, crimson roses in the buttonholes of frockcoats with silk lapels.

By two o'clock the bell rang to clear the course for the novices' handicap, but there was another hour before the race of the day, the Earl of Bristol's Plate for a prize of two hundred guineas. The favourite had gone lame and an outside chance had been scratched, leaving four runners: Cremorne, Prince Rupert, Rainbow and Lalla Rookh. Betting in the ring was heavy, under the shadow of the old grandstand. The withdrawal of the favourite left the race more open. Now it was difficult to put money at long odds on any of the other horses. Prince Rupert was fancied and had shortened to evens by the start. The ring was an exclusively male preserve, crowded by the black silk hats of the wealthy and the bottle-green velvet coats of the heavy swells. The ring was the one place where wealth and crime associated on terms of easy familiarity, the common territory of the aristocrat and the swell mobsman. There was betting in cash and betting 'on the nod' from those to whom the bookmakers allowed credit. Such debts were to be paid by the losers on settling day, the following Monday, in that other famous ring at Tattersalls, near Hyde Park Corner.

Outside the ring at the Brighton course, the professional tipsters drove their desperate trade. A thin, ginger-haired man waited patiently by the gate until each race was over. Then he would wrench off his coat, as in a fit of jubilation, throw it on the ground, and stamp on it in his joy. ' 'ere! 'ere! Got it again! Every winner today! Never mind 'ow I gets the tip, gents, but it's straight from the stable! Who'll say half a crown for the winner o' the next race, writ here in this envelope? Every winner today, gents! Who'll say half a crown?'

Somewhere beyond the stewards' enclosure a bell rang to clear the course again for the Bristol Plate. There was an

immediate hush across the broad downland, where the afternoon sunlight sparkled on the canary yellow and ultra-
marine coachwork of the trim carriages. The four runners
were under starter's orders and the most heavily-backed race
of the programme was about to begin. A single voice in the
ring shouted for a last time, 'Evens the favourite!' And then
there was silence.

The stillness lasted only for a moment. Presently there
came a roar from the stand as the horses thundered forward
and the backers in the ring surged across to the rails to see
them pass. They were away in a few seconds, streaming
across the turf between its white-painted rails, curving above
the sunlit waves, far across the skyline towards Rottingdean.
It was hard to make out the order of the runners from this
distance. Prince Rupert and Cremorne appeared to be in
front, which was not unexpected. Prince Rupert's jockey
rode in a distinctive style, his knees tight to the saddle on
which he seemed to be propped rather than sitting. Cremorne's rider sat straight, the reins in his left hand, the whip
flourished in his right.

The crowd lost sight of them, only the few spectators in
the top of the stand having a clear view of the entire course.
In the ring, men craned over the rails, watching the long hill
coming down from the east which formed the last stretch of
the course, bringing the riders past the stand again. As the
first two horses appeared over the brow of the hill, there was
a universal roar and a waving of papers. Prince Rupert was
in the lead, though not by a great deal, with Cremorne lying
back. Then, as the slope began, it seemed that Prince
Rupert began to tire. Moreover, Cremorne's powerful
shoulders told to his advantage on the hill. The shouting rose
to a crescendo as it became apparent that the leadership of
the race was about to change, and within twenty seconds
Cremorne was past the post, a neck in front of Prince
Rupert.

Far away from the tumult on the downs, the promenades

and gardens stretching out to Hove were almost deserted in the afternoon sun. Sealskin Kite mused in his Bath chair. He needed no one to tell him the result of the Bristol Plate. That was a matter which had been seen to long before. Of course, he was going to be much richer regardless of the horse that won.

'But old men likes things their own way,' he said comfortably to Mole who was pushing the chair. 'And the world must pamper 'em up a bit, hey?'

Mole grinned, only understanding part of the allusion. But the rider of Prince Rupert had become the object of devotion of a statuesque young blonde who went as Helen Jacoby. The things which she did for him would have sent any man quite wild. And then she told him that five hundred pounds was on Cremorne at three to one, and that as she meant to share everything with him for the future, half of it was his. The Jockey Club forbade riders from placing bets on horses but if the rider of Prince Rupert received a present from the beautiful backer of Cremorne, that was beyond the Club's control.

The old man looked at the sea and clicked his tongue.

'Little bit of a bonus, Moley. Little bit of a bonus, hey?'

And the shrewd old Sealskin smiled fondly at the glittering tide.

Above the plumes of the chestnut trees, the London sky was black with the threat of summer thunder. A warm metallic smell of rain hung in the stagnant air. By four o'clock on Monday afternoon Rotten Row and the shaded walks converging on Hyde Park Corner were busy with the parade of horsemen and equestriennes. The fashionable world leant on the white-painted rails and watched the passing show. Among the last parade of the London season there were little foot-pages, heavy swells walking three and four abreast, children playing, severe-looking ladies of considerable age who steered younger ladies away from the wicked old bucks who leered under the brim of every ribboned bonnet.

Among the idlers at the rails there was a stir of attention and a raising of spyglasses every time that a pretty horse-breaker rode past. The lenses scanned every inch of the pleasant prospect from the girls' roguish little wide-awake hats or pertly cocked cavalier bonnets and plumes, down to the Amazonian riding trousers strapped under the instep of coquettish little boots with military heels.

Scandal and fashion had given each young woman her admirers. There was something like a universal sigh as a well-made blonde Venus rode by. With her strong hips, her hair worn in a chignon, blue eyes in a face of doll-like innocence, she was known as Helen Jacoby. Until the robbery of railway gold four years before and the arrest of her keeper, she had been plain Ellen Jacoby. But fashion and a sense of prudence dictated this change of syllable. There was the colt-ish figure of Maggie Fashion, the curtains of blonde hair neatly ribboned, and behind her, like a page or squire, her companion Tawny Jenny. This Asian beauty, Jennifer Khan, was a curiosity even by the standards of Rotten Row. The sheen of black hair lay in a pretty tangle between her shoulder blades. Her olive-skinned face with its high cheek-bones and disdainful almond eyes drew the idlers' glances at once. Unlike her mistress she wore no skirt over the tight, fawn riding trousers. The spyglasses caressed the firm thighs and hips, following wistfully down the Row as if for a last view of the broadened spread of Jennifer Khan's bottom moving suggestively on the saddle.

Beyond the chestnut trees, the riders came out by the tall gates. From Hyde Park Corner, far down Grosvenor Place, carriages of every description waited. There were mail phaetons of the sporting aristocracy, trim cabriolets with high wheels and tall grey horses, open carriages and pairs with parasolled ladies. Among them were a few discreet broughams with their rose-coloured blinds drawn and a terrier or lap-dog peeping out. At the far end there were even plain carts and chaise carts which might almost have belonged to the costermonger trade.

The reason for the unusual crowds in the park and the waiting carriages in Grosvenor Place was universally known. Monday afternoon was by custom 'Settling Day' at Tattersalls. Groups of men stood in casual conversation where White Horse Street turned from Piccadilly. Just beyond was a little lane, busy with men of rank and book-makers of substance who had come to settle their accounts. At the end of the lane, where a livery stable might have stood, there was a cluster of little buildings and a stout rail-ing. Within the railing a gravelled walk circled an area of shaven grass. This simple plot was the famous Ring of Tattersalls Subscription Rooms. The rooms themselves were entered only by the demi-gods of gambling who were members, but any man could see for himself the Ring where bargains were struck and payments made.

Tattersalls was not the betting office of the working man, which was a consolation to Sealskin Kite. The old Sealskin traded on the knowledge that aristocratic betting was done entirely by trust and credit. When settling day came, a man of honour or his bookmaker who laid off money through Tattersalls must either pay or else raise money on the 'accommodation market' at high interest. In consequence, the value of transactions at Tattersalls on such a day as this, when all England put its accounts in order, might have been the envy of the Stock Exchange or the Bank. Notes of hand, backed by the finest names in the country, changed posses-sion by the hundreds. Tattersalls was the guarantor of integ-rity in betting as much as the Jockey Club was in the rules of racing.

From the crowded little lane, men came and went, some-times into the grassy ring, sometimes into the subscription rooms beyond their elegant varnished door. A few yards away the Turf Tavern, where members and non-members congregated to do business, was buzzing with activity.

Bookmakers who had hedged bets with one another to the value of a duke's income, shook hands, drank their ale and came out all square.

There were enough ladies of fashion among the crowd to make the arrival of Helen Jacoby pass unnoticed. She spoke to a man in a silk waistcoat and fawn suiting who touched his white top hat and ran her errand for her. Ten minutes later, she was driven away with a Bank of England bill for £5,000 in her hand. A little of that would go to Prince Rupert's jockey, whose lover she had been by necessity. A little more would go to the girl herself. Most of it would go to the man who kept her and the men who employed him. Who they were she did not know. The name of Sealskin Kite had never been pronounced in her hearing.

Among the others there were perhaps a dozen bookmakers, men who had won and lost in their usual proportions. The proportions were large but they had no cause to complain of that. Those notes which they now exchanged were signed by men known in the House of Lords or the Commons, the army or the city, as figures of probity and trust. They endorsed these banker's draughts and went away secure in the knowledge that payment was safe and trust absolute. Had anyone told them that their businesses and all they possessed belonged, far along a chain of humanity, to an old broker named Sealskin Kite, they would not have understood. Had they taken the trouble to investigate, they would have discovered little more than that Kite was a trader on the exchange in cotton and sugar options.

Where the afternoon sun had moved round to create a pool of shadow by the railings of the Ring, Old Mole stood quietly and watched. He was the man of elegance again in his blue suiting and silk hat, only the hanging yellowed mouth betraying him. Mole had no wish to annoy the old Sealskin by probing the mechanics of the swindle too obviously. But he understood enough. A man who had spent £100,000 backing the four horses equally in the Bristol

Plate must have lost. The winner would have brought him £72,000 and the others would have lost him £75,000. A fool's wager, Mole thought. But suppose the money was not his, that it was stolen banker's draughts to be passed untraceably through the processes of bookmaking and settling, wagered in false names and paid to false names? Why then, thought Mole, a man must make his £72,000 clear for nothing.

And suppose, he thought, that a man like the old Sealskin had cause to know that Cremorne might win. And suppose he backed him with a bill which cost nothing should the horse lose, over and above the rest. Why then, he would be £20,000 more to the good. True, he thought, Mr Kite was not quite as good as his word. £92,000 was short of £100,000. But Old Mole was not disposed to quarrel. Even the short money would allow a man to buy Buckingham Palace or Windsor Castle, he supposed, and still have enough to stiff a doxy or two.

With this latter thought in his mind, Old Mole shrugged himself off the railings and prepared to leave. His attention was drawn at that moment by the arrival of two equestriennes, Maggie with her blonde veil and the young Moslem Venus who attended her. Mole grinned. He was particularly intrigued by Jennifer Khan, the slight heaviness of the Asian girl's hips in the suggestively tight riding trousers. As the blonde girl went to give her commission to one of the runners, Old Mole sauntered past. His hand came down with audible appreciation on the cheek of Jennifer Khan's seat. She swung round, indignation brightening the dark eyes with their slight upward slant at the outer corners. Old Mole grinned delightedly at the response.

'Better than a kiss in the dark, missy!' he said cheerfully.

He walked on, swinging his stick, thinking that even those two doxies, had they but known it, were probably working hard for the old Sealskin. He sauntered down Piccadilly a few yards to the stand between White Horse Street and Hyde Park Corner. Then with a final flourish of the silver-topped stick, he whistled for a cab.

'It ain't to be complained of, Mr Mole,' said Sealskin Kite
wistfully. 'It ain't to be complained of at all. I'm an old man
now and, in course, I ain't much more to expect. But I think
what I've seen. Men go to death and perdition for a trainload
of gold as could never fetch more than £15,000. Men destroy
themselves for half that or less. And they risks their lives to
get it. No, Mr Mole, it ain't quite so much as £100,000 but
it's the rightest little tickle that's been seen in my lifetime.'

He sat, as though he had never moved since the running
of the Bristol Plate, in his Bath chair looking out from Brunswick Lawns across the glitter of the afternoon tide. The two
men were alone together.

'There's them two women, Mr Kite,' said Mole gently.
'They can't be let go free now. Jane Midge seen you and me
when Strap had to get the truth of the Shah Jehan out of her.'

'Shah Jehaney trumpery!' said Kite tetchily.

'They can't be let go free, Mr Kite!'

'No,' said Kite more quietly. 'I don't suppose they can.
Not exactly free. No.'

'They both gotta be snuffed, Mr Kite. You know that,
with all that's at stake. The money. You and me staying out
of trouble.'

'Yes,' said Kite, as if agreeing with some observation on
the warmth of the afternoon or the clouds in the sky. 'Yes,
Mr Mole, I suppose they must. Looking at it all sides up, I
think they must.'

A squat barge with rust-coloured sails was making the
best of the light breeze as it cleared Shoreham harbour with
the tide. Old Mole looked at it absent-mindedly.

'Jack Strap,' he said at last. 'No reason he shouldn't make
a job of 'em, same as that Cosima. Once they been smothered, he can make it look like what he likes. Pretty Jane, a
famished orphan washed up by the sea. And that jack's
woman found at the foot of the cliff, every bone broken by

the fall and the smell of the gin-shop on her. Nasty places, cliffs.'

Sealskin Kite emitted the senile buzzing noise between his teeth which was an invariable prelude to speech.

'T' other one first,' he said quietly. 'That little squeak Stunning Joseph. I shan't sleep quite easy until the day they plays the Dead March in Saul over little Joe. Time enough to snuff a pair o' doxies after that.' He watched the half-hearted ripple of a wave along the shingle. 'And another thing, Mr Mole. None of this is to do with Sealskin Kite. See? The old Sealskin been a bit too close to some of the naughtiness over that Cosima person. Eh?'

'Course, Mr Kite,' said Mole deferentially. 'As you say.'

'When pretty Jane and Missy Bella get quietened by Strap,' said Kite, 'the old Sealskin and Mr Mole ain't to be within fifty miles. Savvy?'

'Leaving Strap to his business.'

'*Pre*-cisely, Mr Mole! Strap knows that until the sad news of their demise is announced to the world, his payment shan't be quite ready for him. 'sides, Jack's a simple boy and he do take his pleasures in such things. No inconvenience to him, Mr Mole. None whatsoever.'

Old Mole was nervous as he pushed forward on the handle of the invalid carriage and eased Sealskin Kite eastward along the promenade. To snuff a spiderman or a solitary doxy was one thing. To snuff Cosima already, then Stunning Joe and the two girls held captive was more than Mole cared for. But as he had said to Kite, not one of them could be safely set free. And then, thought Mole, the crafty old Sealskin himself would never have got so close to the caper if it were not entirely safe. As the solid rubber wheels of the carriage mumbled on the paving, Mole turned tactfully to the other subject which preoccupied him and which Kite had so far avoided.

'Now the money's known, Mr Kite, how much it is and so forth, what's Strap's share of it to be?'

Kite knew perfectly well that Old Mole wished to know of his own share, not Jack Strap's. But he played the game for a moment.

'There's £12,000 to be paid here and there,' he said casually. 'Paid to men for services performed. There's £50,000 I must have for my own trouble, I really must. And there's £30,000 which shall go half and half to you and Strap.'

Mole was shocked and then angered on hearing that he, as Kite's second-in-command, was to get only £15,000 out of almost £100,000. But he knew better than to show his displeasure. Indeed it was Kite who took the initiative, turning his head a little as if just able to see Mole from the corner of his eye.

'That's fair, ain't it?' he asked shrilly. 'That's fair, my dear young sir, to be sure! If you don't think so, Mr Mole, put it to Sealskin Kite like the man o' business he is.'

' 's fair, Mr Kite.' Mole could hardly get the words past the tightening of his throat.

'It's more than any dozen men put together should earn in all their lives!' squealed Kite. 'There ain't an earl nor a baronite in the land as wouldn't stoop to pick up such a sum!'

' 's fair, Mr Kite!' snapped Mole. 'Ain't I said so?'

'Course,' said Kite. 'I only say that £30,000 is half each for you and Strap. Suppose when Strap's work is done he never had the heart to claim his share. Why then, Old Mole, you must be his heir. It's you that holds all £30,000 in trust, you see. And a man could just imagine how Strap, the dear fellow, should never come to ask his portion. You can imaginey, that, Mr Mole? You can imaginey that? Hey?'

Old Mole's heart leapt. The apprehension at so many deaths faded in the excitement of the one which meant most to him.

'Yes, Mr Kite,' he said softly. 'I imagine it all right.'

'I thought you might, Mr Moley! I thought you might, Old Mole!'

And the old man's amusement carried across the sunlit

promenade like the high keening excitement of a rodent to its mate.

Sixty miles away from Kite and Mole in their sunlit afternoon, two other men faced one another in a room from which all hint of summer was excluded. The director's office of the Union Bank was overshadowed by the counting-houses across the street and the huge shape of St Pauls beyond them. Its interior was dark, heavy with mahogany and buttoned leather. A few dim portraits in oils hung upon the oak panelling. Only the reds and blues of the Turkey carpet brightened the place, or the ivory stands, cut-glass ink-wells and polished brass bell upon the director's desk.

The two men were like figures at a death-bed, sombre in knowing that there was nothing to be done which might alter the course of events. From his chair, the director looked steadily at the white-haired figure of Superintendent Gowry, Scotland Yard's most diplomatic senior officer.

'Nothing,' said the director. 'Nothing to be done whatsoever, sir.'

'A crime has been committed,' said Gowry, gently insistent. 'A fraud of the greatest magnitude.'

The director winced. He was a thin abstemious man who knew no stimulant beyond the manipulation of money.

'A fraud was committed by the late Baron Lansing,' he agreed cautiously. 'A very great fraud. He put the bills out a second time, they were endorsed by men who may have done so in all innocence. The names on the notes mean nothing. They may be men of reputation or thieves who assumed such names for the purpose. No, Mr Gowry, there is only one man to whom you can bring home the crime. The Baron Lansing. But Baron Lansing is dead and what remains of his estate would never pay the tenth part of the money stolen.'

'The banks who took on Lansing's clients after his death might prosecute the matter,' said Gowry. Yet his voice implied a statement rather than a hope.

The director's lips moved, a tremor just short of a smile.

'To what purpose, sir? Imagine yourself a banker, Mr Gowry. Accept responsibility for the debt and it will cost you £10,000. No, £5,000 let us say. To be sure there is a cost. But you would pay it gladly, sir, to prevent the world hearing that men have been cheated by their banks. Why, Mr Gowry, there would be such a run upon the funds as would ruin a dozen commercial enterprises by tomorrow morning.'

Gowry nodded and played his last card with the air of a man who accepted defeat even before the hand was dealt.

'The clients, sir, the men whose notes of promise were put out a second time to defraud them? Will they be content to see the matter settled without a public noise?'

This time the director smiled openly.

'To be sure they will, Mr Gowry. To be sure they will. When such bills as these are drawn, even the noblest in the land become shy of investigations. Some of the money is put to innocent purposes and some is not. But you know as well as I, sir, that behind the story-book names endorsed on the cheques there are whores and their keepers, other men's trainers and stable managers, money-lenders and even blackmailers. No, Mr Gowry, when the notes are safely cancelled the men who wrote them in the first place will want only to see the scandal decently laid to rest.'

'Then the banks will pay,' said Gowry gloomily.

'They will,' said the director, 'rather than have it said that one house put a man under the hammer because he was swindled by another from whom the account was inherited.'

Behind the white splendour of his military moustaches, Gowry's old face grew a deeper red.

'Story-book names!' he said loudly. 'Somewhere beyond the story-book names endorsing those notes, sir, there are real men. Real men who have stolen £100,000 as surely as if they'd blown open your vaults to do it! What d'ye say to that, sir?'

224

The director sighed patiently.

'Our banks will stand the racket, Superintendent Gowry. Have no fear of that.'

'And nothing more?'

'Lord Culham, heir to the Earldom of Stephen, Member for West Berkshire, proposes to bring in a bill next session asking the Commons to regulate the transfer of promissory notes.'

'Bills and balderdash!' Gowry was on his feet now. 'And men must go free because they robbed by the pen rather than with a jemmy and cudgel! *Fiat justitia,* sir! Let justice be done though the heavens fall!'

The director tapped his fingers on his polished boot.

'No, Mr Gowry. No man allows the heavens to fall, however just his cause. Justice is dearly bought, sir, if it destroys England's trust in her banks and ruins the good name of a dozen noble families. Ask your own Mr Commissioner of Police. Ask Mr Home Secretary, if you choose. Only let our government grow strong and our finance prosper, sir. Then it can bear such robberies from time to time.'

'And justice, sir?' asked Gowry bitterly. 'What of justice?'

The director rose from his chair and held out a hand to his angry guest.

'Where the heavens fall, Mr Gowry, there is no justice. Pray do not hesitate to tell me if I may serve you again at any time.'

19

A thin mist coming in with the evening tide chilled Stunning Joe through the black worsted cloth of the only suiting which now remained to him. During the past week the little spider-man had begun to show the signs of hunger more visibly, his face having the shrunk and wizened look of a starved child. He had searched the unfamiliar streets morning and after-noon for any sign of Jane Midge. Joe had heard the police-man's words at the door of the room in the Swell Mob ordinary, the promise of safety and protection. He guessed that it was not the law who had her now. Pretty Jane was safe in the keeping of Mr Kite's bullies, along with Joe's affydavy, as he called it.

Hard against his breast, under the thin shirt, Joe had grown accustomed to the shape of the Shah Jehan clasp in its case. As he had protested when they forced it on him for his share of the plan, he could neither sell it nor eat it. Despite that, he thought, it might be the hangman's noose for Kite and the bullies who had taken Jane. Joseph O'Meara lived in a cold twilight world of his own, where the pangs of loss were numb and he saw the future as a time for calculating vengeance. The law might never touch Sealskin Kite, but Stunning Joe could do things which were beyond the law's devising.

By day he watched his chance carefully, stealing scraps of food and comfort as each opportunity presented itself. He was careful, more careful than he had ever been. To be caught and recognised by the authorities was the way to obscene suffering and a death whose horrors would have shamed the meanest creature. But the ordeal of prison had taught him patience. He might not save Jane Midge by wait-ing, for the child could be dead even now. But he believed as an article of faith that he had only to stay alive and watch quietly in order to destroy Sealskin Kite and his entire empire of suffering.

With such consolation in his heart Stunning Joe moved through the summer crowds like a broken child whose ene-mies had no cause to fear him. At night he found the same resting-place that he had known with Jane Midge. The

Chain Pier was deserted after sunset, except for the watch-man who rarely moved from his cubby-hole at the landward end. Against the flush of starlight the graceful suspension wires hung in a series of loops from the iron arches of the decking, holding up the wooden promenade which ran out to the pier-head and landing-stage. Under each of the iron archways through which the steel cables rose and dipped, the pier received additional support by wooden piles rising from the shallows and, higher up, from the shingle of the beach itself. In the darkness, the little spiderman scaled the weed-hung timbers easily, vaulting over the wrought-iron railings and on to the deck of the closed pier.

The four archways of cast iron stood like triumphal gate-ways across the narrow pier, each one a structure of Regency elegance with its cornice and pediment. At the base, the sides of the arch were thick enough to contain small shops or booths where refreshments or souvenirs were sold. The ornamental lamps above the cast-iron arches threw suffi-cient light for Joe to deal with the locks, though not enough to make him visible from the shore. As he had done with Jane Midge, he opened the little booths, taking a pie from one or a neatly ribboned cheese from another. Even in these trivial thefts his skill remained instinctive. He stole carefully, so that the pie-woman would not be quite sure next day if she had not counted wrong. The apple-seller would not see precisely that one pyramid of fruit was smaller than it might have been.

After he had eaten, Joe would find the corner of the arch most sheltered from the night wind. There he would curl himself up and sleep. He woke always with the first cold light of the pre-dawn sky. Before the stirring of the watch-man or the rattle of the earliest stable-door, the little spider-man was down the lichened timbers and moving away across the shingle.

At last there came a night when Stunning Joe felt so weary from his constant searching that he took the only coin in his pocket and paid for an entrance to the pier half an hour before it closed. By this time he was tired of climbing, of walking, and longed only to throw himself down in a quiet corner and sleep the rest of his life away.

He made his way the full length of the pier where the decking, no more than a dozen feet wide, broadened out at the landing-stage. There, across the base of the final arch, he sat and looked out across the dark water towards the French coast far beyond the horizon. He had been there for almost half an hour and the last strollers had gone when he heard a sound. It was not as much as the creak of wood, hardly more than a pressure of a man's boot upon the timber. Crouched in the shadows he kept motionless, only his eyes turning to catch sight of the intruder. The figure standing over him was taller and stronger than the watchman. Its shoulders were those of a coal-heaver and its heavy pouched face loomed six feet above him.

'Why, Stunning Joseph,' said Jack Strap humorously, 'you never meant to give yer friends the slip? Eh?'

Joe pulled himself up slowly until he was standing with his back to the cast-iron flank of the arch. The top of his head was not quite level with the bully's shoulders. All hope of concealment was gone, he knew that. Only his wits could now avoid or postpone his destruction.

'You never found me here by chance, Mr Strap,' he said admiringly. 'You never did!'

Jack Strap chuckled.

'Not quite, little Joseph. Jane Midge told us this afternoon. She'd been asked previous, of course. Only I never had put the question as strong as today. She's pining for you, Joe. We all are!'

She was still alive then, Joe thought. She must be. If they wanted him badly enough they would never have finished her off until they were sure she spoke the truth. And now the only hope for her continued survival was that he should remain alive in spite of all that Strap could do.

'What you after, Mr Strap? What you want with me and little Jane?'

The big man chuckled again in the darkness.

'Hold still, little Joseph. Hold still!'

Stunning Joe knew that he was about to be killed. They would never have sent the towering bully for any other reason. Through his mind the thought passed repeatedly that as soon as he was dead it would be Jane Midge's turn. Now at least he was prepared.

It came like the swish of a sword blade through the darkness, the heavy belt which had given Jack Strap his name. Joe sprang to one side, feeling the thick leather fan his cheek and hearing the heavy metallic impact of brass against the cast-iron arch.

' 'old still!' bellowed Strap. Once again the doubled belt with its lethal brass fitting swung down through the darkness. Joe scampered on hands and knees to escape, splinters from the rough decking of the landing-stage tearing at his bare palms. He was almost clear but the brass weight caught the fleshy part of his right upper arm with the force of a truncheon. Like a wounded animal he slithered and rolled away, a paralysing anguish spreading from shoulder to fingers. One blow to the skull and Jack Strap would finish him.

At the wrought-iron railings he pulled himself up, one arm still hanging as though it might have been broken. For himself he cared nothing. If Jack Strap put him to death now with a single blow, quickly and surely, it would be the end of all his misery. It was for Jane's life that he fought. Pretty Jane under sentence by Jack Strap! Joe thought of the agony and humiliation which would make her death a blessing and he lunged away as the heavy belt scythed down through the darkness again.

'You give me trouble, you bleeding little squeak!' roared the bully. 'You give me trouble and I'll see your dancing orphan weep herself dry afore she gets her quietening!'

They faced one another, Joe with his back to the rails at the end of the pier-head, Strap in the archway of the promenade which led ashore. The width of the arch was no more than a dozen feet, all of it within range of the loaded belt.

'You got no sense, Mr Strap!' Joe panted. 'You never thought that affydavy on her was the only one? There's two more copies. They'll be opened if I can't be found. They got your name in 'em!'

It was a last despairing lie and it failed him at once. Strap grunted.

'You could have six affydavies, with Mr Kite's compliments. When you can't be found and when you're known to be dead and buried off Portland, them papers is just someone's joke. You think they can hurt a respectable broker like Mr Kite? You're dead, little Joseph! You ain't no business to be wandering free!'

Strap was coming for him now, the hideous doubled belt whirring at his side as he wound it through the air like a blade. In a few seconds more there would be nowhere on the little square of decking which was beyond its range. Joe looked helplessly about him, thinking of the sea below. But the wooden piles stretched out under the pier-head. A man who jumped would be broken by them before he reached the churning water. Jack Strap was hardly six feet from him now and Stunning Joe was ready to scream with terror. Then, quicker than he could think, he turned and snatched at the red warning light which hung on the end of the pier-head to guide shipping. It was no more than a large hurricane lamp suspended there. Like a bomb, Joe hurled it at the bully's feet. It shattered and burst into flame, the fire running across the planks as the oil spread.

Jack Strap sprang back towards the archway, cursing the little spiderman but not daring to walk through the fire which now separated them. Worse still, the bully knew that the flames would be seen at once from the shore and that the watchman with his assistants would be there in a moment more. Shouting obscenities and blasphemies, the assassin moved further away, following the last of the promenaders towards the pier-gates.

While fire and darkness flickered alternately about him, Stunning Joe edged to the ornamental rails at the pier's end. He stepped over them, his toes on the thin edge of wood outside. Then he dropped down until his fingers held the rim of wood where his toes had lodged. In a few seconds he was hanging below the pier, lost to Jack Strap and the watchmen alike, moving hand over hand along the dry rusted girders. He reached the first damp timbers where they supported the pier-deck, but the tide still swirled beneath him. Then he launched himself on to the girders once more and made for the next wooden pile. At its foot the shingle was dry and he sprang down in three well-judged leaps. By the time that Jack Strap emerged on to the promenade, Stunning Joe was already hidden by the crowd. He looked back once at the pier-head but the flames had almost died away. Perhaps the *Brighton Gazette* or the *Herald* would spare a paragraph for the quirk of breeze which had lifted a warning lamp and smashed it on the decking. So far as the world was concerned it was no more than that.

As he walked among the swells under the coloured lights, Joe knew what had to be done. There was no safety for him any longer, nor perhaps for the girl. Pretty Jane would die or live as her captors pleased. They would hunt him and destroy him, there was no escaping that. But suppose, Joe thought, suppose that before they did he could succeed in coming face to face with Sealskin Kite? And suppose that before anyone could stop him, he should kill Sealskin Kite as an act of open murder? A man had as well die on the Newgate trap as under the loaded belt of Jack Strap.

With this in mind, he forgot that he had not eaten that day. Just now there was something more important than eating. He walked through the little streets beyond the market and waited until he saw the girl. He had seen her passing there before and knew that sooner or later he would meet her. She scurried, unescorted, in her pink silk dress, almond eyes and profile sharply downcast to avoid the glance of admirers.

'Miss!' he said softly. ' 's me, Stunning Joseph!'

Jolly stopped as though struck by terror.

'I ain't dead, miss,' said Joe softly. 'If you heard that, you heard wrong. That's just a story.'

Jolly relaxed a little.

'What is it, then?' she whispered. 'I never had to do with you before!'

'You're with a jack,' said Joe, still gentle with her. 'Everyone knows. You turned nark. Didn't yer?'

The fear returned to her eyes.

'What's it to you? You've no business. . .'

'Listen!' said Joe impatiently. 'I want to help you, that's all.' He drew out a package from his coat. 'Give him this. Don't open it. Give it him as it is. Tell him that the villain is Mr Sealskin Kite. And tell him there's nothing a jack can do. Mr Kite couldn't even be prosecuted for beating his horse. But tell him not to worry. I mean to have justice, and I shan't need the law to help me.'

They stood together for a moment in the darkness of the street, Jolly's height several inches more than the little spiderman's.

'And what shall I have, then?' she asked quickly.

'A purse of gold.' The solemnity in Joe's voice put the promise beyond doubt. Jolly drew her cheeks in, rounded her mouth, and rolled her eyes in a humorous appreciation of her own good fortune. Then she looked once more at the childlike figure beside her and hurried away.

'Well?' said Old Mole. 'Is it done then?'

Jack Strap looked at his master with large animal eyes. His slow mind had had ample time to ponder the consequences of Joe's escape. Mr Mole's displeasure would, at the very least, be followed by the denial to Strap of the reward promised him. But Mole's anger had sometimes taken far more brutal forms than that. Strap promised himself that first thing next morning he would hunt out the little squeak and finish him.

'Yes, Mr Mole,' he said, his eyes lovingly obedient. 'It's done. Off the end of the pier with no one around. Burnt the face off 'im too so's he'll never be known if washed up. Made it seem like a lamp caught fire, that's all.'

Old Mole looked uncertainly at the bully, but it sounded a safe enough way. The burning of the dead man's face was particularly good, far beyond the resources of Strap's intellect on other occasions.

'Bravo, Jack Strap!' he said gently. 'Then you know what more's to be done. Me and Mr Kite leaves the Bedford Hotel Sunday morning and takes the London train. After that, you snuff them two doxies and follow next day. Take all your time with 'em, Jack. Just as you please. Then dump 'em as arranged like sacks o' coals.'

Jack Strap could hardly be spoken to after that. Whenever Old Mole looked at him, he saw the bully's face creased and his eyes moist as if he could almost have cried for happiness.

Four of them stood round the bare kitchen table, Ruth and Stringfellow at one end, Verity and Jolly scowling at each other across its width. On the scrubbed pine the riches of the Shah Jehan clasp glowed and blazed in purple and green. A sheet of writing in Joe's scrawl lay beside it.

'Right, miss!' said Verity for the third time. 'You got nothing to fear if you tell the truth now. Whatever you done, I shan't be vexed. But it gotta be the truth!'

'Stunning Joe!' she wailed, and the dark enigmatic eyes flashed with the intensity of her anger. 'I know him, don't I? Used to take his serving of greens off Vicki Hartle, didn't he? Regular as Sunday!'

'He's dead!' Verity insisted. 'Died on the hulks, buried off Portland!'

'Well, he says different. So's that paper!' Jolly turned grumpily away as though dismissing the entire affair from her notice. It was Stringfellow who made the peace.

'Lissen!' he said. 'Lissen, Verity! It don't matter if it's him or his ghost. Someone calling hisself Stunning Joe knows the score of this. He knows the clasp was took from Brunswick Square but what was really needed was the case with slips of paper worth a fortune.'

'Notes of credit,' said Verity. 'Banker Lansing's. They gotta be.'

'Right,' said Stringfellow. 'And all the taking of Bella and the rest o' it was to get them bits of paper. Worth a mint o' gold. And if this note's to be believed, it's all down to a broker called Sealskin Kite. Take it all to Mr Croaker. Now.'

'Stringfellow!' shouted Verity. 'Ain't you got the least sense? Me go to Mr Croaker with a note writ by a man that's been dead a month? First off, he'll say I wrote it meself! As for Mr Kite, he may be fly as a monkey but the law got nothing against him. Nothing!'

'Kite's a mobsman!' howled Stringfellow. 'You know that!'

'So far's the law knows, Stringfellow, he's no more a mobsman than is Lord Palmerston or Prince Albert. Can't yer see that?'

'And Miss Bella?' wailed the old cabman. 'What's the law to do for her? They'll bloody kill her, Verity, now they got what they want!'

Verity assumed a confidence he did not feel.

'Not while there's you and me, Stringfellow. Now listen. First we find Sealskin Kite and stop Stunning Joe or whoever it is from murdering him. That's the way to Miss Bella.'

'You'll never find Kite!' sobbed the old man. 'Never! Never!'

That night Verity completed his plans. With the two young women and Stringfellow he had four pairs of eyes, though when it came to a fight he must rely upon himself alone. To find Kite, that was the first task.

It was easier than Stringfellow had suggested. If Kite was in Brighton, he guessed how to track him down. At eleven the next morning, Verity took up his position with a clear view of the corner where Folthorp's Royal Library and Reading Rooms stood near the Pavilion gates. He watched the faces of the men who came and went as the latest prices, telegraphed from the Stock Exchange in London, were posted up. Not one of them resembled Sealskin Kite.

Fearing that the old mobsman had bolted already, Verity crossed to the library and spoke to the uniformed flunkey who stood by the polished brass handrail.

'Message for Mr Kite?' he inquired meekly. 'Mr Kite. Broker on the 'change.'

The flunkey looked disdainfully away and called to someone in the cool temple-like interior of the reading rooms. Then he turned back to Verity.

'Mr Kite returns to Town. Messages directed to Bedford Hotel.'

Verity touched his hat with a gratitude that was entirely unfeigned. Moving almost at a run, he disappeared down East Street towards the flash of sun on water, and turned on to the promenade. The square façade of the Bedford with its columns and awnings shone far ahead of him. With the perspiration soaking his dark clothes Verity panted onward. He would get no further than the porter at the door, he knew that. But that would be far enough. The condition of his plump breathless face was sufficiently convincing for the role he had chosen.

'Message for Mr Kite!' he gasped. 'Ain't gone yet, 'as he? Most important message from gent at Folthorp's Library. Consequential on the posting of the share prices this morning!'

The porter was impressed by the hint of a fortune made or lost. He went inside, leaving the door temporarily unattended. When he returned he was confiding and hopeful.

'Stay today, go tomorrow. Morning train. Message requiring reply?'

Verity shook his head, as if too winded for speech. Into the porter's hand he thrust an envelope addressed to Sealskin Kite. It contained nothing more than a card advertising Glaisyer and Kemp, the chemists in North Street. When Kite read the card, with its puffs for corn solvent or stomachic and digestive candy, he might be irritated but hardly suspicious.

Then there was nothing for it but to wait while Stringfellow and Miss Jolly found him. It had been decided that Ruth must stay in Tidy Street with the children while the two men and Jolly continued the search. Verity was also aware that his colleague Sergeant Albert Samson of the Private-Clothes Detail had been posted to Brighton as his replacement. Samson had appeared as the guard in Brunswick Square several times, another burly figure with red mutton-chop whiskers. Until the right moment, however, Verity had decided not to involve Samson in his plans.

Stringfellow's coach, yellow and as lopsided in movement as its owner, appeared early in the afternoon.

'What you got, then, Verity?' the old man inquired eagerly.

'Sealskin Kite. Put up at the Bedford Hotel till the London train tomorrow morning.'

'And Stunning Joe?'

'Dunno, Stringfellow,' said Verity reluctantly. 'I ain't seen a living soul here in three hours that could be 'im.'

From the darkened interior of the coach Jolly flashed a quick slanting glare at this imputation upon her honesty. Stringfellow too now saw the promise of Bella's safety taken from him.

'She ain't 'ere!' he wailed. 'They couldn't have took her to a hotel like this! Not without someone knowing or her being willing!'

'Stringfellow!' said Verity sharply. 'Don't you see yet? It don't matter where she is. We could search every house in Brighton and she might be a prisoner in London all the time. But if Sealskin Kite's at the bottom of all this, we shall get to her if we get to him. And if Stunning Joe should be alive, as we been told, we shall know for certain by watching Mr Kite. See?'

The cabman mumbled to himself, miserable and unconvinced. After that he sat in silence until the reflected fire of sunset had faded from the channel waves.

'I never seen Stunning Joseph,' he said at last. 'I never seen anyone who could even look like Stunning Joseph. Not all the time we been here.'

'No,' said Verity shortly.

'And you mean to sit 'ere all night?'

'Yes.'

'Why?'

' 'cos I got no bloody reason to do anything better, Stringfellow.'

There was another long and reproachful silence. This ended when Verity heard a quiet sob from Jolly. It startled him from his thoughts. The beautiful enigmatic eyes had glared with anger or glittered with desire. To his knowledge they had never brimmed with tears except when she was being whipped by her keeper. Now the first sob was followed by several more.

'It was 'im!' she wept. 'It was Stunning Joseph! I hope to burn in hell if I never told the truth of it!'

'There, there,' said Verity softly, patting the slim warm arm. 'You been a good girl. No one disbelieves you now.'

From the box of the coach Stringfellow emitted a grunt of scepticism clearly audible to those within.

Only Verity saw the night through without closing his eyes. But unlike the others he was used to such duties and knew all the old soldier's devices for holding sleep at bay. The sea mists of the summer dawn lightened slowly and then the morning turned into the palest and most delicate shade of blue. There was a bustle of activity as the windows of the Bedford Hotel began to open and the awnings were rolled out on their metal frames. By seven o'clock Stringfellow and Jolly were awake and watching too. At eight the cabs for the London train began to leave.

'There!' said Verity suddenly. Two men were approaching a cab, the younger one helping the elder. 'That's 'im! That's Kite! And that other! 'ere, Stringfellow, it's Old Mole! Once for thieving and twice for handling stolen goods! This is it, Stringfellow! It gotta be!'

The old yellow coach pulled out and rattled after the trim cabs. Verity saw the cab carrying Kite and Mole as it turned up West Street away from the sea. Far in the distance rose the cast-iron pillars and glass canopies of the London and Brighton Railway Company's terminus.

'They ain't got Miss Bella with 'em!' howled Stringfellow as he drove. 'Where's she to?'

'Never mind, Stringfellow! Keep after 'em!'

They drew up in the station yard. Verity handed out six shillings to a porter to fetch two tickets for the 8.30 London train. Then he bustled Jolly out on to the pavement.

'Wait with the cab, Stringfellow. If we have to go on the train, drive back to Tidy Street and wait there. I won't let 'em go, Stringfellow! Not now I got 'em!'

Without staying for a reply, he snatched the tickets from the porter, gripped Jolly's arm, and plunged into the crowd on the heels of Kite and Old Mole. In the steamy, soot-laden air of the glass canopy the little engine of the London train waited with a dozen individual carriages. Verity stopped suddenly but his eyes were no longer on Kite or Old Mole. He squeezed Jolly's arm affectionately.

'You *are* a good, truthful girl,' he whispered. 'I ain't a man that sees ghosts. But if that ain't Stunning Joe stood in a doorway, may I be shot!'

He was not mistaken, Verity was positive of that. Beyond the platform, in an archway of smoky brick which led to the crowded refreshment room, the little spiderman stood. In his shabby black and crumpled hat, Joe O'Meara looked a cross between an undertaker's mute and a comic drunkard in a stage farce. He saw neither Verity nor Jolly. His eyes turned steadily to follow the progress of Sealskin Kite, Old Mole and the three porters who carried their luggage. Then Stunning Joe pulled himself upright, following the men towards the London train.

It was the 8.30 'Parliamentary' train, so called from its legal obligation to transport the poor as well as the rich. Behind the dark iron and polished brass of the little engine, with its tall stack and the double domes of its boilers, there were a dozen individual carriages. At their head were yellow and brown first-class coaches, no more than dumb-buffered boxes on wheels for all their quilted seating and new lights. Behind these came the paler brown second-class, and at the end the third-class passengers. The company made slight profit from its third-class passengers. Accordingly, their wagons were low-sided, open to the weather as if they were animal trucks. The seats were no better than planks without backs, set so uncomfortably that many third-class travellers preferred to stand.

As Verity watched the waiting train he saw that another coach had been attached to it behind the luggage van which normally made up the rear of the assemblage. It was the most luxurious of all the vehicles provided by the London and Brighton company, a private saloon coach painted in royal blue and cream. The saloon was hired exclusively by a single traveller and represented a well-furnished drawing-room on wheels. There were cushioned seats round its sides, fixed armchairs and a polished rosewood table. At one end the carriage was partitioned off to accommodate a pair of servants and a water-closet.

Into this privately-hired saloon, Sealskin Kite, Old Mole and their luggage had disappeared. From the shadows of an iron pillar Verity watched Stunning Joe. O'Meara had shown nothing of his plan yet. Perhaps he guessed, as Verity had done, the significance of having the hired coach behind the luggage van. It was to be slipped by its brakeman somewhere between Brighton and London Bridge. At the precise moment the coupling would be unfastened, the coach would ride loose and glide into a platform on the way without delaying the Parliamentary express. The slip might take place anywhere, Verity thought, Reigate or Haywards Heath, or perhaps some out of the way place where Sealskin Kite was to be the guest at another man's country house.

Under the glass canopy of the station roof the steam and soot collected. A porter with a watering-can went up and down the train cooling the iron wheels of the carriages. There was a smell of quenched ashes in the warm air and a perfume of ripe pineapple from the third-class wagons. A warning bell rang and Verity tightened his grip on Jolly's arm.

He had expected Stunning Joe to be dismayed by the sight of the slip-coach. There was no means by which a man could follow Sealskin Kite once the saloon had left the rest of the train. But either the thin-faced spiderman had not understood that such a thing could happen or else he had already allowed for it. Waiting to make sure that neither Kite nor Old Mole would leave the train, he pulled himself up from the platform into the last of the third-class carriages. Verity bustled the girl to the far end of the same carriage just as a snort and a shriek from the little engine announced the train's departure in earnest.

With Jolly on his arm he stood among the shabby men and women at the end of the carriage nearest to the engine. Behind them there was only the luggage van and Sealskin Kite's saloon coach. Through the crowd he had a view of

Joe's crumpled black hat as the spiderman looked from the open side of the coach across the tiles and red brick of the Brighton slums below. They were on the great viaduct where it strode across the dark streets to the north of the town. Patches of pale green downland, with flocks of Sussex sheep grazing, flashed like the images of lantern-slides in the openings of the crowd.

Without warning the sides of the carriage shook as if with the impact of a blow and they were plunged into the darkness of Patcham tunnel. A few feet away the sides of the cut chalk, flecked by whiteness, roared and swirled as the express gathered speed again. Verity felt the girl press more tightly against him. Then the noise ended as abruptly as it had begun and they were out in the sunlight with trees flashing past them and the telegraph wires rising and falling endlessly beside the track.

Verity looked for Stunning Joe. The stunted figure in black had gone.

He had known that Joe might be tempted by such a feat but he had dismissed it from his mind as impossible. Pushing through the crowd, warning the girl to stay back, he found the opening at which Joe O'Meara had been watching the landscape as it flew from them. In the depths of Patcham tunnel there had been two or three minutes of complete darkness, even the lamps of the first-class carriages casting no light towards the end of the train. Now, in the brightness of the summer morning, it was Verity who looked out from the open side of the third-class wagon.

Stunning Joe was just in sight. He had clambered along the foot-board of the coach, reached the luggage van and then trusted to his fingers and toes. The ledge above the wheels of the van was too slight to afford a foothold but with his toes lodged upon it and his fingers hooked over the edge of the curving carriage roof he had shuffled his way almost to the rear end of the luggage van. There was no sign of the shabby hat. Even the little man's coat streamed like a flag from his shoulders, whipping and snapping in the wind.

Verity too had thought that somehow or other he must be on the saloon coach when it was slipped, perhaps by a bribe to the brakeman but not by the means which Stunning Joe used now. Only a madman would follow him that way. And then he thought of the worst thing of all. Joe O'Meara was set for vengeance now. Sealskin Kite was about to die and with Kite's death all hope of finding Bella was at an end. Verity took off his tall hat and his threadbare frock-coat. In white shirt and shiny black trousers he saddled himself on the low wooden side of the third-class carriage.

The other passengers looked at him fearfully. He had expected that they might surge forward and try to prevent what looked like a suicide's last act. Quite the contrary, they drew back and stared at him as though he had been afflicted by some virulent contagion. He swung his other leg outward and stood on the narrow foot-board. The wind tore at his back, billowing the white shirt as if to drag him down to his death where the polished wheels sped on the rail with the precision of knife blades.

'Joe!' he shouted. 'Stunning Joe!' The agile figure ahead either could not hear him or was resolved to go on at all costs. For a moment longer Verity clung there, the wind blinding him with his own tears. They were in a cutting now with trees in full leaf rising above the grass banks. As carefully as he knew how, Verity shifted his grip, pulling himself along the foot-board to the end of the coach.

There was no platform between the third-class carriage and the luggage van, only the chain couplings and the buffers which danced lightly against one another. The gap was no more than two feet-but he knew that he must cross at full stretch while the shingle of the permanent way slashed beneath him at fifty miles an hour and the speeding wheel blades honed themselves to a razor edge in preparation for his least miscalculation. Verity thought of Bella, held the corner of the carriage with one hand, feet straddling the chasm, and swung his weight towards the coupling chain on the luggage van.

The heavy links were oily from use. He felt the weight of metal slip from him and then he caught it again, hanging by it and sobbing from exertion and fright as he trusted himself to his new grip. He was less agile than Stunning Joe but he had a longer reach. By sliding his feet sideways against the planking of the luggage van he was able to use the ledge running above the wheels as a foothold. At the same time there was a sufficient ridge at the meeting of side and roof for his hands to clutch. Inch by inch he moved forward, looking neither to the side or below. Left foot, left hand, right foot, right hand, left foot again, left hand. . . There was a blast from the whistle of the engine but his back was to it and he did not dare to try and look. The end of the luggage van had seemed far away but he was getting nearer now, past the central sliding door with its iron bar and padlock, closer and closer to the end of the train. He could even see the swaying saloon coach which carried Sealskin Kite and Old Mole.

In a moment more Verity had reached the corner and saw the brakeman, the man for either the luggage van or the saloon coach. He was lying motionless and senseless in the open-sided space at the rear of the luggage van. And then he saw Joe O'Meara. The ragged spiderman had leapt nimbly enough across from the luggage van to the narrow buffer-platform of the saloon coach. Neither of its occupants could see him or had the least idea of what was going on. Stunning Joe had detached the coupling chains which held the saloon coach to the end of the train and was in the process of slipping the carriage. The draw-bolt connecting the saloon coach with the rest of the train was held fast by a catch in the coupling of the luggage van. Attached to it was a rope which the brakeman of the saloon coach would use when the moment came to draw open the catch and release the bolt from the coupling. With the chains already hanging loose, Stunning Joe had found the rope and was pulling the draw-bolt clear.

Verity shouted again, but the towers of a gothic fortress reared above him and the train drove at full speed into what seemed like the dungeon of a great castle. Tunnel walls roared at either side. The red warning lamps on the rear of the luggage van threw a shadowy glare upon the scene. Verity saw the bolt coming clear from the coupling on the luggage van and, as though in a nightmare, he leapt for the little platform on which Stunning Joe stood. But Joe had sprung aside and gone before ever the burly figure of the policeman fell sprawling on the tiny wooden space.

By the time that Verity got up, the spiderman was out of view, scrambling round the side of the saloon coach to find an entrance. The carriage was still riding close to the train until the gap between it and the luggage van grew suddenly wider. For another mile the coach would continue to lose speed until it came to rest, still somewhere beyond the far mouth of Clayton tunnel.

So, at least, Verity reasoned. Stunning Joe would hardly get to Kite in that time. Even if he did, Kite was protected by Old Mole. Already, he thought, Miss Jolly would have alerted the brakeman on the last carriage of the train as to what was happening. It was only a matter of hanging on.

Only then did he realise that the lights at the rear of the luggage van were receding far more quickly than he had expected. The saloon coach was travelling after the train but, perhaps because of a gradient, it was losing speed. He guessed that it would never clear the far end of the tunnel. Indeed, they were half a mile from full daylight. At intervals, high above the line of the rails a faint pool of light from the ventilation shaft far above marked the distance of the track. A splash of yellow oil-light from the windows of the saloon coach showed the rough chalk surface of the narrow tunnel on either side.

From the little platform with its buffers and coupling chains it was possible to glimpse the interior of the coach through a small roundel of glass, like a miniature porthole.

Verity moved cautiously across to it, expecting to see the entrance of Stunning Joe.

There was no sign of him. Old Mole lounged in a buttoned-leather chair, the back of his cropped head towards the tiny window. A wreath of greenish-grey cigar smoke hung in the lamplight above him. Sealskin Kite lay on a wall-sofa with a tartan rug wrapped about him. He had drawn the rug up so that it encircled his head as well as his body. Peering out from this improvised shawl the wizened senile face might have been that of a little old lady. Neither man spoke. In the pale illumination of the new Warner carriage lights set in the ceiling they looked like a carefully arranged display at the waxworks.

At that moment Old Mole stood up. The scrub-haired mobsman seemed puzzled by the slowing down of the coach and more so by the sudden silence of the engine. He walked to the window and lowered the glass, but the tunnel wall was so close that he glimpsed little more than the rough chalky surface with its contours of soot as the coach rumbled past.

In the sulphurous air of the tunnel Verity's eyes smarted and he felt his chest heaving in the foul smoky fog which he had breathed. He clung to the hand-hold on the little platform as the coach trundled onward and successive spasms of coughing convulsed him. Then he edged outward, clutching the corner of the wagon, and looked along its side into the thick, soot-laden air.

'Stunning Joe!' he shouted as the air swept past him. 'Joe O'Meara! Where are yer?'

The echoes of his voice down the long dark tunnel were lost in the trundling of iron wheels and the rush of a warm breeze. He could just make out that a door at the far end of the coach was swinging open in the space between the carriage and the tunnel wall. He pulled himself back to the roundel of glass, knowing that a single blow from the open door would dislodge his precarious hold on the side of the coach. Then through the roundel of glass, as though he were

245

watching a dumb-show acted far beyond his reach, he saw
Stunning Joe. The spiderman stood, confronting Kite and
Old Mole. In his hand he held a railway key, a right angle of
rounded metal used for securing carriage doors. Using this
he locked the door through which he had just come and
which led to the servants' compartment and water-closet.
Mole stepped forward but before he could reach the little
man, O'Meara had opened the nearest window and dropped
the key outside.

Verity expected that Mole would have finished Joe for all
that. Instead, the mobsman and his master now put on a
bizarre pantomime of terror, almost ignoring O'Meara in
their desperation. Old Mole ran from door to door, trying
each and finding it locked until he came to the side where the
tunnel wall swept past a foot or two away. Sealskin Kite was
on his feet, the muscles of his face working with the horror of
a promise made by Stunning Joe. Joe himself had got one of
the old man's arms twisted back and held him firmly enough.

Kite screamed at Old Mole, the saliva flying from his lips.
But the mobsman had the door undone and was forcing it
open against the pressure of streaming air. He looked back
once at Kite who scrabbled and scrambled in Joe's grip.
Then he was gone.

Verity heard rather than saw what happened. Old Mole's
shout came to him as the mobsman tried to jump between
the coach and the wall of chalk flying past. In the darkness
there was a wild animal cry as the door swung back, crush-
ing fingers or unbalancing the mobsman on his perch. The
sound ended as Old Mole hit the wall of chalk and his body
rebounded under the slicing wheels of the coach. The terrible shriek faded down the dark tunnel as Verity clung to
the little coupling-platform and prayed.

Now he was certain of the bitter vengeance which Stunning Joe had planned. It was the revenge of a man doomed
to destruction, who valued his own life only as a weapon to
turn against his destroyers. In the darkness beyond the oil-

246

light's glimmer Verity heard a sound deeper than thunder. The walls of chalk speeding past seemed to shudder as at the approach of an avalanche. There was a wild shriek in the distance, and the first red glare of Joe O'Meara's vengeance.

In the dark nightmare of the tunnel events moved with macabre logic. At the Brighton end, the signalman in his sham medieval lodge above the tunnel's mouth had signalled 'Train in' as the 8.30 Parliamentary express roared into the earth. At the Clayton end the second man would have telegraphed back 'Train clear', as he saw the pillar of smoke and heard the engine of the 8.30 thunder into the light again. Now, already within the tunnel, the following train, the 8.40 express to London Bridge, bore down on the slipped saloon coach in the darkness. Even if the driver should see the coach in his path, it would take almost a mile before each brakeman on each carriage of the express combined to bring the train to a halt.

Verity beat desperately on the little circle of glass and shouted at Stunning Joe. Either the spiderman heard nothing of the cries or else chose to ignore them. His thin strong fingers were locked on Kite's right wrist and left shoulder, forcing the old man to his knees. Kite was screaming and babbling, promising and praying by turns, cursing and imploring, drooling in a last terrible self-abasement.

Verity's own fear was steadier and more certain. With Kite dead the only hope of finding Bella would be lost. It mattered little after that whether she was put to death like a criminal at execution or had already been abandoned to starve in her chains. He must get to Stunning Joe or stop the express. Nothing else would do.

There was no way into the coach from the buffer-platform on which he stood, and no way down either side of the carriage with the doors swinging open. He dared not risk jumping down from the platform on to the track. It would be a jump into the path of the moving coach, under wheels which sliced their way down the rails. Even at ten miles an hour they could cut a man in half.

Before he had thought clearly what he was going to do, he balanced on the low guard-rail, gripped the edge of the roof and pulled himself on to the top of the saloon coach. The roughness of crusted soot was like pumice under his hands and grit between his teeth. Above him the curve of the tunnel roof flew away in a stream of warm air. Gauging the sway of the coach and the curve of its roof to either side of him, he pulled himself forward. The wind rushed at his feet, carrying the drifts of engine smoke over his head and swirling it away down the long receding arch. Down this narrow perspective of the track he could see the next London Bridge express clearly enough now. Like a child's toy the flame of the furnace lit the cylindrical outline of the boiler, the windshield beyond with the driver standing at his controls.

There was no time to argue with Stunning Joe, he knew that. But at the rear of the coach was the individual brake which every carriage had. A signal from the driver's whistle and the application of the brake separately on every wagon was the only means of stopping any train. Verity lowered himself gingerly to the rear platform, seized the metal lever where it rose from the planking and pulled it with all his strength. He felt the wheels lock and heard the scything of metal on metal but to his dismay the coach slid onward with its speed little diminished.

Unless the express could be stopped there was no hope for the occupants of the saloon car, whatever their speed. Now that he was at the rear of the carriage, he thought, he could jump down without fear of being killed under its wheels. Taking a breath he floundered on to the shingle between the rails, rolling and knocking the breath from his body. Then, in a mime of despair he picked himself up and ran, arms raised and outspread, towards the thunder of the London Bridge express.

With every second, he thought, with every yard he covered he would increase the time for the driver to avoid a collision. In the distance the engine still looked like a toy but then, as in the illusion of a stage magician, the toy became a machine and the machine became a monster, its pistons galloping towards the catastrophe which lay ahead.

'Stop!' he shouted, standing in its path with his arms still outspread. 'Stop!'

It was almost upon him, the tall stack with its banner of fire rising like a tower of hell in the darkness. He sprang aside and spreadeagled himself against the wall of chalk, feeling for the first time that it was wet as if the hill streams found a natural course here. Then the terrible pistons and the iron wheels were thrusting and flashing by him while he shook in abject fear. Panes of light from little windows flickered past. He had a shadowy vision of the driver turning in the light of the furnace, the first brakemen rooted in astonishment at the sight of him.

Then the London Bridge express had gone by and the echoes in the tunnel began to subside to a long rumbling. A second later the shrilling steam of the whistle sounded and there was a long screaming of metal on metal, the last demonic cry as the locked wheels of the express slid uncontrollably towards their impact.

It came to him as a splintering of matchwood, far away. The demonic cry was still and instead there was a puff of fire and the first wails of human grief.

Verity ran until he saw the faint daylight, yellow in the smoke, which marked the Clayton end of the tunnel. But it was not daylight that glowed ahead of him. The rear of the London Bridge express had come to rest safely enough and heads were peering from carriage windows. Beyond that the smoke was white in the redness of fire. The powerful engine had hit the saloon coach in its path, mounting on the wreckage like a splendid beast of fable rearing vindictively above its prey. The tall stack was crushed against the roof of the tunnel and the scattered coals from the furnace had set light to the varnished matchwood of the coach.

It was several minutes before Verity reached the ruins of the saloon coach, averting his eyes from the remains of Old Mole as he passed. The mobsman was so disfigured that only the fragments of clothing distinguished him from a stray animal caught in the darkness. Under the engine's roar of steam and flame the chassis of the saloon coach, derailed by the impact, had slewed across the width of the tunnel. Several men from the train and the tunnel's mouth had reached the debris. Verity, his clothes torn and blackened, his face smeared by soot and the blood of several grazes, joined them.

The oil from the lamps had started several pieces of varnished coachwork blazing like pine kindlings. In the firelight Verity saw the body of Sealskin Kite, open-eyed in the last moment of despair before the rending and burning. He looked for Stunning Joe. Had the little spiderman jumped clear at the last moment, knowing that Kite would never have the agility to scramble down and throw himself from the path of the express? Perhaps he had.

Then Verity saw two men standing over a shape in the periphery between darkness and flame. If Joe had thrown himself clear, it had been to no advantage. All the same he walked across.

'Almost gone,' said one of the men, as if deprecating the dying spiderman's unpunctuality.

Verity thrust himself through and looked down. The body, twisted and broken, could never be moved during its owner's lifetime. It was a kindness to let Joe O'Meara die as he was. The threshold of life and death was so uncertainly defined that Verity could hardly determine whether Joe was still breathing or not. Then there was movement in the dark little eyes and Verity knelt beside the spiderman in the light of the flames.

'Lissen, Stunning Joe,' he said softly. 'Lissen if you can hear me. It's me, Verity. Whitehall Police Office. Can you hear, Stunning Joe?'

As if there was pain in even so slight a movement, the dark eyes turned in Verity's direction.

'Joe,' said Verity, his lips close to the little man's ear. 'I got the message you sent me. I got the message Miss Jolly brought. And I meant to be even with Sealskin Kite and his friends.'

Now the eyes registered nothing.

'You gotta tell me, Joe. If you know of it you gotta tell me. There's a young person took by the villains to be foully put to death. If Kite said anything before he died, where she might be, you gotta tell me. Please.'

The spiderman's lips moved and there was a faint breath behind their shape.

'Jane Midge. . . took. . . left with Jack Strap to be snuffed.'

'And another young person,' Verity persisted. 'Bella Verity. You and me both got accounts to settle.'

Stunning Joe made a slight movement as though, if he had been able, he would have shaken his head. The breath came again through the slow movements of the lips.

'Left Jack Strap. . . snuff 'em. . . too late.'

'No, Joe, no! Where are they?'

In his desperation Verity could almost have shaken the dying man.

'Snuffed,' said the silent lips.

'Where?'

This time the voice broke into a harsh crackle.

'Brunswick Square.

'They can't be, Joe. The law's there. In the house and out.'

The lips moved again.

'Trains.'

'Trains?'

And then, though the lips were still, Verity understood.

'Drains!'

He wanted to thank the little spiderman, promise him that Jane Midge should be safe after all. But Stunning Joe

O'Meara had received all the thanks and promises he ever would. Verity stood up and strode towards the daylight at last.

He was in a long cutting, the tunnel entrance in sooty, yellow brick rising like a second castle with the signalman's lodge above it. The folds of the Sussex downs, now wild and open, rose beyond the trees on either side. Verity found the flight of steps which led from the tunnel mouth to the field above. He climbed them, crossed the bridge and came to a little village with an old church, a tavern and a dozen cottages. The idlers had begun to gather already, drawn by the gangers and officials hurrying down the embankment. Beyond these was a boy in a pony-cart. Verity approached him.

'Right, my son! I'm a private-clothes officer. Scotland Yard. You have me in Brighton by ten o'clock and these two sovs is yours!'

21

'C'mon, Stringfellow!' said Verity urgently. 'That horse of yours must be able to go faster 'n this!'

Between the shafts of the yellow hackney coach Lightning moved in his elderly shambling gait. Stringfellow snarled at the animal and Lightning laid back his ears, as if to return the threat, then resumed a sedate progress down Western Road. Verity had stopped long enough at Tidy Street to dismiss the boy with the cart and put on his best frock-coat over the torn and blackened shirt. The old cabman whimpered with frustration and the growing fear for his missing daughter.

'Can't be Brunswick Square!' he wailed to Verity, beside him on the box of the coach. 'How can it?'

Verity gestured furiously at the horse as if to shoo it forward.

'I dunno, Stringfellow. I dunno how it can be. All I do know is that Joe O'Meara said as much with his dying words. A man like that don't deceive. Not when the parties have taken his own young person, Jane Midge. Not when he's killed himself to be even with them.'

They turned at last into Brunswick Place and came out into the square itself with the sea stretching peacefully beyond it. It was a scene of great tranquillity, not a sign of movement near the tall white houses except where Sergeant Albert Samson stood like a sentry at the door of the corner building. Verity got down from the box and called back to the cabman.

'Go to the station, Stringfellow! They'll have stopped the first train beyond Clayton and I daresay Jolly 'll be fetched back with the rest. Bring her here quick as you know how. I gotta have another pair o' hands.'

'I got hands!' roared Stringfellow.

'All right,' said Verity more gently, 'but you ain't small enough to be put through windows like her. Go on, Stringfellow! Fetch her for Miss Bella's sake.'

With consternation still visible in his face, the old man rattled the harness and Lightning ambled off down the elegant Georgian vista. Verity marched determinedly towards his colleague, Sergeant Samson, and stood glowering before him. Under the tall private-clothes hat, Samson's face reddened beneath its luxuriant ginger whiskers.

'Go away, Verity!' he said indignantly. 'You got no business to speak to me on duty! Go away 'fore bloody Croaker comes round!'

'Mrs Verity and a young person is held prisoner in that house, Mr Samson. Jack Strap's been left to murder 'em both!' In his fear for Bella, Verity's voice rose to a shrill plea for help.

'Look,' said Samson reasonably. 'I was happy in London, what with Croaker and your mob in Brighton. Things was easy and peaceful. Me and Fat Maudie was having a bit of a time. Then you have to get yerself suspended and I'm sent for to stand like a bloody Haymarket doxy outside someone's front door. You done enough damage, my son. Go away!'

Verity was appalled to realise that Samson had not the least idea of what had been going on.

'Listen,' he said. 'Mrs Verity been taken away by Sealskin Kite's men. Kite's dead an hour since. So's Old Mole. And so's Stunning Joe O'Meara what was s'posed to be buried off Portland but been walking round alive for a month since.'

Samson's eyes scanned Verity's face, as if for some sign of lunacy or deep deception.

'With his dying words O'Meara swore that his young person, Jane Midge, and Mrs Verity is prisoner here in Brunswick Square. Jack Strap was left behind by Kite to murder 'em both. And in case you don't believe me even now, Joe O'Meara give this to me!'

From the capacious pocket of his frock-coat, Verity drew the jewelled length of the Shah Jehan clasp. Samson looked at it, stupified for a moment, and then recovered his wits.

'Gimme that!' he squealed indignantly. 'That's stolen property!'

Verity took a step or two backward, dangling the green and crimson stones tantalisingly before his colleague.

'Not without I see the inside of that house!'

He expected Samson to lunge after him. Instead Samson stepped up to the front door of the house where Cosima Bremer had been found dead. He knocked loudly. Presently the door opened and Constable Meiklejohn's face appeared.

'Who's in there, Meiklejohn?' Samson asked loudly, for Verity's benefit.

'Me and Constable Betteridge,' said Meiklejohn. 'Why?'

'You been in every room and cellar today, same as usual?'

'Course we have, Mr Samson. Why?'

'You seen Jack Strap murdering a pair o' young persons?'
Meiklejohn's face creased with incomprehension.
Samson turned to Verity.

'See? And don't tell me now it was some other house in the
square after all, 'cos the rest is all occupied by persons of
the first quality that's lived here for years. Now, give me that
jool and then go away!'

Verity continued to glower.

'What's all this, then, Mr Samson?' said Meiklejohn peevishly from the doorway.

'Nothing,' said Samson sharply. 'Go back inside.'

The door closed and Samson turned again to Verity.

'Happy now, are yer? Let's have that jool!'

'When I seen the drains,' said Verity defiantly.

'Drains?' Samson looked at him dumbfounded. 'This
bleeding sea air done something to your head, my son!
When you seen the drains? Why?'

'Stunning Joe swore as he died that Jack Strap and the two
young persons was down in the drains.'

'And you believed 'im?' Samson assumed the sympathy of
a visitor towards a patient in an insane asylum, 'Jack Strap
ain't in any drain. Come to that, Jack Strap ain't in Brunswick Square. Me and Meiklejohn been watching, turn and
turn about. Two suffering days and nights. Let's have that
jool off yer. Then go 'ome and see if Mrs V. don't come back
of her own sweet accord. All right?'

'No,' said Verity stubbornly. 'I see down the drain first.
Then you get the jool.'

Sergeant Samson sighed. In common with Constable
Meiklejohn he sought only the simple things of life: a snug
billet; Mr Croaker off his back; a bit of a time with Fat
Maudie. The flushed stalwart figure of Verity now stood between him and all these things.

'All right,' he said, 'suit yerself then. See the beastly
drains.'

He glanced down into the basement area and led the way

there. A little distance beyond the kitchen door there was an iron manhole cover about twelve inches across. He got his fingers under the edge and heaved it back with a heavy clang.

'The drains,' he said. 'All right? I couldn't get down there. You couldn't get down there. Let alone a hulking bully like Jack Strap.'

Verity peered into the darkness. But Samson was right. He doubted if the opening would even admit Bella, however willingly she had submitted to the indignity. Samson let the round iron cover fall back into place.

'You ain't half a caution, old chum. Now, let's 'ave that jool safe and snug.'

Verity handed over the glowing gems of the clasp. The two men went up to the pavement again. He turned to Samson, as if for a last word. But Samson had drawn himself up piously to attention. He spoke from the corner of his mouth.

'Watch yerself, Verity!'

Verity turned, almost expecting to see Inspector Croaker behind him. It was only Madame Rosa, the tall imperious figure in black, thrusting towards the steps of the Brunswick Academy next door. Verity waited until she had gone inside.

'Stunning Joe never lied to me, Mr Samson. I know what a liar is!'

'Verity!' Samson pleaded. 'Go away! Bloody Croaker's due on his rounds any time now.'

'Brunswick Square, he said, Mr Samson. Not an hour since.'

'Go away!'

He left Samson to his guard and walked away towards the sea, puzzling out the design of sewers. All the houses had the same iron drain-cover in their basement areas. Evidently they ran into a common culvert somewhere under the pavement. And where would that go? From the slight incline, he guessed that it must run down towards the sea. Probably into the sea. He walked to the promenade, leant over the rails, and saw an iron pipe about eighteen inches across. It ran low beside a wooden groin to an outfall at the level of low tide. The outfall was covered by water just then.

So there was a sewer and storm-drain running under Brunswick Square. It must be one of the main arteries of the Brighton sewer system by the time that it came this close to the sea. It would be properly lined with brick and that meant that it had to be maintained. A man would hardly crawl up the outlet pipe from the mark of low tide. There was another opening. There had to be.

Verity crossed back to the square and found it easily enough. It was a large round of iron set into the pavement at the corner of the houses and Brunswick Lawns. Although the iron was heavy he succeeded in lifting it and laying it back on the stone. A small crowd gathered.

'Crack in the wall of the drain,' he said hopefully. 'Nothing to concern yerselves about. Company business. That's all.'

He swung down into the blackness and found the iron staples which offered a rough ladder. A stream of water rippled a dozen feet below. He lowered himself until he was standing in it, darkness everywhere except from the shaft overhead. It was just possible to make out the brickwork arch of the drain, about four foot high and wide enough for a man to make his way through so long as he could go forward at a stoop. In his pocket there was a box of lucifers. He struck the first and felt for the other tool which he had snatched up in Tidy Street: a candle-end from beside his bed.

It was like an obscene parody of the ordeal in Clayton tunnel. As the candle cast its uncertain light on the low brick curve of the drain, he sloshed his way through the evil stench of the stream running round his boots. On his left, at regular intervals, were the twelve-inch outlet pipes from the individual houses. He tried to count them, as if to determine when he reached the corner at which Samson stood. But it hardly seemed to matter. No one in his senses could believe that Jack Strap was down here with a pair of captive girls.

And at that moment he saw her body. The shape was indistinct at first, something long and dark floating half above the stream. By accident, it seemed, the corpse was wedged across the drain, as if destined to remain there until it had decomposed and the bones had fallen into dust. Verity gave a hopeless cry and floundered on. Presently he stood over her and the anguish gave way to nausea. He turned back and stumbled towards the manhole through which he had dropped down ten minutes before. The candle fluttered and went out but that was unimportant now. He could see the grey gleam of light and he was there in a few moments more. Pulling himself up he stood blinded for an instant in the glare of sunlight. Then, his boots wet and his clothes soiled, he strode up the square to Sergeant Samson.

'You gotta lantern, Mr Samson?'

There was a new determination in Verity's features which caused visible unease to his colleague.

'Meiklejohn got one inside I daresay. Why?'

'Cos there's a body under your feet, Mr Samson. That's why.'

Samson looked aghast.

'Never Mrs Verity?'

'No, Mr Samson, but it might well be for all the notice you took.'

'Who, then?'

'The late Madame Rosa of the Brunswick Academy,' said Verity grandly. Samson's face relaxed.

'Thank Gawd for that!' he said sincerely. 'I thought you was serious for a moment.'

Then he looked at Verity's face again and his tone changed.

'Now you see here, Verity. I had about enough of all this. Joe O'Meara what's been buried a month is walking the streets and catching trains to London. Madame Rosa what passed you and me a few minutes since has actually been dead in the drain for the last week. Anything else?'

'Yes,' said Verity quietly. 'You ever seen Madame Rosa's face, with her veil lifted?'

'No,' said Samson defensively. ' 'ow should I?'

'I once had occasion to see her unveiled, Mr Samson. And I just seen her again. Down there. Now, get a lantern.'

Self-consciously, Samson knocked on the door and spoke to Meiklejohn. The constable went in and reappeared presently with a bull's-eye lantern.

'Right,' said Samson. 'Meiklejohn, you stand guard outside this door and don't flutter a bleeding eyelid till I get back. See?'

' 'ere, sarge! I was on all last night. 's me turn for kip now!'

'Stand 'ere!'

Samson removed his hat and his dark frock-coat. Then the two sergeants set off down Brunswick Square towards the open cover of the main sewer. Verity led the way down, taking the lantern and shining its yellow oil-light along the wet brickwork ahead of them.

'Now,' he said at last. 'Take a good look.'

'How can I say?' pleaded Samson. 'I never saw her face before.'

'But you have seen a dead body, I s'pose?' Verity snapped. 'And you got sufficient acquaintance with the law to know that murder ain't encouraged by the authorities?'

But even in the thin light of the lantern, Samson's face was radiant with optimism.

' 's all right!' he gasped. 'Can't be Madame Rosa. Can't be anyone from round here! Look at them pipes from the houses! You'd never get a body through one of those. She's been swept down by storm water from miles away.'

Verity snorted derisively. He beckoned Samson onward. They stepped over the body of the old woman and Verity played the lantern on the brickwork of the wall ahead of them. Something was visibly wrong. At first it seemed that part of the roof of the low tunnel had fallen in. Then, as they approached it was clear that several of the bricks round one of the pipes leading from a house drain had been knocked out. The resulting breach in the wall was about two feet across, quite enough to launch the woman's body on its last journey.

'C'mon!' whispered Verity. He was leading the way through the gap into the chamber beyond. It was tall and narrow with a thin circle of light round the edges of an iron cover above. They were now beneath the basement area of one of the houses.

Ahead of them the domestic culvert ran into the foundations of the house itself, under the kitchen floor presumably. Here too the brickwork had been disturbed. Though the bricks themselves had been replaced it was easy enough to lift them out, revealing a gap big enough to admit a man's body under the basement floor. There was a space under the joists and boards in this case, sloping like the square outside. At the higher end the builders' rubble and broken bricks lay piled up almost to the level of the floorboards. At the other extreme there was a cavity about four feet high against the foundation wall of the adjoining house.

Daylight shone through occasional cracks in the walls. As Verity turned the lantern in a semi-circle he heard a sudden shuffling of stone and the squeak of rats. At the level of the foundations the partition wall between the two houses was pierced by a narrow gap at one end, as if to facilitate inspection of the premises by officials of the gas and water companies. Somewhere above him, then, there might be a convenient trapdoor or at least a place where the floorboards could be easily moved. He was so preoccupied in examining the joists and boards that he almost cried out with fright and disgust as his feet blundered into the soft fetid shape on the rubble.

Disgust gave way to horror as the lamp showed him the

blue embroidered band of Bella's crinoline. The dead face looked up at him. Surely, even the ravages of death could never have altered her to the swollen idiocy on which he now looked. He could think of this only as a stranger in Bella's clothes. Then, with Samson at his side, he found two floor-boards so loosely nailed back into place that he could knock them up again with his clenched fist.

The two men heaved themselves up into an unfamiliar kitchen. Its shape was approximately that of the Baron Lansing's, except that it occupied the entire basement area. Moving softly to the stairway, Verity pressed the latch and led the way up to the ground floor. It was a sparsely furnished house with none of the buhl and velvet which Cosima Bremer had enjoyed. However, there appeared to be a more sumptuous room on the first floor glimpsed through a half-open door. It was a woman's dressing-room and, as they drew closer, Verity could make out the tiny sounds of skirts being put on or off.

There was no doubt that they were in the Brunswick Academy. Every glimpse from the windows confirmed the position of the house at the top of the square looking directly down towards the sea. The sergeants edged their way into the doorway, still unobserved. Verity stood there, fascinated by the figure before him.

Madame Rosa's black bombazine was unmistakeable. But like the contrivance of a freak-show, there emerged from the bulky skirts and bodice a cropped and grizzled head. The pouched face was dusted with rouge and coarse with ill-shaven stubble. A wig with a veil attached lay on the table. It was Samson who recovered his wits first.

'Oh dear, Jack Strap! Ain't you a pretty thing, though? 'f I'd a-seen you like this first off, why I don't s'pose I should 've had a glance to spare for Miss Maudie!'

Strap turned upon the two men with a roar. In a single gesture he ripped the skirts and bodice clear, standing in trousers and shirt as if prepared for battle. He snatched up a

261

chair by one leg and charged upon Verity, whirling the piece of furniture like a claymore. Verity sprang aside in time, but Jack Strap was upon Samson as the chair smashed harmlessly against the door. The bully seized Samson by a leg and an arm, lifted him and launched him horizontally through the air towards the window. There was a shattering of wood and a rending of curtains as a small occasional table broke Samson's fall. Shaking his head stupidly, he picked himself slowly out of the wreckage, while Strap turned upon Verity again.

The bully had hold of Verity by shirt and trousers and was slamming him back repeatedly against the wall. Verity's fists beat on the pouched face but Strap seemed to feel nothing. And then, as the breath was beaten from his body, Verity's arms fell limp and the light from the window began to grow black. He tried to shout for Samson but the words came only as spasms of breath from his exhausted lungs.

Then Samson was back in the fight, clutching at a leg from the broken chair and bringing it down on Jack Strap's head. But Samson was too short to deliver the blow effectively. Strap shook his head, as though to dislodge a troublesome insect, and then began to beat Verity against the wall again. Satisfied that one of his adversaries was out of action for the time being, he left Verity to slide down the wall to the floor, and swung round on Samson. From the waist of his trousers, the bully had drawn his brass-weighted belt. The time had come to finish Samson once and for all. Whirring the weighted leather at his side he closed upon the dazed policeman.

Samson staggered back, stumbling over fallen furniture in an attempt to get beyond Strap's range. It was Verity who got first to his knees, then to his feet, and attacked the enemy from the rear. To hold him back from Samson, he leapt upon Strap's shoulders, hanging there with his arms locked round the bully's throat. Strap hardly seemed to notice. He moved forward, driving Samson into a corner of the room.

As they passed the dressing-table, Verity snatched up a large bottle of lavender water and began to beat the massive skull with the thick glass. And still Strap hardly appeared to notice. With Verity's weight riding on his back, he whirred the loaded belt faster and faster as he prepared Samson for the *coup de grace*.

His arms thrown up before his face, Samson was crouched in the corner beyond all possibility of self-defence. Strap had begun his career as a fairground fighter, taking on three men simultaneously in the exhibition ring. It would have needed the greater part of the Private-Clothes Detail to match him now.

And then Verity came to his senses. He stopped beating Strap on the skull and loosened his grip on the leathery throat. Very gently he undid the top of the lavender water and poured the contents of the bottle down over the bully's face and into his eyes. Strap thrashed about him with a bellow of fury, fists scrubbing at his eyes to wipe away the blinding pain. Samson edged away from the corner in which he had been trapped. He grabbed a fallen curtain, ran a running noose round Strap's ankles and brought the bully down by a tremendous heave.

As Verity fell on his adversary's back, Samson took the handcuffs from his belt and managed to snap one of them round Strap's right wrist. The second wrist defied all his efforts. It was Verity who reached out and drew the bed closer until the free cuff could be locked round its iron frame.

'Samson!' he shouted. 'Get Meiklejohn! All of 'em! Anyone yer can! Call from the window!'

He jumped clear and left Samson in the room with his prisoner. His last glimpse was of Samson shouting through the open window, while the half-blinded bully bellowed and roared his way round the room, towing after him the iron bedframe to which he was now shackled. Verity opened the door of the only other room on this floor and found it empty. On tiptoe he went up the next flight of stairs. He had no

263

idea who, if anyone, might be in the attics above but it was quite possible that Strap was not the only one of Kite's men in the house. And if Kite and Old Mole had ordered the deaths of Madame Rosa, her maid, and Cosima Bremer, they would not have hesitated to add his own to the list.

He opened the first attic door. The sunlit little room contained three beds, presumably used by Madame Rosa's pupils during term. Otherwise the apartment was empty. He opened the next door and saw two empty beds. Where else could she be? He took a step forward into the room. And then, worse than anything that Strap had done to him, there was the sudden shock of an atrocious impact on his skull. He slid down in an explosion of light and a slow darkness closed above him.

He had no idea how long he had been lying there. As he drifted towards consciousness again there was such pain in his head that he could not bear to move it. Bella's voice came to him, weeping and far off.

'Oh, Mr Verity! Oh, Mr Verity!'

He opened his eyes and saw that he was lying on the little bed nearest to the door. Bella was looking down at him.

'Mrs Verity!' His voice rasped and thickened however much he tried to prevent it. 'Bella!'

Her hands were clasped in consternation.

'Oh, Mr Verity! We never thought it was you! We never meant it for you!'

To one side of him, on the floor, was a length of metal pipe.

'Mrs Verity!' Admiration and reproach were finely balanced in his voice.

'Oh, Mr Verity! Poor, dear, Mr Verity!'

There were two other people in the room. He saw, in double vision, the adolescent figure of Jane Midge. Then, as his eyes cleared, he made out Meiklejohn working with a hacksaw at another length of piping. He looked back at

Bella, scandalously attired in nothing beyond bodice and pantalets.

' 'ere Mrs Verity!' he said excitedly. 'Where's yer clothes?'

'They took the dress for the servant girl,' she said primly. 'The big man and that other one with dark cropped hair.'

'Old Mole,' Verity said thickly. 'Meiklejohn! What's been happening while I was lying here?'

'Nothing much,' said Meiklejohn sawing determinedly to free Jane Midge. 'Half of Brighton constabulary is in the square outside. That's all.'

'And Jack Strap?'

'They caught him just below, on the promenade. Pulling a bed behind him. He's cuffed and ironed, in the lock-up.'

'And them bodies?'

'Madame Rosa and her maid. While you was decoyed to the beach that time, seems that Sealskin Kite's lot took over this house and coopered the pair of 'em. On'y Strap was to pretend to be the old girl coming and going. That way they could keep Mrs V. and Midge prisoners here. And they could come and go through the foundation wall to get from this to next door.'

Verity lay there, too exhausted to discuss the matter further. In any case, he knew all there was to know by this time.

A dress was found for Bella and early in the evening they were taken home. In the corner of the square stood the yellow hackney coach with Stringfellow and Jolly on the box. Verity followed Bella inside after the cabman's tearful reunion with his daughter. All Bella's tears of joy had been shed on her husband's recovery. She sat in the coach with him, calm and contented.

'I never would a-done you such damage, Mr Verity,' she said softly. 'You know that.'

'There, there, Mrs Verity!'

'Only it was that nasty Strap person we was expecting. And I got this bit of lead pipe free yesterday. And though I couldn't quite reach the door, being chained to the iron pipe by an ankle, I could make the lead one reach there. So, of course, when the door opens and someone comes through. . .'

'There, there, Bella! There, there!'

They passed the evening crowds and the quiescent tide, but their eyes rested tranquilly on one another. Presently, however, Bella sat back and wrinkled her pretty nose.

' 'ere, Mr Verity! Where you say you been exactly?'

22

Three times Verity had stood to attention in front of the desk to receive Croaker's reprimands. But this time there was a difference. The lime-washed office of the Brighton constabulary was familiar enough, but the face behind the desk had changed. Brushing his white cavalry commander's moustaches compulsively, Superintendent Gowry seemed to pierce the plump sergeant with the gaze of his calm blue eyes. Gowry was the supreme 'Governor' of the Private-Clothes Detail, a stickler for discipline. But, unlike Croaker, the ex-artillery supply officer, Gowry had been a fighting soldier. As such, he had been trained in the old-fashioned military ideals of decency and loyalty towards the men who served under him.

'Sergeant,' he said quietly, 'it is a matter of great regret to me that I should be compelled to perform this duty in Mr Croaker's place.'

'Yessir,' said Verity as contritely as he knew how.

'Mr Croaker, gallant officer and leader of men that he is, will remain an invalid for the rest of the month. Both arms and one leg in plaster.'

'Sir?'

'Your inspector's valiant attempt to apprehend Jack Strap in Brunswick Square, as the villain was fleeing towards the promenade, is an example of courage to you all. Indeed, had you and Samson not been so remiss as to attach the man to a potential weapon, the injuries might have been avoided.'

'You mean Strap hit Mr Croaker with the bed, sir?'

'Yes,' said Gowry shortly. 'Mr Croaker was furthermore the victim of a cowardly assault by a masked villain, still unidentified, during the search of Brunswick Square and the discovery of Fraulein Bremer's body there.'

'Well I never, sir!'

'Be that as it may, Mr Croaker is now *hors de combat*.'

Verity's honest face creased in total incomprehension. Gowry looked at him coldly.

'Which brings us to the matter of your suspension, sergeant.'

'Yessir.'

'You were in the wrong, of that there is no doubt,' Gowry's fingers played indecisively upon the desk as he sought for words. 'I find you wrong in leaving your post. I find you foolish, as I hear from Mr Croaker, in merely pretending that your wife had gone off with another man in a cab. Never once did you offer evidence of the gravity of what had happened in fact.'

Verity opened his mouth protestingly but Gowry waved him to silence.

'However, sergeant, the ordeal you have suffered and the courage you have shown must be weighed in the scales likewise. Your suspension is lifted, your pay is restored. There will be no board of inquiry.'

' 'umbly grateful, sir.'

'You have saved two lives,' Gowry continued. 'The evidence of Strap and the dying testimony of O'Meara has thrown the fraud in reverse. A good deal of the money, though perhaps not all of it, will be recovered from the thieves, alive or dead.'

'Very gratified to 'ear it, sir.'

Gowry opened the folder in front of him. It was Verity's dossier.

'Not much here to sing about. Eh, sergeant?'

'No, sir. 'fraid not, sir.'

'Reprimands, warnings, insubordination,' Gowry's fingers flicked through the pages, 'assault, suspicion of complicity, complaint by a young person Cox.'

'Yessir.'

'To which I must make my own addition,' said Gowry solemnly.

'Yessir.'

'Commander's commendation for valour.'

The blood surged to Verity's head and his plump cheeks glowed with the pride of recognition at last.

'Dunno what to say, sir!' he gasped.

'No need to say anything,' Gowry's quill was scratching on the cerulean blue paper. 'Mr Croaker would have known how to reward you, had he been here.'

'Oh yes, sir,' said Verity heavily. 'I 'spec he would all right.'

Gowry closed the folder and looked up.

'Two weeks compassionate leave in respect of Mrs Verity's recent distress. Absence to commence at noon today.'

'Sir!'

The dark eyes in the plump red face were nearly brimming with tears of jubilation. Under the sturdy right arm the tall hat was dented by the pressure of excitement as he held it smartly in its place.

Gowry pushed back his chair and stood up. He held out his right hand.

'Oh, damn it,' he said reasonably. 'Don't go round with a swollen head acting like a conquering hero, sergeant. But congratulations! Well done, man!'

Verity stood before the superintendent, as bewildered

268

now as he had ever been after Croaker's reprimands. So much had been given him. But he had still to ask a favour of Gowry, a request which he had promised himself, promised Bella, even promised the soul of Stunning Joe.

'Sir,' he said shamefacedly. ' 'ave the honour to make a request, sir. With respect, sir.'

Gowry sat down again, the lines of his white-whiskered old face suggesting that he sensed ingratitude on Verity's part.

'Request, sergeant?'

'Yessir. For a young person, sir.'

Gowry looked at him bleakly.

'Miss Jolly may think herself extremely lucky. . .'

'No, sir! Not 'er, sir. Poor young dancing orphan, sir. Jane Midge that was kept prisoner with Mrs Verity.'

'What about her, sergeant?'

'Well, sir,' said Verity awkwardly. 'She's not old, only fourteen, and she been a real brave soldier. Being an orphan and having to flash her legs in a gaff ain't her fault, sir.'

'Well, sergeant?'

'Well, sir, what it means for her is Mrs Rouncewell, ex-police matron, sir. Steam laundry down Elephant and Castle. I gotta great respect for Mrs Rouncewell, sir, but. . .'

'But what, sergeant?'

'Jane's on'y a pretty child yet, sir,' said Verity firmly. 'She been brave and she done no wrong to speak of. It ain't the place for her, sir, not with persons of fallen virtue. And there's no call for a child like Jane to be birched over and over, or have that opening medicine put down her, same as Ma Rouncewell has to do with hardened creatures, sir.'

'Then come to the point of your request, sergeant.'

'Just this, sir. You being who you are, sir, p'raps you might know of a respectable lady and gentleman that'd be glad of a clean, honest girl to be took in and made useful. She been a faithful girl, sir, as well. Faithful even to Stunning Joe O'Meara in her way.'

Gowry sighed, as if the problem were hopeless, but Verity knew that he had won his point. The superintendent, former cavalry officer on active service, had the old-fashioned strengths and weaknesses of his kind. He would cut his way murderously through a press of dark-skinned enemy in a colonial skirmish. And then he would stand close to tears at the sight of an abandoned child of the battle or a fine horse in its death agonies.

'Mrs Rouncewell ain't took her yet, sir,' said Verity gently. 'She's still in the other room.'

In a moment more Jane Midge stood beside him at Gowry's desk. It was Verity's idea that she should keep on the dancing clothes in which she had been abducted. Gowry glanced up at the cut of her straight brown hair with its narrow slant of fringe, the firm pretty features of her pale face. When she touched her lower lip with her teeth it might equally well have been apprehension or knowing impudence. But the thin silk of her tight harem pants showed all too clearly the muddy bruises left by Jack Strap's belt. Gowry's face tightened with anger at what he saw. Then he looked up gently at her.

'Can you sew, Jane?'

The girl nodded.

'Will you sew for Mrs Gowry? Should you like to be her milliner, Jane? To read to her and keep her company? And perhaps, one day, to learn to play and sing for her?'

It was plain to Verity that Gowry had no clear idea of the proper duties. But the girl curtsied and cried out her answer.

'If you please, sir!'

Verity sighed with satisfaction. He knew his commander well enough to guess his reaction when the sight of such distress was set before him. Of all the couples whom he knew, Superintendent Gowry and his wife were the most likely to bring up the dancing girl in the best way of all, like their own lost daughter.

There was a reverential hush in the little kitchen at Tidy
Street as Verity described the interview with Superintendent
Gowry. It was Stringfellow who spoke first, after Verity had
finished.

'Always told yer,' he said smugly. 'Mr Gowry's a gent.
Croaker's not. That's the difference between 'em. Show me a
man that's ridden into battle with his men, and I'll show you
a gent. That Croaker was nothing but commissariat supplies
for the artillery. Any wounds he ever got was in the backside, running away.'

He got up, lolloped over to the cupboard and pulled the
cork from a bottle with his teeth. It appeared to contain
horse linament but when poured into glasses the smell was
more palatable. He raised his own glass to Verity, Bella and
Jolly in turn.

' 'ere's to me old sojer. 'ere's to a true brave girl. And 'ere's
to the prettiest little nark that the constabulary ever 'ad!'

He drained the glass and refilled it hastily before Bella
could speak the unease that was in her gaze. They all drank
toasts and then luxuriated in the sense of unaccustomed
ease. Two weeks' leave by the sea was a holiday beyond
anything which they could have afforded under normal
circumstances. Ruth, the servant-maid, and even Jolly,
were still bemused by the good fortune which had spread to
them as well.

They were still sitting round the wooden table in the kitch-
en when there was a hammering on the street door. Ruth,
her brown eyes widening prettily under her cropped fair
curls, scurried to answer it. They heard her voice saying
coquettishly: 'I'll see if Mr Verity and Madam is at 'ome.'

'Mrs Verity!' hissed Verity. 'This gotta stop! She ain't to
talk like that! 'alf Paddington Green is laughing its head off
over us!'

But Ruth returned with something like an appearance of
fright in her soft young face.

' 's a gentleman!' she gasped. 'To see Mr Verity personal!'

271

There was a sudden bustling about. Verity snatched up his frock-coat and put it on. Then he walked into the little front parlour while Ruth ushered the visitor in. He was a young man dressed in black who made a particular effort at refinement of speech and manners in the presence of humbler families. As though beginning a formal dance he executed a florid little bow in front of Verity.

'Hoskins,' he said solemnly. 'Steward of the Household to 'is Excellency the Earl of Stephen.'

They sat down and Hoskins explained the reason for his visit. Verity was uneasily aware of the shifting floorboards just outside the door and the silent presence of witnesses each pushing for position to overhear what was passing between the two men inside.

'Lord Stephen,' said Hoskins, ' 'as the honour to be director of the London and Suburban Bank. A bank what stood to lose almost £10,000 by the late notorious fraud of Mr Kite. Fortuitously, seeing as so much of the money been traced back and recovered, the loss shan't come to even half what it might have been.'

Verity made an agreeable little sound of pleasure at this disclosure, and Hoskins continued.

'In consequence of a felicitous outcome, 'is lordship desires to make a show of appreciation towards your good self and the young person Jolly also instrumental in the matter. To wit, one hundred pounds to yourself and fifty to the young person.'

Verity looked solemnly at his visitor.

'The young person, Mr Hoskins, shall have whatever she's given. There's no bar to her taking it. But I mayn't. A man mustn't be rewarded for doing what's only his duty. You know that.'

Hoskins hardly bothered to disguise the contempt in his eyes.

'His lordship anticipated some such objection. Is there a boy?'

'What sort of a boy?' inquired Verity suspiciously.

'A boy Verity, o' course.'

'Oh,' said Verity, 'a son, you mean? There's only Billy. He's three.'

Hoskins nodded.

'Among his many other benevolences, Lord Stephen is a governor of the 'ospital school. He anticipated some such difficulty as you made but felt it could hardly extend to depriving your own son.'

'Billy Verity ain't deprived of nothing!' said Verity indignantly.

'Quite so,' Hoskins waved the objection away. 'I therefore been instructed to tell you that when the governors of the school meets again, Lord Stephen's nomination for the coming year shall go to Master Billy Verity.'

Verity stared at the young man, not understanding.

'Nomination?'

'Your son,' said the steward, 'shall receive the finest education in the land without a penny cost to yourself. He shall be a great man, if he has it in him. A man of learning, a soldier, a judge.'

'I dunno what to say, Mr Hoskins.' He struggled with the imagined portrait of Billy in judicial ermine.

'You don't need to say,' replied the steward. 'Lord Stephen's nomination shall be made. You must be a hard man, Verity, if you would deny such a gift to your son.'

'Course I wouldn't,' said Verity, bewildered and undecided. 'Course I never would.'

The rest of the conversation, the departure of the steward and the arrangements to be made for Billy when he should attain the age of six were lost to him. After the commendation of Superintendent Gowry this latest news left him numb.

'And you won't deny it to your own flesh and blood, Mr Verity! Not if I know it!'

For the sixth time since they had clambered into bed in the Tidy Street room, Bella voiced her determination in the matter.

'A great man, 'e said. A judge!'

'And why shouldn't your son be a judge?' she cried. 'Why shouldn't he be a great man if he gets the chance?'

There was an ominous shifting from one of the two cradles at the foot of the bed.

' 's all right, Mrs Verity! Ain't I said it's all right?'

'You was lucky,' said Bella complacently. 'You was lucky you didn't take the hundred pounds. What your son shall have is worth a good many times more 'n that.'

'A man don't take rewards for doing his duty, Bella! Mr Hoskins can't see it, p'raps, but your pa brought you up to know better!'

The starlight was glistening on the Brighton slates just as it had so many nights before when he had woken in the room alone.

'And fifty pounds might go a long way to put young Jolly right,' said Bella insistently, 'now we give her a roof.'

' 's only for two weeks,' said Verity gently, touching Bella's face.

'Mr Stringfellow says she'll be no inconvenience back in Paddington Green. Pa says it'll stop you thinking nastiness about him and little Ruthie up in them attics.'

'Whatcher mean?' Verity sat upright in bed.

'Nowhere else for young Ruth to sleep, 'cept in the attic next to his. But you got no cause to think nastiness about it, William Clarence Verity. No cause whatever! There's what they call a chap-y-rone now, Jolly being in with Ruthie.'

'You mean Mr Stringfellow got both them young persons up there with him in the attics?' The agony in his voice was distinct and shrill.

'You gotta nasty mind, William Verity! Pa done everything in the world for you and your offspring. 'f it wasn't for his little 'ouse, you wouldn't have a roof over the heads of any of us!'

It was the second time that they had quarrelled over the attic accommodation since Ruth's arrival. As on the previous occasion Verity heard, in the faint noises of the sleeping house, Stringfellow's fruity chuckle of appreciation. There was a series of sounds which were identical with those made by the cabman's hand when it patted Lightning's flanks. Two separate female giggles followed simultaneously and a throaty old voice said: 'Clever little 'orse!'

'It give your mind a turn,' said Bella severely. 'I know it do. Having to do with criminals and nastiness give your mind a turn. Now all you can do is talk nastiness about poor papa!'

'No!' said Verity hastily. 'No, I never!'

'Mr Stringfellow says Jolly won't be any more inconvenience to him than Ruth.'

A sigh of female contentment breathed high over their heads and there was a shifting of iron springs. Too weary to continue the argument, Verity slid down between the sheets again. Presently he began to drift into sleep, aware that Bella's outburst was over and that she was moving softly towards him. After a little while he stirred and felt that she was as naked and marble smooth as Jolly had been on that other night which seemed to him now so long ago. His hands moved contentedly upon her and Bella snuggled tighter against him.

'Oh, Mr Verity,' she breathed, the world lost to her in their happiness. 'Oh, Mr Verity, what a good brave sojer I've got!'